*Aurealis Award Finalist*
*Best Young Adult Novel*

# Like rain, only softer

White was everywhere. On the ground, clinging to the branches of the trees. I looked down at my feet. I was standing in white, and it was cold. The air was cold too. When I breathed, it hurt.

It wasn't even daytime. The light was wrong. The sky was orangey-grey and I couldn't see the sun. Was it night? Then why were there no stars? No moon? Was it an eclipse? Had the sky been sucked away?

Soft, wet drops hit my face and landed in my still-open mouth. Like rain, only softer. The air was full of white drops, like feathers or petals, floating through the air.

I walked down the steps, watching the gorgeous white dust dancing all around me. I caught some on my tongue and felt it dissolve. I shivered. It tasted like cold, wet air. I loved it.

"Snow," I said out loud, proud of myself for figuring it out. "It's snow."

# FIREBIRD
### WHERE FANTASY TAKES FLIGHT™

| | |
|---|---|
| *The Blue Girl* | Charles de Lint |
| *The Changeling Sea* | Patricia A. McKillip |
| *Crown Duel* | Sherwood Smith |
| *The Dreaming Place* | Charles de Lint |
| *Ecstasia* | Francesca Lia Block |
| *The Faery Reel: Tales from the Twilight Realm* | Ellen Datlow and Terri Windling, eds. |
| *Firebirds Rising: An Anthology of Original Science Fiction and Fantasy* | Sharyn November, ed. |
| *The Green Man: Tales from the Mythic Forest* | Ellen Datlow and Terri Windling, eds. |
| *Hannah's Garden* | Midori Snyder |
| *The Hex Witch of Seldom* | Nancy Springer |
| *The Hidden Land* | Pamela Dean |
| *Primavera* | Francesca Lia Block |
| *The Secret Country* | Pamela Dean |
| *A Stir of Bones* | Nina Kiriki Hoffman |
| *Tam Lin* | Pamela Dean |
| *Waters Luminous and Deep: Shorter Fictions* | Meredith Ann Pierce |
| *The Whim of the Dragon* | Pamela Dean |
| *The Winter Prince* | Elizabeth E. Wein |

# Magic
## or
# Madness

Also by Justine Larbalestier

*Magic Lessons*

# Magic
## or
# Madness

by
Justine Larbalestier

razOr
bill

Magic or Madness

FIREBIRD/RAZORBILL

Published by the Penguin Group
Penguin Young Readers Group
345 Hudson Street, New York, New York 10014, U.S.A.
Penguin Group (USA) Inc., 375 Hudson Street, New York, New York 10014, U.S.A
Penguin Books Canada Ltd, 10 Alcorn Avenue, Toronto, Ontario,
Canada M4V 3B2 (a division of Pearson Penguin Canada, Inc.)
Penguin Books Ltd, 80 Strand, London WC2R 0RL, England
Penguin Ireland, 25 St Stephen's Green, Dublin 2, Ireland
(a division of Penguin Books Ltd)
Penguin Group (Australia), 250 Camberwell Road, Camberwell,
Victoria 3124, Australia (a division of Pearson Australia Group Pty Ltd)
Penguin Books India Pvt Ltd, 11 Community Centre, Panchsheel Park,
New Delhi – 110 017, India
Penguin Group (NZ), Cnr Airborne and Rosedale Roads, Albany,
Auckland 1310, New Zealand (a division of Pearson New Zealand Ltd)
Penguin Books (South Africa) (Pty) Ltd, 24 Sturdee Avenue, Rosebank,
Johannesburg 2196, South Africa

Penguin Books Ltd, Registered Offices: 80 Strand, London WC2R 0RL, England

10 9 8 7 6 5 4

THE LIBRARY OF CONGRESS HAS CATALOGED THE HARDCOVER EDITION AS FOLLOWS:

Larbalestier, Justine.
  Magic or madness / by Justine Larbalestier.
      p. cm.
  Summary: From the Sydney, Australia home of a grandmother she believes is
a witch, fifteen-year-old Reason Cansino is magically transported to New
York City, where she discovers that friends and foes can be hard to
distinguish.
  ISBN 1-59514-022-0 (hardcover)
  [1. Magic—Fiction. 2. Space and time—Fiction. 3. Grandmothers—Fiction.
4. Mental illness—Fiction. 5. New York (N.Y.)—Fiction. 6. Sydney
(N.S.W.)—Fiction. 7. Australia—Fiction.]  I. Title.
  PZ7.L32073Mag 2005
  [Fic]—dc22
                                                    2004018263

Firebird/Razorbill paperback ISBN 1-59514-070-0
Printed in the United States of America

*For Scott Westerfeld and our two favourite cities*

# Note To Readers

The chapters from Reason and Tom's point of view are written with Australian spelling, vocabulary, and grammar. Those from Jay-Tee's viewpoint are written U.S. style. You will find *make-up* with a hyphen in the Australian chapters and without (*makeup*) in the American, and can thus enjoy English in two of her glorious (confusing) varieties. If a word is unfamiliar, turn to the glossary, which will explain that a *jumper* is in fact a *sweater* (and vice versa). However, the book has U.S. punctuation throughout, so as not to totally confuse the poor American copy editor.

Please note that *Great Expectations* is by Charles Dickens, *not* Shakespeare. Literary history is not one of Tom's strong points.

# 1

# Reason Cansino

It would be easiest to just walk out the front door. But I'd been on the run since before I was born—I knew a lot about running away. Sometimes the simplest plan is not the way to go. If you're expected to run away, then wait awhile, go at night, go out a window or the back door, go over the roof. Leave the way people don't look for you to be leaving. (People rarely look up.) Plan ahead. Accumulate supplies and know your escape route. Avoid breaking the law or annoying anyone. Best to keep the number of people chasing you to a minimum.

My name is Reason Cansino. I was named Reason because my mother, Sarafina, thought it was prettier than Logic or Rationality or Intellect and had better nicknames, too. Not that Sarafina has ever called me anything but Reason.

My mother believes in all those things: logic, reason, and the rest, and in mathematics, which fortunately wasn't on the list of possible names. I'm grateful to have a head full of numbers, but I wouldn't want to answer to the name of Algebra, Trigonometry, or Calculus.

Not many people have ever known my real name: the doctors

and nurses at the hospital where I was born, police, private detectives. And *her*, of course, the wicked witch, my grandmother, Esmeralda Cansino.

All my life we've been on the run from her, Sarafina and me. She caught us once when I was ten, but we got away. It was dumb, I guess, but I thought that was it: she found us, we escaped, end of story. She'll never find us again.

Wrong.

Sarafina always said, "Expect the best, but prepare for the worst."

I'm good at the first part, crap at the second. Despite having lived all my life being made ready in case the wicked witch should find us—Sarafina taught me what to say, what not to say, filled my head with detailed plans of Esmeralda's house ("What if she moves somewhere else?" I asked. "She can't," said Sarafina), how to get in contact with each other if separated, all of that.

Even so, I never really believed it would happen. Not *twice*. It was a game we played, Sarafina and me, nothing more.

I loved our life together. I'd seen brolgas taking off at sunset, their white feathers stained pink, purple, and orange by the light, making vast ripples radiate through the wetlands, sending lily pads rocking, frogs leaping from pad to pad, and lazy crocs slipping flash quick into the water. I'd seen a platypus clear as the air after rains have finally wiped the dust and dirt of a drought away, swimming slow and easy at dawn in water so still, so glass-like, you can see reflected the fine hair on your face.

In that life, I'd never seen a movie, or been in a shopping

centre, or held a remote control. I'd never lived anywhere for more than five months, or in a town of more than a thousand people, or had any friends. I'd never had to memorise a phone number because we never had one or knew anyone to call.

Sarafina turned our constant motion into a game, a lesson, a whole different world. I learned more in an hour spent with her than I'd learned in my two months at a proper school. Sarafina made anything fun and everything fascinating. When it was time to move on (if we weren't in an abandon-everything-and-run hurry), we would toss a coin onto a map and go where it landed or find a name of a town that appealed to us (Wanneroo? Borroloola? Or how about Jilkminggan?). Would we go to a nine-letter town like Fassifern (I love nines) or a prime-number town like Warhope? Or a town at an angle of exactly 45 degrees (more nines) from where we were?

One time we just walked in a straight line—using a compass and the stars to verify the straightness—into the bush, even though it took us through dense scrub, flooded creeks, and over steep ravines, until, at last, we came to a settlement. We were so pleased to see people living there on our straight line (the settlement was so small it wasn't on the map) that we stayed for almost four months. A lifetime!

Sarafina taught me how to read, how to run, how to hide, the music of numbers and of the stars above, and the patterns, the spirals in the flowers and termite mounds, the fruits and the scrub, the grasses and the trees.

Together we'd learn how to start a fire by banging rocks

together or, better, with the sun and a magnifying glass; how much water was necessary for an all-day trek (as much as we both could carry and then some); when it was time for a car; how bad was bad enough to go see a doctor (broken bones, high fever, vomiting that wouldn't stop); when to leave a pub before a stoush got out of hand; when to hitchhike and when to walk; how to gather water-lily roots, witchetty grubs, and wild honey.

*That* was our life together. As soon as I turned eighteen and was free from Esmeralda's custody claim, we were going to travel even further—the whole world—start up north (Indonesia, Malaysia, Thailand, Cambodia) and just keep on going. We'd explore the world as thoroughly as we had Australia. For the rest of our lives.

How could I possibly have wound up in the witch's house? In the city, separated from my mother?

But there I was, sitting in a plane for the very first time, headed towards her.

## 2
# With the Witch

She wore high-heeled shoes that were black, with sharp, pointy toes. If she kicked you, it would hurt. The shoes were so shiny I could see them clearly even though the floor of the cab was dark. It was as if they were made of glass.

"How was the flight?" Esmeralda asked again. "Did they treat you okay?"

I scrunched even closer to the door and turned my face to the bright glare of the window, determined not to look my grandmother in the eye.

"Are you hungry? I don't suppose they gave you any food on such a short flight."

I was starving, but I certainly wasn't going to tell her that. I wasn't going to say a single word to Esmeralda *ever*, even if she kicked me with those witchy shoes. I slipped my hand into my pocket to hold my lucky ammonite, tracing the coiled chambers with my thumb. Sarafina had given it to me. It always made me feel braver.

"Do you like cake? Ice cream? There's plenty at home. We could have some afternoon tea. Thought you might enjoy that."

I wasn't going to eat any food she'd touched, not even if it was chocolate. I had my own stowed in my backpack, which rested on the floor between my feet. I'd eat it as soon as I could get away from her.

It was horrible her being so close. At the airport, she'd hugged me before I could stop her. Esmeralda smelled like make-up and a sharp perfume that made my nose wrinkle. She smelled wrong. Fortunately, in the taxi all I could smell was sweat and petrol and most of all stale cigarette smoke. (The driver had asked if he could smoke and Esmeralda had said no.)

I could feel her looking at me, as if she was trying to will me to look at her. It wouldn't work. I knew too much about my grandmother. Asking me lots of questions in what she hoped was a concerned-sounding voice wasn't going to trick me.

"If you want something else, we can stop off on the way. You can have whatever you want, Reason."

*I want my mother to be how she was before,* I thought. *I want to not be in this taxi with you. I want you to shut up!* I felt the anger rising in me, but I knew better than to *ever* lose my temper.

The sun was shining and the sky (the slice that wasn't hidden by buildings) a brilliant blue, but even so, the view out the window was grim. I hadn't seen a single tree since we'd left the airport. Instead of vegetation there were grassless footpaths, giant signs with advertisements on them for hundreds of things I'd never seen before, ugly grey or dirty brown buildings without verandahs or any signs that people lived in them. I'd forgotten how ugly Sydney was.

There were so many cars and trucks that the traffic kept having to stop. A cyclist in bright green-and-yellow shorts so tight they looked sprayed on zoomed past us. We'd left the airport ten minutes ago, but we didn't seem to have gotten very far. So many cars! I'd been here once before when I was ten (the last time she'd caught us) but didn't remember there being this much traffic. And it was Sunday. What would it be like on a weekday when everyone was rushing to get to work?

"If there's anything you need," Esmeralda began again, "we can go shopping. Much better shops here than in Dubbo. I can take you . . ."

I didn't listen to the rest. I was sick of hearing her voice thick with pretend concern, asking the same questions over and over again. Even if she did sound like my mother, hearing Esmeralda talk just made me want to scream.

I closed my eyes and ran through the Fibonacci series silently, noting primes and factors along the way. In my hand I could feel my ammonite, my fossilised millions-of-years-old shell.

Fibonaccis are my favourites. They can take you a long way. Forever, in fact. Fibonaccis are numbers, special numbers that keep getting bigger and bigger as you go. The Fibs are kind of like lies—they keep creating more Fibs endlessly or until you get tired of the whole thing.

When you run out of Fibs you already know, you can always make another by adding the last two together. It all starts with 0 and 1, which you add together to get . . . 1 again. Then add

the last two (both 1s) to make 2. It keeps going on like that—
every number equals the two before it added together:

0, 1, 1, 2, 3, 5, 8, 13, 21, 34, 55, 89, 144 . . .

I wondered how far away Sarafina was. Last night, she'd
been transferred to a "special" hospital in Sydney. Nuthouse,
more like. Kalder Park was its name. The doctor said they
could look after her much better there. What did that mean?
That they were going to leave off drugging her and tying her
down? Or that they were going to do it even more?

The traffic started moving faster. I saw some green at last:
a park with more grass than trees and great big brick chim-
neys covered in pigeons. Flying rats, Sarafina called them.
According to her, the more pigeons in a town, the less healthy
it was. So far they were the only birds I'd seen here. It figured.

"We're not far from home now," Esmeralda said. She
shifted, crossing her legs the other way. "This is Newtown."

I shuddered. My mother had told me so much about
Esmeralda's house. About the things that happened there. In
the weeks before Sarafina'd hurt herself, she'd been even more
insistent about my knowing its layout, about reminding me of
what my grandmother had been—I looked across, keeping my
eyes at the level of her feet—what she still was.

I should have seen that Sarafina was losing it. I should have
gotten her help before she hurt herself. But I was afraid
Esmeralda would find us. I glanced at her pointy-toed shoes.
Too late.

I hoped the hospital where Sarafina was now, Kalder Park,

lived up to its name. She would hate being stuck in some concrete place with no trees, no bush, no sky anywhere in sight. She hated hospitals. And this was even worse: a loony bin.

They hadn't let me see her last night in Dubbo and this morning they were moving her here to Sydney. I just wanted to say goodbye, tell her the plane trip wouldn't be too bad. Neither of us had ever been in a plane before. I was worried Sarafina wouldn't like it. One of the nurses told me that statistically you're much more likely to be killed in a car than a plane. I told her I reckoned that was because people ride in cars far more than in planes, and she said, "Even so, planes are safer. They get serviced after every single trip. Heaps more than any car."

I wanted to tell Sarafina.

"The hospital where your mother is," Esmeralda began. She was still looking at me. I could feel it. "It's fairly close to the house. You'll be able to visit her as often as you want."

Rubbish. Unless they let me live in the hospital, I wouldn't be seeing Sarafina as much as I wanted.

We were in a narrow but very busy street, the dirty grey footpath as full of people as the road was of cars. There were no houses, only shops crammed all in a row with no spaces between them, selling T-shirts, antiques, books, buttons, tiles, clothes, computers, hats, and bags.

There were lots of traffic lights and we caught every red one. There hadn't been nearly so many in Dubbo when we'd driven in from Nevertire in the ambulance with Sarafina unconscious in the back. I wanted to ride with her, but they wouldn't let me. The ambos had driven through every light whether it was green or not.

That had been Friday, two days ago. I hadn't given anyone our real names, but Esmeralda still found us, still had me sent to her.

I blinked, not wanting to cry. I started the Fibs again, not letting them slip away so easily this time.

## 3
## In The Witch's House

The house was huge, as big as a pub, looming over its tiny front yard and the narrow street, making the rest of the houses look puny and insignificant. I stared up at the wrought-iron balcony, clutching my backpack to my chest, not wanting to go in. It was even bigger than Sarafina had said. I tried not to think about the cellar underneath.

Fibs, I told myself. What was the next one? Fib (47): 2,971,215,073 (a prime factor). Add it to Fib (46) to get Fib (48): 4,807,526,976.

I followed Esmeralda's shiny shoes, dazzling in the sunlight, through the low wrought-iron gate, along a short tiled path, between squat rosebushes and a tangle of tiny native violets. The tiles on the porch were maroon, black and cream, arranged in a pattern of hexagons and seven-pointed stars. The doormat said Welcome.

As she opened the heavy wooden door, it let out a loud groan. I almost jumped.

"I keep meaning to oil it," Esmeralda said.

I squinted. The house was almost as light inside as out. I'd always imagined it dark and dank, smelling of blood and bones. Instead I smelled fresh flowers, books, and timber.

I was standing in a long, wide corridor of reddish brown polished wooden floorboards that shone almost as brightly as Esmeralda's shoes. I looked down at a blurry reflection of myself.

The ceilings were ridiculously high. I wondered how she managed to change the light bulbs. At the end of the corridor I saw the bright shining surfaces of what was obviously the kitchen. Everything was so bright and shiny, so clean.

Esmeralda turned. I lowered my gaze just in time.

"Do you want something to eat now? Or should I show you your room? There's an en suite."

Fib (49) is 7,778,742,049.

Esmeralda let out a sound that could have been a sigh. "Your bedroom, then."

As soon as Esmeralda left the room, I jammed a chair under the door handle. I felt shaky but pleased with myself. I'd managed to get through the whole ordeal without looking at Esmeralda or saying one word.

I sat down on the bed. It was hard to believe. I was in Esmeralda's house and Sarafina was in the loony bin. I was in the house my mother had run away from at the age of twelve. I'd heard about this place my whole life. It wasn't what I had expected. A clean, airy witch's house?

And a clean, airy bedroom. I looked around carefully. This was to be my room. Bare and unornamented, no pictures on the wall, no rugs on the floor, and plain white curtains at the windows. The floorboards shone like the ones downstairs. There was a side table beside the bed as well as a desk, bookshelves filled with books, a couch, and a stand with a television resting on it.

I was half tempted to turn it on. I'd seen so little television in my life—only horse racing, cricket, and footie in pubs, and only five minutes at a time. Sarafina always said I wasn't missing much, though she hadn't seen much more than me.

The room was large, with two glass doors that led out onto a balcony, a big one that ran along the front of the house. I leaned out over the lacework iron railing, looking up and down the street. None of the other houses were as big as this one, but each had a balcony, however small.

It would be pretty easy to climb down to the street from here. A couple walked by below, wheeling a baby in a pram. One of them looked up at me and waved. *Hmmm,* I thought, waving back, *and pretty easy to be spotted doing it.* I needed a different escape route.

I walked the length of the balcony, came to another set of glass doors. The room I glimpsed through them was a mirror version of my own, though more sparsely furnished. The bed had a mattress but no covers. Another guest room. For a moment I wondered if it was waiting for another prisoner like me. Someone else trapped in Esmeralda's web.

I went back to my bedroom, continued my recce. There were two more doors to open. The first led into an enormous walk-in wardrobe. I stepped inside, stretched my arms out, and spun around. I didn't come close to touching the shelves. It was bigger than any of the *rooms* I'd ever stayed in. How could one person need this much space?

When I opened the second door, I was dazzled by gleaming white tiles.

"Bugger."

It was the biggest bathroom in the world. It had a bath, a huge bath that you could practically do laps in, and a *separate* shower. A skylight in the ceiling flooded the white tiles with sunshine. I had never seen anything like it. There were no windows, though. It was a dead end.

I'd never lived in a house before. I'd never had my own room before, let alone one with a balcony and a bathroom. And here, in my evil grandmother's house, I had all those things. I would have swapped it all in a nanosecond to be with Sarafina.

There was fresh lavender on the dressing table and in the bathroom. The smell was very soothing. Too soothing. Sarafina had taught me lots of chemistry, including the properties of herbs and flowers. Lavender could confuse and induce forgetfulness. I shredded it, stem, flowers, leaves, flushed them down the toilet, then washed my hands.

Neatly folded on the bed was a pair of blue-and-white cotton PJs with matching dressing gown and slippers. They were grown-up looking, no little-girl ribbons or flowers or bows. I liked them.

I sniffed at the pyjamas and gown carefully. I couldn't quite identify the scent. It was lovely and didn't make my eyes water. Better to be safe than sorry, though. I threw them into the bathtub and turned on the hot water. Piping hot. Good. Heat would soon dissolve any oils or perfumes. It was summer; they'd dry quick enough.

Next I pulled the sheets off the bed and shoved the mattress up against the wall. I was sweating by the time I was done. I didn't find any ritual objects: no bones, teeth, amulets, or small figures.

None of those things would really work, of course, but my grandmother believed they did and would have been disconcerted to find them gone. Sarafina had taught me how to keep the upper hand. Besides, things like that are creepy.

I let the mattress fall back onto the bed and remade it.

There were lots of books. More books than in some of the country libraries I'd seen. I grew tired just thinking about flicking through each one to check for dried herbs and flowers. It was so long since I'd had a proper night's sleep.

I sat down on the bed, staring at the bookcase. The titles I recognised were books I'd always wanted to read: *The Magic Pudding, The Wizard of Oz, A Wizard of Earthsea, The Nargun and the Stars, The Hobbit,* brightly coloured books of fairy tales, all of them about magic. Sarafina would have hated those books.

I knew my mother was not like other mothers, and not just because she'd gone mad and tried to kill herself. But it was worth giving up a few stupid books: other mothers weren't as interesting or fun as Sarafina. They didn't teach you number secrets or go walkabout with you. I missed her.

I lay back on the bed and looked up at the white ceiling. It was so hard to keep it in my head that I was really here. My brain kept running through everything Sarafina had ever told me about this place, about her mother.

Esmeralda believed magic was real, truly thought she was a witch, and did *terrible* things in her cellar because of this belief. Growing up with Esmeralda had made Sarafina hate the very idea of magic. She hated fairy tales, bunyips, hobbits, the Harry Potter books (which I'd also been longing to read), all of it.

Most of all she hated Esmeralda.

Esmeralda had kept Sarafina locked in her bedroom for years. She wasn't allowed out until she admitted magic was real. But instead of giving in, Sarafina had run away.

In Esmeralda's house you had to move counterclockwise. It kept the magical energy running in the right direction: widdershins.

There was no electricity in the house because it interfered with magic. There was no cooling in summer, no heating in winter. No telephones, no television, no radio. No nothing.

Esmeralda had sex with every man she met in order to steal their vital energies. Some of them died.

She sacrificed rats, guinea pigs, cats, dogs, and goats. She ate human babies that she bought from their impoverished mothers.

I felt sick thinking about it. I closed my eyes to stop from crying. I missed Sarafina so much it made me ache all over. Looking at the books, wanting to read them made me feel that I was betraying her. I wouldn't touch the books. Even the fact that the house *did* have electricity (probably added since Sarafina had run away), that I had already turned light switches on and off, made me feel guilty.

The books, the pretty room, the balcony, the bathroom, the

television, the blue-and-white robe and slippers, the electricity—
I knew they were all bribes, tricks. Esmeralda wanted to turn
me against my mother, make me believe in magic.

There was a knock on the door.

"Reason?"

For a second I thought it was Sarafina. Every time I heard
Esmeralda's voice, I was shocked again by how much she
sounded like my mother.

"I'm going to the shops. Is there anything you want? You
should eat something."

I didn't answer. I knew not to touch my grandmother's food.
Firstly, it was disgusting: Esmeralda liked to eat snails, frogs,
livers, brains. Secondly, in the old days she'd drugged Sarafina's
food to make her compliant.

I'd stocked up. At the hospital I'd bought three Violet
Crumbles, two Mars bars, and four sausage rolls. Even cold, sossi
rolls were my favourites. I figured I could make the food last at
least a couple of days. I wasn't going to stay any longer than that.

I listened to Esmeralda's footsteps going down the wooden
stairs, creaking loudly, then I crept out onto the balcony to
wait for the sound of her leaving. The heavy wooden door gave
its almost human groan. I ducked my head behind the railing,
watching as my grandmother walked down the street.

I looked at my watch: 4:35 PM. I'd give myself twenty minutes to check out the house as carefully and quietly as I could.
Everything I did from now on was practice for my escape.

# 1
# in the Witch's Bedroom

I **tiptoed to the top** of the stairs. I told myself I was searching for escape routes, but the plan of this house was etched in my brain. I knew there were two ways out the back: from the balcony outside Esmeralda's room and from the kitchen. All I needed to do was check them, see if I could climb down from Esmeralda's balcony onto the fig tree, and run away, as Sarafina had eighteen years ago.

Figuring out how best to escape was my priority, but I also wanted to search this house, find all its secrets. My mother had taught me to be curious, to ask questions, to explore. I *had* to compare the reality of Esmeralda's house with the plan, to compare the stories Sarafina had told me with the places where they happened.

I had to see Esmeralda's room, see what she wore, what she kept on her bedside table, what secrets lay hidden in her dressing table.

And, well, I wanted to hassle Esmeralda. She truly believed in her bones and amulets. That's the problem with believing in magic: it backfires. Even though I knew it was bulldust and that her witchy stuff had no power, I could still muck Esmeralda around because *she* believed in it absolutely. Sarafina had taught me well. I knew just what to do.

Most of all, even though the very idea terrified me, I *had* to see the cellar I had heard so many terrible stories about. Magic couldn't kill anything or anyone, but knives could.

Sarafina had also made it clear that there were times when curiosity had to be put on hold, times when curiosity could get you into trouble. The cellar most likely fell into that category, but, well, how could I resist? How could I not explore every room in the house that I had been warned about my entire life?

But not *known*. Plans, no matter how accurate—and Sarafina's were accurate—gave no sense of what a house is like. The corridors, the rooms, the stairs were all where they were supposed to be, which was definitely reassuring. But they were so vast!

Somehow Sarafina had never made that clear. Or maybe I just couldn't imagine a house this big. Unless it was a pub divided into lots of cramped little hotel rooms upstairs—none of which was ever quite clean—and a big, smoky bar smelling of stale beer below. I always preferred camping or staying in caravan parks. Though you could meet amazing people in pubs.

I crept along the corridor, trying not to make the floorboards squeak, then opened the door to Esmeralda's room. It was double the size of the one she had given me but much, much more cluttered. It was a mess. I felt claustrophobic standing in it, as though something were about to fall on me. Paintings and photographs filled every available centimetre of wall space, so crowded they looked likely to drop from the wall if I trod too heavily.

Three hundred and sixty-five of them. The number popped into my head as it always does. Counting for me is like breathing.

Though it's not really counting: I see numbers first, then the thing. *Twelve,* my brain will chime, then I'll see that there are twelve bananas in a bowl, snails on a wall, or ants on my foot.

The floor was as cluttered as the walls, strewn with shoes and piles of newspapers, magazines, books, disposable coffee cups, and other things I couldn't quite identify. It was impossible to put my whole foot down without disturbing things, so I tiptoed. Too many layers for an accurate count. Sarafina would have estimated, but unless the things have all the same dimensions, like lollies in a jar, I need to see what I'm counting.

I stared at all the photos and paintings until my eyes stopped at what looked like a photo of my mother as a baby. Curly black hair, big brown eyes, fair skin, clutching a rattle and sucking her thumb. I turned the photo over and opened the frame. Lying against the back of the photo was a pale yellow dried flower I didn't recognise. Smaller than my thumbnail, with five petals.

I tried to pick it up using thumb and forefinger, but the tiny, faded thing crumbled to dust in my fingers. For a few moments the air smelled faintly sweet where it had disintegrated, almost like jasmine. Whatever Esmeralda *thought* her little flower had been doing, I'd stopped it. When I wiped my fingers on my shorts, there was no trace of dust at all.

In the only other photo I could be sure was Sarafina, she was six or seven, wearing blue corduroy overalls, climbing on a metal jungle gym. There were eight other kids swarming all over it. I wondered if they'd been her friends. I'd never known

Sarafina to have friends. I'd never seen a photo of her when she was a kid before.

When I opened the back, there was another flower, just like the first. I didn't touch the pale yellow, just tipped it out, watching the tiny flower disintegrate as soon as it touched the air. A gentle fragrance was in my nostrils, then gone.

In a way, Esmeralda's chaos was a relief. It showed how completely different she and Sarafina were. The eerie similarity of their voices had shaken me, but looking at her room proved that was all they had in common. My mother was the neatest, most organised, tidiest person alive, and Esmeralda, judging by this room, had to be about the messiest.

The bed was covered with twenty-seven books, thirty-four newspapers, and eighteen magazines. I couldn't see how Esmeralda could read that many things at the same time. Nor how she managed to get into the bed, let alone sleep in it.

The bedside table had three drawers: the first two were crowded with fifty-one newspaper and magazine cuttings, eighteen pens, 332 paper clips, nine rubbers, five sharpeners (though no actual pencils), a letter opener, and a box of twelve ink cartridges. No order there for me to disturb. No flowers either.

The third was locked. I tugged, but it wouldn't give. Jemmy it? Old-fashioned locks were usually simple to get past. I pulled the bobby pin from my hair and twisted it straight, inserted it into the lock, and pushed at the catch—it clicked.

The drawer held an old-fashioned key as big as my hand.

Nothing else. It looked sinister, all alone in there. *Here lies the key to the gates of hell.* I smiled to myself, imagining what Sarafina would say to that. The key's teeth were big and simple, but the other end was a mess of metal curves that wound round and round each other. When I traced them with my finger, I tingled. There was no beginning, no end. Infinity.

I just bet this was the key to the cellar or to *something* I wasn't supposed to see. I pulled it out, put it in my pocket, where it dug into my thigh, and shut the drawer, using the bobby pin to relock it.

Every chair, the end of the bed, the half-open doors to the walk-in wardrobe and to the balcony were all draped with clothes. The wardrobe itself was bursting with them. I couldn't understand how anyone could need, want, or for that matter *wear* that many clothes. Most of the clothes looked almost identical. I examined thirty-eight—*thirty-eight*—black jackets, finding no difference except in the number of buttons. I felt the linings carefully. One had a single black feather in the inside pocket. I put the feather back upside down, as Sarafina had taught me, imagining how freaked out Esmeralda would be when she discovered it. I wondered what Esmeralda thought the feather would do.

Unlike the rest of the room, there were patterns here. The wardrobe was stuffed with clothes, but it was ordered. All the white shirts together, the black jackets, the brown skirts. It didn't look like the wardrobe of a person who would leave empty coffee cups all over the floor. It also occurred to me that while Esmeralda's room was a disaster, it wasn't actually dirty.

There was little dust. The sheets on the bed seemed clean. The whole house was clean.

The bathroom was crowded with bottles of gunk, make-up, and I had no idea what else. Strangely, many of the bottles looked like the kind of no-name brand that my mother always bought. I took the lids off some and sniffed at them. They smelled a lot better, though.

There were seven towels hanging to dry from the various hooks and railings and two scales. The large, metal one with sliding weights was clearly for weighing yourself, but what was the small electronic one on the countertop for? I turned it on and dropped a tissue on it: 1.1882 grams. Talk about precision. To weigh tiny dried flowers, maybe? It had never occurred to me before that magic might need scientific precision, since it was all make-believe anyway.

In a neat row in front of the mirror were five hairbrushes. How could anyone possibly need more than one? I picked up the biggest. The handle and back of the brush were made of a yellowy white stuff. It was smooth but definitely not plastic. Ivory? There was kind of a dip in the middle. I pushed it, and the back of the brush popped open.

It was full of teeth. Thirty-three of them.

"Bugger."

Five of the teeth had fillings in them. Definitely human.

Eight had scattered across the counter, making a sound like restless fingernails. I gathered them up, feeling queasy, and shoved them back into the brush. It snapped shut with a click.

The teeth felt exactly the same as the brush itself. Is something still ivory if it's made from *human* teeth?

This really was my evil grandmother's house.

Suddenly I felt like I was going to chunder. With careful steps, I retreated into the bedroom and out onto the balcony, inhaling fresh air and grasping the reassuringly cold and solid iron of the railing. After a few moments, the chunderous feeling in my stomach began to fade.

The backyard was dominated by one of the biggest Moreton Bay fig trees I'd ever seen. Sarafina had described it as a big tree, but *big* didn't cover it. It was taller than the house. Much taller. Its enormous canopy spread out to cover the entire yard and beyond. Some of its branches had been lopped to prevent them growing through the railing and into the bedroom. But it still seemed to threaten the house.

I'd seen what happened when trees were allowed to grow unchecked. In the country there are lots of old broken-down houses with trees growing right through them unstoppably, until all that's left is a sad, rusted, corrugated-iron skeleton, overrun by the tree that has eaten it.

The cut-back branches were really close. They'd been lopped off recently, giving off that new-cut-wood smell. Above me some of the branches still touched the house, as if plotting its downfall.

Instinctively I liked the tree. For one thing, Sarafina had escaped from this very balcony on its branches. You could be the worst climber in the world (which neither I nor Sarafina was) and still get from balcony to fig tree to back lane and then . . . away.

I wished I could leave right then. I wanted to, badly. But I wasn't ready. I had no supplies, not enough food, not enough money. I'd taken all the cash Sarafina had hidden in the lining of our suitcase—$250. It had seemed like a lot, but today, having seen how much the taxi ride from the airport cost, it seemed like nothing. I had her bank card, in the name of Suzanne Alexander, but it was new and I didn't know the pin number. I'd tried the usual ones and they hadn't worked. I'd have to ask Sarafina when I saw her.

I knew where I was and how to get from here to Central, where buses and trains would take me out of Sydney. I also knew the name of Sarafina's hospital—Kalder Park—but not where it was. I couldn't possibly run away until I'd seen her, told her what I was doing—*I'm going to run away just like you did, Sarafina, make my own way in the world*—and promised to come back for her when I was eighteen and no one could stop me.

But not yet. Any fool can walk out a door, climb out a window. Running away is not about simply getting out of the house. It's about not getting caught two days later.

I checked my watch. Esmeralda had been gone twelve minutes. Did I have enough time to check through more drawers? Or to go downstairs to the cellar?

It wasn't really a question. After finding those teeth, I *had* to see the cellar. But what was I going to find there?

# 5
## into the Cellar

The cellar door lock was small and modern, with a dead bolt. No way would the infinity key fit. Part of me was relieved. I didn't know how far the shops were; Esmeralda could be back any second now. I did not want to be caught down here.

I asked myself why I needed to see the cellar. What was I hoping for? Proof that my mother's stories were real? *Sarafina Was Here* written in blood on the cellar wall?

I'd seen enough in Esmeralda's room to know that she was exactly what my mother claimed. *Human teeth.* And yet . . .

Was this *really* the house Sarafina had escaped from all those years ago? There was electricity, hot running water, and it was beautiful—even Esmeralda's chaotic room. Except that it was laid out *exactly* as Sarafina had taught me. The cellar door was where it was supposed to be, right here, behind the stairs.

I reached for the handle. It turned easily. I let go fast, stung. My heart beat faster. The door was unlocked. *Bugger.*

How much time before my grandmother returned? I looked at my watch again: eighteen minutes had passed.

Why not check out the backyard? My escape route. If

Esmeralda came back too soon, I could climb the tree, sneak back into my room through hers.

I reached for the door handle again, my hand shaking. *Stop it.* What could possibly happen if I was caught down here? Okay, lots of things. *Bad* things.

But would they really? The authorities knew I was here. A social worker was supposed to come by to see me once a fortnight, check on how I was "adjusting." It was perfectly safe, I told myself, only half believing it, to explore the house . . . even if I was caught.

A tremor went through me. I tried not to think about the thirty-three teeth, the flowers that had dissolved into nothing. What if Esmeralda made me do the things she'd made my mother do? She couldn't, I told myself. Sarafina had been a little kid. By the time she ran away, Sarafina was still only *twelve*. I was fifteen.

Esmeralda couldn't do anything vile to me *too* soon, and I'd be gone before long.

They weren't the most comforting thoughts, but they were enough to make me open the door. I groped for a light switch. Nothing but a cold stone wall. The light from the hallway didn't reach very far down the stairs. I could see only the first ten steps, nothing of the cellar below. It was very dark and cold: the first stone step chilled my bare feet. This was how I'd imagined the whole house. Dark and bone-penetratingly cold, even in summer.

I descended until the light ended in front of me. The darkness had a sharp edge, like a curtain. *Here be dragons.* I edged my left foot forward, let my toes curl around the stone. What if I took another step forward and there was nothing there? Would I fall all the way to the cellar floor? Or keep falling and falling forever?

*Stop it.* These were the kinds of fears that Sarafina always chided me about. There were enough *real* things to be scared of.

I took a deep breath, kept my left hand firmly on the stone wall, and edged forward. My foot found another cold stair. I felt for the stone in my pocket, my lucky ammonite. Sarafina had given it to me when she first taught me about the Fibonacci series. Each segment spiralling out from the centre, equalling the area of the two previous ones, infinity in a fossilised shell, a golden spiral. It was beautiful. I carried it with me wherever I went. Normally it comforted me, yet this time I didn't feel any less nervous.

I went down the rest of the way slowly, a step at a time. There were so many, I started to think the stairs would never end. When my soles finally slapped the uneven stone of the cellar floor, I yelped, "Bloody hell."

For a moment I couldn't move. I was in *the* cellar.

My mother's stories flooded into me. All those things Sarafina had seen—they had happened down *here*. She'd been tied to a chair here, been made to watch Esmeralda slit the throat of Le Roi, Sarafina's fat ginger cat. Now I was in that same cellar. I half expected to feel the squish of cat's blood and innards under my toes.

I tentatively felt for a light switch, half hoping I wouldn't find one. Did I really want to see this place? Of course I did. I *had* to. Anything was better than standing here in the dark, imagining what was in front of me. Especially now that my eyes—finally—had started to adjust to the darkness. The cellar was crowded with dark shapes.

A loud groan came from upstairs and then a *boom*. The front door opening and closing.

I froze. Esmeralda. *Bugger,* I thought. I'd left the cellar door ajar. What if she came down here? I had to hide. But all those dark shapes. What if they still had *their* teeth?

What were they, anyway? Not anything living. (Which immediately made me think of something *dead*.) Whatever they were, they didn't move. There was no sound of breathing other than my own. *Dead things,* I reminded myself, *can't hurt you.*

The floorboards overhead creaked loudly. Quickly I threaded my way between the shapes, stumbling on the uneven stones under my feet, afraid that I would bump into the strange shapes. I scraped my knee on concrete, lost my footing, and steadied myself against something that felt like smooth, rounded glass. My heart beat in my fingertips.

Above me, the door creaked open wide. I ducked down, not sure if I was actually hidden.

There was a click, and the cellar was instantly bathed in dazzling light. My eyes watered, but I forced them open.

Wine racks everywhere, holding hundreds and hundreds of

bottles of wine. Enough to hide me, unless she was searching for me.

Footsteps down the stairs. I crouched even lower, holding my breath, praying Esmeralda wouldn't see me. I heard the scraping of wine bottle against brick. Then steps back up the stairs. The lights went out. The door closed.

I breathed again.

My night vision was gone, but I was more sure of my footing now that I'd actually seen the cellar. All I had to do was get back to my room without being busted. No worries. No harder than crossing the Nullarbor Plain naked with only a teaspoon of water.

In my haste I banged my shin on the bottom step. Stupid. After a second it began to throb.

I climbed the cellar stairs fast. At the top I saw a light switch glowing faintly. How had I missed it the first time? I knew exactly what Sarafina would have said about letting my fears make me miss the obvious.

I stood close to the door, listening. Noises coming from the kitchen. Now or never. I grasped the door handle, afraid she'd locked me down here, but it turned.

I slipped out, tiptoeing along the hall, then up the stairs and into my room, shutting the door and pushing the chair back into place under the door handle. I threw myself on the bed, out of breath and sweaty, my right shin throbbing. But the witch hadn't caught me.

Something sharp dug into my hip. I reached into my pocket

and pulled out the infinity key. What *was* it the key to? I put it away in my backpack. Whatever it opened was important. Why else would Esmeralda keep it in a locked drawer?

My head was filled with a hundred confusing thoughts. The legendary cellar had turned out to be an exceptionally well-lit wine cellar, crowded with endless bottles. Sacrificing animals down there would be pretty difficult. There'd barely been room to move. It didn't smell of blood. Nor of antiseptic for getting rid of the scent of blood. It smelled only of dust.

The house had electricity. There were telephones and radios and televisions.

I couldn't believe Sarafina had lied. I *knew* she hadn't. Sarafina didn't lie, though it was true that sometimes she could be, well, confused. Besides, there were those teeth, the dried flowers, the key. Maybe Esmeralda was doing her "magic" somewhere else. But she still kept a few things here. Carefully hidden or locked in drawers.

The welfare people must've looked around before they'd allowed me to stay here. Esmeralda had to hide what she was. So she'd cleared the magic out and scrubbed the house cleaner than it had ever been.

I looked around "my" room one more time. It was *gorgeous*. It was a shame this was Esmeralda's house. It was a shame I couldn't live here with Sarafina. It was a shame I couldn't stay.

# 6

# Through The Window

My bed was moving, a giant hand shaking it hard. I tried
to wake up. My whole body was heavy, thick with sleep.

A rattling sound, like chains. A giant's chains?

No. It was the windows and doors. *Oh, bugger,* I thought,
*Esmeralda's coming for me.* Then I was awake and sitting up, my
eyes wide.

It stopped. Esmeralda wasn't there. Hadn't burst through
the door wielding an axe.

I jumped up and ran out onto the balcony. Maybe it had
just been a semi-trailer passing by? But there was no truck disappearing from view. And I couldn't see how any truck big
enough to shake the whole house could fit down the narrow
street. An earth tremor, maybe?

It was 7 AM. The adrenaline leaving me, I smiled. I'd had
hardly any sleep, but it didn't matter—I'd survived my first
night in the wicked witch's house (and possibly an earth-
quake).

Alive, but also hungry and lonely. At least I could do something about the first. I dug the last sossi roll and half a Violet
Crumble out of my backpack, all that remained from my dinner

last night. So much for my supplies lasting. I ate it all in seconds, still feeling hungry afterwards.

Was Esmeralda up yet? I couldn't imagine how she could have slept through that rattling. I pressed my ear to the door. The sound of footsteps coming up the stairs made me jump back. Had Esmeralda been waiting for that exact moment?

She stopped outside my door. I held my breath. The floorboards creaked. I looked at the gap under the door. A white envelope appeared.

I heard her going back down the stairs. I breathed again, pulled the letter out. It was thick. My name was on the front in big, slanting, even handwriting. I placed it on the desk unopened.

Then I washed my hands.

As soon as I was sure she wouldn't hear, I crept out to the top of the stairs, listening to the sounds coming from the kitchen. The back door opened and closed, creaking loudly on its hinges. The whole house shook again. *What on earth?*

I tiptoed down the hall, picked my way carefully across Esmeralda's messy floor and out onto her balcony. Peeking down through the lacework railing, I couldn't see her anywhere. The fig tree blocked a lot, but not the path she'd take from back door to garage door. She couldn't have gotten to the garage that quickly. Besides, it was a roller door—I'd've heard it. Maybe she hadn't gone out back at all? I crept to the top of the stairs and listened intently. Nothing. The house was quiet.

I checked every room: library, lounge and dining rooms, even the laundry and downstairs bathroom, ready to run back upstairs at the slightest noise. They were all, including the cellar, empty. Esmeralda wasn't anywhere.

Was there a hidden passage? Could she be watching me right now? Sarafina had warned me that the house was strange, that her mother had a habit of appearing from nowhere. *Esmeralda has many ways,* Sarafina had said, *of convincing you that magic is real. You have to remember that it's just tricks. Mirrors and light. Nothing supernatural.*

I wondered, as I had many times before, if it was possible that Esmeralda simply used the word *magic* for all those things that science hadn't yet explained. Even for some that *had* been explained. Lots of things my mother'd taught me didn't entirely make sense. She explained them in terms of patterns and numbers, but I could imagine someone with less knowledge of mathematics would think them magical. It isn't magic that on so many flowers—from buttercups to orchids to passion-flowers—the number of petals is a Fib, just science.

To make sure the house was empty, I did one of Sarafina's tricks, one of the ones that didn't entirely make sense to me: I stood still, closed my eyes, just as she'd taught me. Squeezed the ammonite in my pocket and thought of the stars at night. Hundreds and hundreds of stars as far as I could see, too many to count at a glance. I let my fear and anxiety slip away. When I was relaxed, or as close as I'd managed since Sarafina had gone to the hospital, my head was filled with Fibs and a spiral grew inside me, radiating out, making me its centre as it moved through the house. It touched no living thing bigger than a skink.

I opened my eyes again. There wasn't anyone in the house but me.

Sarafina called this process meditation. When you meditate, your brain chemistry changes. You become more sensitive to the patterns of other people, of animals. Not just their brain, but the energy they expel just by living. In a meditative state you can feel entropy, the process of decay, and know whether anything living is nearby. Rocks, bricks, wood don't have brains, so they expel energy at a much slower rate. Their patterns are more static. Not magic, science.

It never failed.

A house empty of people. I could feel it. The only buzz came from the electrical appliances, the plants, cockroaches, spiders, ants, lizards, and skinks. Nothing human but me.

With Esmeralda gone, I could check out the downstairs escape route, through the backyard. I walked into the kitchen. Seeing the reality was a lot different from looking at the plan. It was bigger than a kitchen had any right to be, and it was *all* escape routes: a back door and lots of large open windows.

And a note from Esmeralda stuck to the fridge:

*Gone to work (speed dial 1). Might be able to duck back for afternoon tea. Otherwise I won't be home till late. Rita will be by at 11 AM to clean. She's a love. She can tell you anything you need to know about the house. She'll make you lunch and dinner, but if you get hungry before that, help yourself to anything in the kitchen.*

She'd signed it with *love*. I tried not to gag. I wondered if
Rita was another freak who liked to hurt animals and people
and used magic as her excuse. On the counter were two
wooden blocks full of knives.

I turned the handle on the back door, but it resisted stub-
bornly. I tried to rattle it, but it wouldn't budge. Turned it the
other way. Nothing. But I'd just heard Esmeralda open it. It
didn't feel like it was sticking—it was locked.

I lifted the raincoat from the hook on the back of the door.
No key hung behind it. The coat was heavy and damp. Weird.
It hadn't rained. I touched the lining. It felt like fur. But it was
January, the middle of summer. Why on earth would a winter
coat be hanging there? It was 7:30 AM and already boiling.

I searched through the pockets, finding no key but plenty of
coins. I dug them out, hoping for lots of two-dollar ones. But they
were wrong: not heavy enough, too thin. None of them had the
queen on them. United States of America, they said. Useless.

I looked in the large fruit bowl, but it held only fruit: sugar
bananas, a big juicy-looking mango, and some weird kinds of
fruit I'd never seen before, including three that were red and
hairy.

I loved mango. I looked at it longingly. Surely Esmeralda
couldn't tamper with a mango? But Sarafina had warned me
not to touch *any* of Esmeralda's food. Best not to risk it.

Why would anyone lock the door but leave the windows
open? Was Esmeralda hoping for stupid thieves or ones who

were too short to climb in?

I climbed onto the counter, unlatched the window over the sink, and pushed it as wide as it would go. I sat on the sill, surveying the yard.

I remembered the infinity key; maybe it unlocked the back door. It was the right size. Didn't matter, though, more fun getting into the yard this way—quieter too. Trees and bushes were crowded thick along the fence; the neighbours couldn't possibly see me. Perfect.

# 7
## Treetop

Tom watched as the girl dropped softly to the balcony and looked around. If she was a thief, whatever she'd taken was small enough to fit in her pockets. Not that she had many pockets. She wore only a T-shirt and shorts. Her feet were bare.

Moving about the backyard slowly, peering at everything, she wasn't acting like a thief. Was she looking for gaps in the fence? Or did she think there might be buried treasure in Mere's backyard? Tom would've thought a thief would be in way more of a hurry.

He couldn't see perfectly from up in Filomena—too many branches and leaves. The girl kept popping in and out of sight. He didn't want to draw attention to himself by moving about too much. If she'd stolen something from Mere, he would stop her.

Then he lost sight of the girl altogether. He was sure she hadn't climbed the fence—he'd have heard. And Mere's garage door was the noisiest in Newtown. He closed his eyes, listening, feeling for her, seeing the world around him through his eyelids, divided into its integral shapes: triangles, diamonds, circles, rectangles, and squares. She was so quiet.

*Ah,* Tom almost said out loud. *Climbing up toward me.*

He climbed down several branches, shifting as quick and quiet as a lizard to the top of the fence between Mere's and his father's place, arranging the bottlebrush so the girl wouldn't be able to see him, but he could still see her.

The top of the fence was far more precarious than the solid, wide branches of the tree. He couldn't lean on the bottlebrush for support. Too noisy. He had to keep perfectly still, both his hands clinging to the narrow fence.

Though he knew he shouldn't, Tom closed his eyes again, feeling for her—following her angular but graceful lines as she eased herself up the tree trunk. Filomena wasn't an easy climb. Well, once you were up into the branches, it was dead easy. Getting up was the tricky part. The trunk was huge; even the lowest branches were far from the ground. The girl hadn't looked very tall.

She'd been smart enough not to try the thick hanging roots that temptingly resembled rope but would rip straight from the tree and cover you in bark, twigs, leaves, figs, dead bugs, and, if you were really unlucky, bat shit if you tried to use them. Tom felt the friction of her fingertips and feet against the old bark, like a grasshopper walking on hessian. She found her way with toes and fingertips, using the strength of her legs and back to propel her upward. The girl's eyes were closed, Tom realised, the hair standing up on the back of his neck.

She's done this before: not a normal thief. Was she like him?

He opened his eyes. She was getting closer. He heard her T-shirt catching on one of the smaller branches.

He saw her hands first, then her head and shoulders. *She's gorgeous,* was Tom's first thought. *She looks just like Mere,* was his second. *She's not white,* his third.

If she looked like Mere and climbed like *that,* then Tom was certain she was like Mere in other ways too, which meant she *was* just like him. Why had Mere never told him she had relatives? He'd thought he knew all Mere's secrets.

The girl sat with her back against the trunk, facing him, wiped her hands on her shorts, then her sleeve against her face. She was sweating and grinning widely, dead pleased with herself. Tom found himself grinning too.

She stood carefully, avoiding the branches above. She stepped from one branch to the next, ducking to avoid being smacked in the face, until she reached the thick branch that stretched out over the back lane. Once she was over the back fence, she peered down.

"Hello," Tom said. He tried to sound as friendly as possible, worried she might jump down and run away.

The girl started, almost lost her footing. "Bugger."

She grabbed a branch above her head to steady herself and looked down.

"Hello," Tom said again, a little louder this time. "Over here."

The girl turned. The expression on her face was a mixture of surprise and annoyance, as if she'd been caught, yet she didn't run.

"Hi," Tom said. He pushed aside some of the bottlebrush so she could see him.

"Oh, hi," the girl said. She moved closer.

"I saw you climbing out Mere's window. I was wondering what you were doing."

"Bugger," she said again. "How? How'd you see me?"

"I was up here. In this tree, I mean." Tom blushed, having no idea why. If anyone should be blushing, it should be her. "Mere lets me climb it."

The girl paused. "You mean Esmeralda?"

"Oh, yeah. I always forget that's her full name. No one ever calls her anything but Mere. Are you two relatives? You look just like her. I mean, except that you're dark." He blushed again. "Not that that's a bad thing or anything." *Shut your mouth, Tom.*

"Esmeralda's my grandmother."

"No," Tom said with total disbelief. Of course she was related to Mere, so Mere must have kept things from him. Not just that she had a child but a granddaughter too. "Bull. No way. That's impossible."

The girl said nothing, looking at him as if he were from some faraway planet.

"Your *grand*mother."

"Uh-huh."

"Wow." Tom realised that Mere had never told him how old she was. It shook him. What else didn't he know about her? If she was a grandmother, then she was *much* older than he'd thought and how was that possible?

"Don't you have a grandmother?" the girl asked.

"Huh? Yeah, of course. I've got two of them. But they're really old and they don't wear gorgeous clothes and they're not beautiful."

"Esmeralda's old. She's forty-five."

Tom didn't quite believe her. He'd thought Mere was maybe thirty. Tops. If she was that old already . . . Tom shook his head, not wanting to think about how long Mere had left. Maybe that's why she hadn't told him. "Anyway, that's not grandmother old. My *mum's* forty-two."

The girl shrugged as though it were perfectly normal to her, which he guessed it would be. He wondered why Mere hadn't told him about her granddaughter. Or the child who was this girl's mother or father. Did she have other children? Other grandchildren? Was the girl going to be studying with Mere too?

"Can I join you?" he asked, even though he didn't need her permission. He was allowed to climb Filomena whenever he wanted.

"Sure," she said, and then looked uncertain, like maybe it was a bad idea. Too late. Tom was already standing on the same branch as her.

He grinned and she grinned in return. She was even prettier up close, with shortish wavy light brown hair and dark brown eyes that had gold and reddish flecks in them. Her eye-lashes were black and about a metre long. Tom tried to think of something to say to her, but he was lost imagining what she'd look like in a Schiaparelli ball gown. Emerald green. *Mustn't stare,* he reminded himself, though *she* was staring back at him.

"I'm Tom," he said at last, extending his hand.

"Reason," she said as they shook hands. It made the branch under them shake, and they both wobbled. They giggled and sat down, scooting closer to the trunk of the tree.

"Your name is Reason?" asked Tom. He wasn't sure he'd heard her right.

"Uh-huh. People call me Ree."

"Weird name."

"Yeah. My mother's mad."

"Yeah? Mine too."

"No," said Reason. "I mean *really* mad."

"Yeah," said Tom. "Mine too. She kept trying to kill herself. Then one time when I was little, she tried to kill me and Cathy too. So she's in Kalder Park now."

"Wow. My mother's in Kalder Park! Sarafina tried to kill herself too." The girl seemed amazed by the coincidence, which struck Tom as weird. If she was Mere's granddaughter, she should know it wasn't a coincidence.

"Mum would never take her meds," said Tom. "She thinks they put devils in her head."

The girl nodded, then said softly, "I miss her."

"Yeah," said Tom. "Me too."

They sat quietly for a while. When the silence started to make Tom uncomfortable, he asked, "How come you call your mum by her first name?"

"Huh?"

"You called her 'Sarafina,' not 'mum.'"

"She doesn't like it, I guess." Reason shrugged. "I've always called her Sarafina."

"Weird."

The girl just shrugged again. Clearly, she didn't think so.

"Are you going to be living with Mere now?"

She hesitated, then said, "Uh-huh."

"Cool. Great house, eh?"

"Yeah. It's huge."

"Biggest one in Newtown. I mean, take a look at my backyard."

They shifted out along the branch until it started to bow under their weight. Tom's backyard was less than a quarter the size of Mere's. He wondered if Reason knew that Mere owned it too, as well as the house on the other side of hers.

"Are you from Sydney?" he asked, though he didn't think so. Her accent sounded more bush than city.

"Nah. I'm from . . . well, we moved around a lot. Never stayed anywhere very long. We were in a settlement not far from Coonabarabran for five months. That was the longest."

"The bush. Huh. You been in a city before?"

"Been to Dubbo. And here once before. There was a big custody case when I was little, but we weren't here long."

"Do you like Sydney?" Tom asked, though he couldn't imagine anyone *not* liking it. Especially compared to Dubbo.

"Well," said Reason, "it seems really big. Crowded. The houses are so close together. Really narrow streets."

Tom waved her words away. "But what do you think of the Opera House and the Harbour Bridge and the Tannie Gardens?"

"The what Gardens?"

"Botanical Gardens."

"Haven't seen them."

"You're kidding? Well, we gotta climb higher," he said, shifting closer to the trunk. "You can see the bridge from the top." He pulled himself up to the next branch. "Ugh." Tom flicked it away and wiped his hand on his shorts. "Bat shit. Be careful."

"Flying foxes!" Reason said, sounding excited. "I thought I recognised that smell."

The view from the top of Filomena was spectacular. They were a *long* way up. Higher than the top of Mere's house. Up here the wind moved the tree and they had to stay close and hold on. Tom assured Reason it was safe.

Several times he accidentally touched her arm. Reason's hair blew into his eyes. He wished the flying fox smell wasn't so intense. He wondered what her hair smelled like.

He pointed out the city skyline, showed her the tops of the Harbour and Anzac bridges. It was a perfect day. The sunlight glittered on the harbour and the tall glass buildings. It was amazing. Tom could tell she was impressed.

They turned around slowly, admiring the view that stretched forever in all directions. Tom pointed out all the parkland, all the trees.

"Huh," Reason said. "I thought cities were all concrete and glass, not parks and flying foxes."

"Haven't you seen the bats at night? Or at least heard them squeaking?"

"I haven't been here very long."

"When'd you get here?"

"Last night. Afternoon, I mean."

"This a surprise visit? Did Mere know you were coming? Can't believe she didn't tell me. It's going to be cool having you around," he said, barely taking a breath. "Right now the neighbourhood's mostly littlies or uni students. Most of my friends live ages away."

Reason smiled. Tom hoped it was because she liked the idea of hanging out with him.

"Do you go visit her?" she asked.

"Visit who?"

"Your mum. In Kalder Park."

"Yeah," said Tom, his voice a bit quieter. "Not as often as I should. I don't like it. She's all . . . you know."

Reason nodded as though she knew exactly what he meant. "Is it far from here? Could we walk?"

"It's not that far. But easier to get Mere to drive you or take the bus."

"Have you got a map? Could you show me?"

"Sure. We could go together if you want. Might be better to have someone to talk to afterwards. Dad never really wants to talk about it. Visiting mum's about the only thing that shuts him up." Tom shook his head. "Hey, where's your dad?"

"Don't have one."

"Did he bugger off?"

"Nah. Mum got pregnant, but she never found the bloke to tell him. So I've got no dad. She says they only slept together the one time. Wasn't like she really knew him or anything, so why track him down and tell him? She couldn't see the point."

"I guess," said Tom. He couldn't really imagine it. "Was he an Aborigine?"

Reason laughed. "What do you reckon?"

Tom blushed again. He could be such an idiot. "Should we go find you a map? My dad's got a mini *Gregory's*."

The route to Tom's place didn't involve them stepping foot on the ground once. He pointed this out to Reason, who nodded as if to say, Well, of course, and Tom instantly felt like a total dag.

From the fig tree, they crept along the top of the fence between Mere's and Tom's. They had to push their way through bushes and trees. Reason giggled and Tom lost the dag feeling.

"You can go for blocks and blocks using only trees, fences, and roofs. I can show you if you want."

"That'd be great," Reason said with what sounded to Tom like genuine enthusiasm.

From the fence they swung up onto Tom's balcony. He was suddenly aware of how small his house was compared to Mere's. His room must seem tiny to Reason. He watched her staring at the samples, fabrics, and sketches strewn about his room. It must look really messy. To Tom it was his workroom. As far as he was concerned, everything was where it was supposed to be. Every random-looking piece of cloth had found its place in the chaos, a spot where its texture and color balanced all the others. He could find any of them with his eyes shut.

"You have a sewing machine?"

"Yup," said Tom, grinning. "I can make any kind of clothing you can name."

He pointed to one of the drawings pinned to his notice board. "See that?" Tom was proud of his sketches. He looked at it, admiring the way he'd caught the flow of the fabric. The ruching on the sleeves was more complicated than he'd've liked, but you had to please the client. At least he'd managed to talk Jessica out of the bow on the back. He grinned to himself. He'd told her it'd make her arse look fat.

Reason peered at Tom's work of art. She didn't seem very impressed.

"Check this out, then." Tom went to his wardrobe and pulled out the dress. This would impress her. It was the same one as the drawing, though the colours differed. Jessica had said scarlet and then gone and picked a silk that was more maroon. Very annoying.

"Designed it. Made it," he announced.

"And you *wear* it?" Reason laughed.

"Nah," said Tom. "Jessica Chan gave me a hundred bucks to make it. She paid for all the material and stuff too. Final fitting's today."

"A hundred bucks?" asked Reason with an odd expression on her face. Tom winced. He should've realised a hundred dollars wouldn't seem much to her.

"When I finish high school, I'm going to study fashion and then I'm going to become a world-famous designer and make clothes for movie stars. I'll get a *lot* more than a hundred dollars a dress then." *Now I sound like a total wanker,* he thought.

"Can you make normal clothes?"

"Like what?"

"You know, like jeans or shorts or T-shirts. Normal stuff."

"Sure. But why would I? Do you want me to make you something?"

"Could you make me pants with lots of pockets? All the way down both sides. Really big pockets, you know? Like army pants. Not for decoration."

"Sure," Tom said. "I can make anything." He didn't care that it sounded boastful. It was true.

Reason's stomach rumbled very loudly. They both laughed.

"Are you hungry?"

Tom led them downstairs to the kitchen, conscious with every step of how crap his house was compared to Mere's. There were only two rooms and a bathroom upstairs. Downstairs there was a lounge room, a kitchen, a tiny laundry, and a toilet. He felt stupid worrying about it, especially as Mere owned this house too.

Tom poured them glasses of orange juice and made cheese-and-tomato sandwiches. They took their sandwiches and juice up to his room, Tom with the *Gregory's* under his arm. They pushed fabric aside and sat on the floor. Reason wriggled a bit as if she was uncomfortable.

"Are you sitting on something? There might be pins, sorry."

"Nah, it's fine." She settled and took a bite of her sandwich. "Good sambo. Actually tastes like tomato."

"Yeah. Dad grows them in the backyard."

"Best kind."

They got stuck into them. Reason ate as fast as he did and the sandwiches disappeared in no time.

"How'd you get that?" Tom asked, pointing at the big graze on Reason's shin.

"Tripped on the stairs in the cellar."

"Yeah, those stairs are treacherous. Do you like living with Mere?" Tom washed the last bite of sandwich down with the rest of his orange juice.

Reason shifted again. "I've only been there one night."

"Yeah, but you've known her your whole life and—"

"We're not close. I only really met her once before and I was little. Don't really remember."

"You never met your grandfather?" Tom wondered what

kind of a man Esmeralda would choose to have a baby with. Had she been married? He couldn't picture it. Tom had never seen her go out with a man.

Reason shook her head. "So where's Kalder Park?"

"Oh, yeah," Tom said, grabbing the directory and turning to the map of all Sydney. Reason's eyes widened.

"Pretty big, eh?"

She nodded.

"So that's Kalder Park," he said, pointing, "and that's where we are."

"Not so far."

"Well, I reckon it'd take an hour and a half to walk. Lot quicker if you had a bike. I bet Mere would get you one."

Reason grunted. "I like walking."

The doorbell rang.

"That'll be Jessica. Wanna stay? She loves having an audience. She's hilarious, very Patsy."

"Patsy?"

"You don't know Patsy? From that old show? It's not on anymore. Really good, but. I've got the DVDs. We could watch them together sometime. So, you wanna stay?"

"Nah. I better get back. Does your dad's room have a balcony?"

Tom grinned. "Sure."

From the front balcony, they looked down on Jessica, who was wearing high heels and a shoestring-strap dress made of nearly transparent layered chiffon. Tom tried to imagine what

Reason would look like dressed like that. He couldn't. He'd make her something much classier. An emerald green dress, cut on the bias, simple. No bows, no ruching, nothing extra.

Tom leaned over the railing and called to Jessica, "Just a second." He turned to Reason. "Are you in one of the front rooms?"

"Uh-huh."

"Well, then, just step across."

Jessica pressed the buzzer again. "Coming," he called. "I better go, Ree. Hey, wanna hang out later? Or tomorrow?"

Reason nodded. "Sure. That'd be great."

Tom ran down the stairs, his feet barely touching them. His life had just gotten a million times better. Not only was Reason gorgeous, but odds were she was magic, just like him.

# 8
## In The Witch's Kitchen

I hoisted both legs over Tom's railing and then jumped across to my own. An old man watching from the street called out to me to bloody watch myself. I waved to him and laughed.

I now had a bag of almonds, a street directory, three escape routes—I could leave via Tom's house if I wanted—and a clear idea of how to get to Kalder Park. A most excellent morning.

I lay on the bed smiling, thinking about Tom. I'd never introduced myself to anyone using my real name before. I'd never claimed to have a nickname and he'd called me Ree just like I told him, as if it really was mine. It felt strange, but I liked it.

I liked Tom too. He talked a million miles an hour and he blushed constantly. Fair-skinned people make the best blushers, and Tom's skin was so fair it was translucent. I'd been able to see the blue veins below his skin, as though I could see right through him if I stared hard enough. I bet there was no way he could lie and get away with it—he'd turn bright pink. I trusted him.

He had a nice smile and a sense of humour, and I'd figured out long ago that looks didn't have much to say as to whether you were a good person or not.

Tom was definitely funny looking. White-blond hair paler than his skin, even, and skinny. Really skinny. The kind of skinny that made people worry if he was eating enough. Skinny like I used to be before I started getting lumps and bumps.

That's what Sarafina called them. I'd known about puberty—what menstruation was, why it happened, about breasts, hips, pubic hair, reproductive organs—for as long as I could remember. Sarafina was very determined that my head be full of facts. Information. Reason. Even so, she called them lumps and bumps. Sarafina felt the phrase was more descriptive of their power to disrupt. Plus when I called them that, it made her laugh, which wasn't always easy.

Especially not now. Tom's mother too. It was oddly comforting that we were both in the same boat. But how strange was that? Tom hadn't seemed a bit surprised, though. Maybe lots of mothers in Sydney went mad.

I'd heard about the dangers of city living all my life, and not just from Sarafina. There were lots of people in the bush who were sure that everyone in the cities was nutty and had to go off to special loony doctors to get fixed, except they never were because mostly madness is unfixable. It was all the thieves and pollution and murderers and rapists in cities that drove you mad in the first place and until that was fixed, how could city people not end up insane? In the face of such theories, Sarafina usually made pointed comments about circular logic.

Cities had not driven Sarafina mad. She hadn't lived in one

since she was twelve. I had no idea why Sarafina had changed the way she had and no idea how to fix it.

I felt bad about stealing the bag of almonds from Tom's kitchen counter, especially when they'd dug into my arse (which I knew I deserved, but still) while we ate the sandwiches in his room. But I couldn't risk running out of food and I wasn't sure what he'd say if I'd asked for them. It would've looked strange, what with Esmeralda being rich and all.

I felt bad too that we weren't going to be friends for very long. I could imagine what it would be like to stay here, to become friends with Tom. I'd never had any real friends. We'd moved too often, and besides, Sarafina wasn't wild about me making friends. Friends were people who knew things about you, like that you were on the run and that your real name wasn't Sarah or Velma or Jessie.

Tom knew my real name. I'd already had an urge to tell him things I'd never told anyone before, like that I only called Sarafina "mum" in front of strangers. It was like the fake names I had to use. I wanted to ask Tom why he didn't think it was strange that everyone called their mother the same name: mum. Maybe I'd come back some day and we'd be friends again.

I opened up the directory. I'd planned my escape all the way to Central. Maybe hitchhiking would be better? But I had no idea how you went about it in a big city. Catching a bus was probably a lot more sensible. But $250 wasn't going to go far. How was I going to get more? I thought of Tom again. A hundred bucks to make a dress. I wished I could do something like that.

Sarafina and I had made money working out people's taxes for them, doing accounts, number stuff like that. I'd also babysat, picked fruit, coached kids in maths and science, cleaned, helped Sarafina out while she tended bar.

Sometimes it was hard finding work in country towns, and we'd gone for long stretches on instant noodles and what wild grub we could find. Lots of people out bush ended up coming into cities looking for work. We never had. In the end something had always turned up.

It would be a lot harder making money without Sarafina.

I looked up and noticed another envelope sticking out from under the door. Wasn't she supposed to be at work? I placed it with the first: on the desk, unopened.

A tapping woke me. I dreamed crows were pecking at my hands. I opened my eyes. No crows. I was indoors. Lots of light. I got out of bed groggily, not quite sure where I was until I saw Tom standing on my balcony tapping at the glass.

"Ree," he called, squinting in. "Reason."

I opened the door, and he took a step back to lean against the railing. The day was still brilliant, blue and shimmering. The air was motionless and hot. I blinked, brushed a fly away.

"Hi, Tom."

"Jessica's finally gone." He rolled his eyes. Some red thread clung to the front of his T-shirt. "Hey, were you asleep? Did I wake you? Sorry. But it *is* only three in the afternoon. Do you normally sleep during the day?" Before I could reply, he continued, "Wanna hang? You seen much of Newtown yet?"

I shook my head, trying to wake up and follow his volley of questions. I stepped out on the balcony, shutting the door behind me. I'd just remembered the almonds, didn't want him spotting them.

"We could go swimming."

My eyes felt gritty. I wiped the remaining sleep away, rubbing my hands on my shorts. "I fell asleep. Didn't sleep so good last night. New place, you know?"

Tom nodded. "Aren't you used to that, but? Travelling around so much and all?"

I shrugged. I *was* good at sleeping anywhere, just not in wicked witch houses, but I was hardly going to say that. I looked up. There wasn't a cloud in the sky; it looked like it would never rain. It'd never occurred to me that drought could happen in cities as well as the bush. Not that there seemed to be a drought on; all the plants were way too green for that.

"So you want to go swimming? It's hot as."

"Not swimming." I wanted to explore more.

"We could go see a movie at the Dendy."

That was more tempting. I'd never seen a movie on television, let alone in a real cinema. I'd always wondered what they were like. But there wasn't time. I shook my head.

"But you want me to show you around sunny Newtown?" he said, sounding anxious that maybe I didn't want to do anything with him after all.

"That'd be grouse," I told him, smiling. It *would* be, plus it'd

be quicker and easier to find my way to King Street with Tom
to guide me. From what I'd seen, the streets around here were
narrow, winding, confusing.

I could remember some things from when I was in Sydney
five years ago: the smell (musk incense and chamomile tea) of
the foster home they'd put me in until the case was heard, the
endless questions about Sarafina and our life together, which
I'd answered just as she'd taught me. I remembered the nice
woman who was my lawyer. She'd seemed young, had worn
jeans and a T-shirt until we went to court and suddenly she
was all make-up and suits. At first I hadn't realised she was the
same person. She'd given me Mars bars and promised I'd get
to stay with Sarafina. She was right, I did, but not because of
the court case.

I'd only seen the streets of Sydney from car windows as I
was shuttled back and forth from my foster home to the courthouse. Until Sarafina had gotten us away and onto an interstate bus. I was pretty sure I could recognise the place the bus
left from. An old street with sandstone arches, close to where
all the buildings got tall and close together. There'd been a
park, just across the road. And lots and lots of pigeons.

"Now?" Tom asked. "You wanna go now?"

"Sure," I said, fixing my thoughts on the present, on *this*
escape. "Can we go like you said? Not touching the ground?" It
was probably a bit daggy, but it sounded like fun.

Tom grinned. "Only way *to* go."

There was a loud knock on my bedroom door. "Reason!"

"That'll be Mere," Tom said, turning around. "Coming," he called out. Before I could stop him, he was across the room and opening the bedroom door, me trailing behind, a protest not quite escaping my lips.

"Hi, Mere," he said, kissing her cheek, not seeming at all embarrassed at being busted in my bedroom. "How're you going?"

I didn't avert my gaze, turn around, or run away. Esmeralda was looking right at me and I was looking back.

I didn't turn to stone. (Not that I ever thought I would.) I squeezed the ammonite in my pocket, then rubbed my thumb over its smooth surface. It wasn't as comforting as I needed.

She hadn't changed much in five years. Except that now she looked even more like Sarafina. A short Sarafina with wavy hair. She was wearing one of the black suits from her wardrobe. I hoped it was the jacket with the upside-down feather.

"You two have met, I see." Esmeralda smiled at Tom; the smile faded a little when it got to me. I looked for malice, but there was only sadness in her expression. She reached out a hand as if to touch me, but let it drop. She half smiled again, apologetically. I almost said, "sorry," myself. Almost returned her smile.

"She can make you believe almost anything," Sarafina had told me. "She should have been an actress."

"We met in your fig tree." Tom grinned at me. "We were both climbing."

"Filomena doing good again?"

Tom nodded, looking sideways at me, his cheeks growing pink. "That's what we call the tree," Tom explained. "I know it sounds lame, but she seems almost human sometimes. You know, when the wind's blowing and . . ." He trailed off, his face completely red.

"I was going to ask Reason if she wanted afternoon tea." Esmeralda glanced at her watch. "I've got half an hour before I have to be back at the office. There's chocolate muffins, cinnamon rolls, and lemon tarts. Want some?"

"Brilliant," said Tom.

I nodded, though there was no way I was going to eat any of it. I wondered how long I could get away with saying nothing. I followed them down the stairs, trying to take up the Fibs from where I'd left off—Fib (55): 139,583,862,445—and rotating the ammonite through my fingers.

Esmeralda spoke softly, close to Tom's ear. Tom nodded and they pulled apart. Esmeralda asked him something about his studies. Apparently she was tutoring him. H. S. C. Black Arts? I hoped not. I didn't like the idea of Tom being involved in her "magic." Tom asked Esmeralda if I'd be joining them. Joining them doing what? I wondered. Not that it mattered. I'd be gone before too long.

They were comfortable together. Though Tom seemed to have a crush on her—his cheeks kept going red. But Tom's cheeks seemed to go red all the time no matter what.

I sat on the stool next to Tom's, leaving no room for

Esmeralda to sit near me. He was examining the array of
cakes, trying to decide which one to have. The cinnamon rolls
were almost as big as my head. I could smell the butter, and
they dripped with cinnamon sugar.

Esmeralda was opening the windows wider. A cool breeze
was starting to blow. It felt wonderful sliding past us.

"Southerly's starting to hit," she said. "Can you run and
open the front door, Tom? Use the stop. Nice to get some air
through."

"Sure," he said, jumping up.

"Help yourself, Reason," Esmeralda said, sitting opposite
me and taking a cinnamon roll. Her hands looked young, as if
they'd never seen the sun, the fingernails long and even,
painted a browny red. Like blood, I decided, though really the
colour was more like that of the earth up north.

Tom returned, plonked himself down. "Chocolate muffin,
please." He picked out the biggest one and bit in. "Mmmm,"
he said with his mouth full. "It's pretty blowy out there.
Clouds coming in. Might be a storm."

The sound of the wind in the tree, in *Filomena,* was getting
louder. There was a sharp noise as branches scraped the side of
the house. I found it comforting that the weather could change
as fast in the city as it did in the bush.

Esmeralda nodded. "One's predicted, but for later."

"Should I open the back door, too?" I asked, standing up. I
directed the question to Tom, so technically I still hadn't spoken to Esmeralda.

Tom looked at Esmeralda. I couldn't quite read the expression on his face. I put my hand on the doorknob.

"No need," Esmeralda said.

I turned the handle, but it didn't move. Just like before. "It's locked," I said to no one in particular. "I wonder where the key is?" In my backpack, maybe?

"I'm not sure," Esmeralda said. "The lock sticks. I keep meaning to get it replaced. In the meantime I go out the front door and use the side passage."

I'd heard her go out the back door that morning. Why was she lying? Sarafina had told me that she lied about everything. The more Esmeralda knew, and the less everyone else did, the more powerful she felt. Her "magic" was all about having power over other people. Even in the petty matter of the whereabouts of a key. I shrugged and sat down. I'd try the infinity key on the door later.

"You should have a muffin," Tom said, taking another for himself. "They're fantastic."

"Not hungry," I said, though as usual I was starving. "Still full from all the sandwiches at your place."

"That was hours ago!"

Esmeralda looked at me, her brow creasing. "You haven't eaten much since you got here, Reason. You sure you won't have some?"

"Maybe later." I didn't look at her when I said it, but there was no escaping that I'd answered her question.

"There's potato salad in the fridge and a quiche. Bought

them with the pastries. And cheese and chorizo and lots of other things. Help yourself," she said, standing up and pushing her stool under the counter.

I thought of the frogs and brains and liver and snails Sarafina had told me about. But somehow I couldn't imagine them in her huge stainless steel fridge alongside the cheese and cake.

Esmeralda reached out a hand as though she was going to pat my shoulder but instead brushed a few imaginary crumbs from her skirt. "I have to get back to work, might not be home till late." She paused. Her eyes were wide looking at me, hopeful. "I know you've been through a lot. I've tried to give you some space. . . ." She trailed off. "Maybe we'll talk later?"

I looked down and muttered.

She bent forward but instead of kissing my forehead kissed the air. I heard the light smack of her lips against Tom's cheek.

"See you both later," she said, dashing out the front door. It slammed behind her. For a second I wished she *had* kissed me and instantly felt that I'd betrayed Sarafina. All because of some pretty-looking cakes. *Don't let her charm you.*

"Bye!" Tom called before turning to me. "Want to have the quiche now?"

I shook my head. "Not hungry. You still going to show me around? Not touching the ground once?"

"Sure," Tom said. He grabbed a lemon tart and wolfed it down as we climbed out the window.

# 9
# Cemetery

"So how do we get across?" Reason asked.

It had taken them barely ten minutes to get here from Mere's. Reason did *not* climb like a girl. Tom was dead impressed at how easily she kept up with him despite the wind as they climbed along tree, fence, wall, roof, ladder to this corner where they now perched on the low brick fence around the microscopic front yard of Elohtihs Ruo.

Every time Tom saw the plaque—all fancy cursive writing and a picture of a rose-covered cottage bearing no resemblance to this one—he cracked up. Elohtihs Ruo! He bet whoever'd first come up with Emoh Ruo was pretty cranky, ropeable even. Around here the other houses with plaques mostly had try-too-hard names like Bates Motel or Burning Palms Cottage with a picture of upturned hands burning. None came close to topping Elohtihs Ruo.

He and Reason looked at the park on the other side of the road; all the rain this summer had made it ridiculously green. A Newtown mums' group (including some token dads) were packing away a picnic, which involved much running after hats and rubbish and even Tupperware picked up by the southerly, holding skirts down and hair out of eyes while trying to round up their children crazily running around fuelled on sugar and barometric pressure, committing mayhem and interfering with the uni students' already crap cricket game (they were using a tennis ball, a plastic bat, and for the stumps an upended esky, which kept blowing away). Beyond them was the cemetery wall, the church spire, and a jungle of trees, riotous in the wind.

It all seemed impossibly far. Squat bottlebrush trees lined the footpath, none of them strong enough to support his or Reason's weight. Not that any of the branches spread out far enough over the road. There was no way of getting across without touching the ground. Tom regretted his wild claim. He'd been half hoping for another opportunely placed ladder. Or a crane or *something*.

"Well, okay, I admit it. I exaggerated a tad."

Reason's eyebrows went up. "A tad? No *way* can we get across."

"We don't *have* to go to the cemetery." Tom had spent the whole windswept journey selling Reason on the glories of the cemetery, as well as hinting at the certain something he wanted to show her. He was pretty sure she didn't know about it.

She and Mere didn't exactly seem to know each other well. He wondered what that was about. Reason seemed great, and he knew that Mere was, so why weren't they getting on like a house on fire? Reason had gotten quiet as soon as Mere showed up, had hardly looked her in the eye. She hadn't touched any of her food either, though she must have been as hungry as he was.

And on top of that Mere had whispered to him not to mention things to Reason, giving "things" a slight emphasis so that he knew she was talking about magic. He'd raised his eyebrows, but Reason had been right there, so Mere couldn't explain. Why would she tell him not to mention it? Reason was her granddaughter and seemed to be magic herself; surely she'd know all about *things?* Unless she wasn't magic? Tom found that hard to believe; there was something about her, about the way she'd climbed that tree.

As it happened, he hadn't said a word to Reason. That was just standard cautiousness. It wasn't something he talked about with anyone but Mere. His dad knew, but he wasn't magic, and the idea of it scared him. Especially the way it was with his mum. They almost never spoke of magic. Tom wasn't even allowed to tell his sister. Mere had been very firm about that. As far as she was concerned, it was bad enough that his dad had to know.

But Tom'd planned on dropping Reason a few hints. Like taking her to the graveyard. He figured Mere wouldn't mind as long as Reason brought the subject up.

"We *do* have to go, Tom. You made it sound amazing. I want to see."

"I could carry you," he offered. She couldn't weigh that much. Not that she was likely to say yes.

Reason giggled. "Okay. That counts. You didn't say we'd *both.* be able to go blocks and blocks, you just said me."

Tom liked her reinterpretation. He also liked the idea of getting to hold Reason. *Best day ever.* He grinned and slid off the fence. "Okay, my unworthy feet are on the ground. Shoulder carry or piggyback?"

"Which is easier for you?"

"Piggyback," Tom said. The grin was not going to leave his face anytime soon.

"Ready?"

She sat down on the fence and put her arms around his neck. Their faces were very close. He slipped his hands under her thighs, filthy pleased with himself, and took an unsteady step forward. He let out a grunt.

"You right?"

"Yeah," Tom said, talking almost normally. *Heaven,* he thought, stepping slowly to the curb.

He looked both ways to check for traffic. Australia Street could be busy. A truck drove by, then two sedans, lastly two erratically riding cyclists, tennis rackets slung over their backs, having a shouted conversation about someone with the unlikely name of Chip. Tom looked both ways again, pausing briefly at the feel of her cheek against his when he turned his head left. Warm, delicious.

"No cars, Tom. Let's go."

"Right."

*Think about the road, Tom.* He sprinted across, feeling Reason's cheek still resting against his, her breath mixing with his. It would be dead easy for them to kiss. Her warmth and closeness outweighed the annoyance of her hair flicking into his eyes. Tom kept running across the park.

"Hey," Reason said.

Tom decided that with the wind, he could pretend not to have heard her. He could feel the tension of her muscles shifting; she definitely wanted down.

"Hey!" she shouted, her mouth in his ear. "You can let me down now."

"It's okay," Tom said, still running. "You're not heavy."

"Tom! Let me down. You're too bony. My legs hurt."

Reluctantly Tom dropped Reason to the path. They were both wobbly for a second. Reason rubbed her thighs, looking up at him with a grin. "Made it. Ta."

"No worries." Tom dodged a bit of newspaper flying past. He looked up. Clouds were hurtling by; the sun kept disappearing. He saw jagged lightning flash briefly in the south. "Come on. Storm's not far off."

The delight on Reason's face pleased Tom so much that despite his resolve to kill his inner dag (*must not be too enthusiastic*), he clapped. Reason clapped too.

"Bloody hell," she said. "You'd hardly know you were in the city. It looks like a country graveyard. Only, I don't know, spookier."

"Isn't it great? You step from the street and the cars to this, and whoosh, everything's changed. This place is so old they don't even bury people here anymore."

Most of the graves were more than a hundred years old. Wherever you stepped, there were gravestones and statues falling to pieces. Where there weren't graves, there were trees, lots of overgrown trees, their roots pushing up, knocking over more tombstones.

"Used to be even bigger," Tom said. "The whole park—you know, where they were playing cricket and everything? That used to be part of the cemetery too."

"You're kidding," Reason said, eyes wide. "We were walking on top of lots and lots of dead people?"

"Yup. See all the gravestones along the cemetery wall?"

Reason turned to look at the orphaned gravestones, long separated from their plots, sides touching, backs to the wall, like they were facing a firing squad. There were hundreds of them along the entire length of the high cemetery wall, made, like most of the gravestones, of sandstone. Their inscriptions so worn you could hardly identify so much as a single letter, though Tom liked to peer at them and guess.

Sandstone wears fast. Tom had wondered why people used it all over Sydney since it practically crumbled in seconds, but then Mere had explained that sandstone was pretty much the only local stone. Granite and marble and other harder stones all had to be imported.

"It's normally much quieter." The wall kept out sound, as well as blocking any view of the surrounding houses and most of the tall buildings on King Street.

"What, when there's not a gale blowing?"

Tom grinned. It was *way* more than a bit blowy now. The sound of the wind through the trees, their branches waving wildly, assaulting each other, was a steady roar, almost drowning out the sound of thunder in the distance. The intense heat of the day had all been blown away—it was almost comfortable now.

"You should see this place when the sun's blazing through the trees." He stretched his arms, taking in the dilapidated tombstones, the twisting trees, the church. "Everything glows. It's like there's a force field around it. The light's brighter, no sounds from outside. You can't even hear the cars passing by."

Reason shivered. "Perfect for ghosts."

Tom held out his hand, and she took it unselfconsciously. He led her along a well-trodden path. "Come on, I'll show you the most famous resident. If there's a ghost here, it'd be her. The story's excellent. And then"—he paused dramatically— "the mysterious thing I have to show you. Watch out for the dog shit." He stepped over it, pulling her after him.

They passed a couple, huddled together on a tombstone that had been knocked flat to the ground, trying to light a cigarette that kept going out in the wind. Reason said hi and they both nodded at her.

"I swear most of the people buried here drowned in Sydney Harbour," Tom said, pointing to the nearest drowned-in-the-harbour inscription. "The early settlers weren't much chop at swimming."

Reason giggled. "They still aren't. I met these English backpackers at Woolgoolga on the beach, and they didn't know how to swim. They just lay on their towels and turned pink, too scared to put more than a toe in the water. Weird, huh? Wasn't even stinger season."

Tom nodded. "There's this French girl at school. . . . Hey, do you know what school you'll be going to?"

"Nope."

"Hope Esmeralda doesn't send you private. If you go public, you might be at the same school as me. Wouldn't that be great?"

Reason nodded, not looking as enthusiastic as he'd've liked, but he figured that was the thought of school, not the thought of school with him. He wondered again if Reason would be studying with him at Mere's.

"Anyway, the French girl couldn't swim. Tried to get out of it when we were all doing our Bronze Medallions—"

"What are they?"

Tom looked at her, startled. "You know, lifesaving certificates? Jump in the deep end with all your clothes on and tread water for forever? Fake rescue someone?"

Reason shook her head. "Never did any lifesaving."

"Really? I thought all schools taught it."

"We moved around a lot."

"But you can swim?"

"Yeah. Of course!"

"Right, then. So the French girl was trying to get out of it, but they made her have lessons. So we're at the deep end pretending to drown and then saving each other, and she's in the shallow end screaming her head off, sounding like she *really* needs to be saved."

"Did she learn?"

"Yeah. But she's pretty crap. Doesn't like putting her head in the water. Worried about getting her hair wet or something. Almost there." He stepped off the path, where three gravestones stood packed close together with no discernible graves in front of them.

"So is this it?"

Tom shook his head. "Not yet. Have to tell you the story first."

"Story?"

"Have you read *Great Expectations?*"

"Nope. Never heard of it."

"It's by an old English guy. Shakespeare, maybe? Whatever. I haven't read it, saw the movie, but. There's this old nutter, Miss Havisham. When she was young, she was going to be married, but on her wedding day the bloke never showed up. She was rich, so the whole house was decked out with flowers and there was this huge cake and stuff. And everyone was just sitting around waiting for him to show, but he never did.

"She went into shock. Totally lost it. Never took off her wedding dress or let them clear away any of the wedding gear. Not the cake or the flowers or the food or anything. It crumbled and decayed, was covered in the thickest dust and cobwebs. Stayed like that till she was really, really old."

"Ugggh." Reason shivered. "But that's just a book, right?"

Tom nodded. "But it was based on someone real. That's it there." He pointed to a marble cross under a small copse of trees. "At the bottom, that's her. The real person Shakespeare based the book on. She lived right here in Sydney. That's her father, James Donnithorne Esq., at the top with the big important lettering."

Reason crouched down. You had to get close to make out the smaller letters. She held her hair out of her eyes and read out loud, "'Eliza Emily. Last surviving daughter of the above. Died 20th May 1886.' Yet another loony lady," she said. "Sydney's full of them."

Tom crouched down beside her. "Yeah. Just like our mums. Except, you know, ours have better hygiene: my mum changes once a day, not once a century."

"Did she hurt you badly?" asked Reason. "When she tried to kill you?" She looked concerned, which made Tom squirm. He didn't much enjoy people feeling sorry for him.

"No, Dad got there first. She was waving a knife around saying that she'd kill us. She cut Cathy, but Dad reckons it was an accident. Cath's got a scar on her shoulder, it's tiny, but."

"Cathy's your sister?"

"Yeah." Tom stood up, then Reason. "She's studying at film school in America."

"Wow."

"Pretty cool, huh?"

Reason nodded.

"She's studying at NYU. That's New York University in New York City."

"Long way from home."

"When I finish high school, I'm going to go study there too," Tom told her. "Or maybe London. Or Milan. I wanna study fashion. I'm going to make beautiful clothes for women and have my own label like Chanel or Balenciaga or Schiaparelli."

"Wow," said Reason, sounding impressed, though Tom could tell she'd never heard of any of them.

"Don't worry. I'll still make you normal clothes. I've already started on your cargo pants." Reason looked blank. "The pants with all the pockets? You know? That you asked for?"

"Oh, right," Reason said. "Ta. That was quick."

Tom shrugged. "I'll show you the sketches tomorrow probably, then we can go fabric shopping."

They were still staring down at Eliza Emily's grave. Tom was imagining what her wedding dress had looked like, how it would've changed as it disintegrated. He fashioned the acute triangles in his mind until they became a dress of silver-grey cobwebs that hung from head to toe. Kind of fairytale goth, only with more elegant lines. Bias-cut 1930s à la Vionnet. The material would be designed to dissolve slowly. Sleeves melting away first, then maybe the back. He'd have to design an elegant slip dress to go underneath. But where would he get a fabric like that? Could he learn to make it himself? How about sleeves made from real cobwebs?

Reason punched him lightly on the shoulder. "Hey, Tom. Where's the mystery thing you promised?"

"This way." Tom led her past more trees, graves, and the roped-off area where they were trying to get native grasses growing again.

"Drowned in Sydney Harbour. Only sixteen years old." Reason pointed to a broken-up grave whose tilting headstone featured two engraved anchors. "That's five."

"See the anchor over there? The real one?"

Reason nodded, looking across at the little alcove and the fenced-off grave with the anchor lying on top.

"This huge ship, the *Dunbar*, went down in the olden days and that's where most of the people are buried. *All of them* drowned in Sydney Harbour."

"How many?"

"Hundreds."

"Bloody hell."

Tom nodded. "The anchor really is from the *Dunbar*. They dredged it up from the bottom of the harbour. You want to look at it or are you ready for the thing I told you about? It's just over here."

"The mystery," Reason said.

He led her to a tall monument next to a large palm tree. At its top was an angel holding a book in one hand and a sword in the other. Her wings were longer than her body. All four sides of the monument had names and dates on them, the oldest at the top.

"Oh," Reason said, staring at the names. Almost everyone shared the same last name: Cansino. "They're my relatives?"

Tom nodded.

Reason circled the monument, staring, openmouthed. "They're almost all women."

Tom nodded again, amazed that she really didn't know anything about her family.

"With the same surname."

"Yeah. See? Here's one of the few men." He pointed to the first male name, Raul Emilio Jesús Cansino, right at the top. "He's a Cansino. I'm thinking he's where the name comes from, but after him there are only a few men and their last names aren't Cansino. All the women, though—"

"All the same as me," Reason finished. "Cansinos." She was tracing her fingers across one name: Sarafina Maria Luz Cansino. "My mother wasn't the first Sarafina."

Tom shook his head. "Nope. Look, there's an Esmeralda. See how the names get repeated? Lots of Milagros and Luzs and that's not counting the middle names. See how none of them are described as 'loving wife' or 'daughter of'?"

"Just 'mother of.'"

"That's right. This is the only tombstone that tells so little about how they're related. Weird, huh?"

Reason was looking intently at the inscription for Esmeralda Milagros Luz Cansino—born in 1823—a strange expression on her face.

"What?" Tom asked.

"She died so young."

Tom glanced at the dates, working it out. "Eighteen. They died a lot younger in the olden days. You don't know much about your family, do you?" Why was she surprised? Of course they died young. Tom was disappointed. Maybe he'd been wrong about Reason.

She shook her head. "Not really. Just what Sarafina told me: everything she knows about my dad, which is not much, and about growing up with Esmeralda. She didn't talk about family history."

"Huh."

Reason moved to the next name. "This one was only twenty, and this one twenty-one, fourteen, five—ha!—look at this: *Gone before her time.* What about the rest of them? Were they all *on* time? Next one, nineteen, then twenty, twenty-five." She glanced at each set of dates for a split second before announcing the age. As fast as Esmeralda would've done it. She *had* to be magic too.

"Wow, Ree," Tom said. "You're really good at maths!"

Reason looked at him as if he was a bit slow. "That's not maths, that's just arithmetic."

"Whatever. I've never seen anyone add so fast. You definitely are Mere's granddaughter."

"Actually, it's mostly subtraction." She moved to the next side. "Twelve, sixteen, twenty-seven, twenty again. Tom, look, they *all* died young."

"Not all." He pointed to John Matthew Douglas

O'Shaughnessy. "Sixty-five," he said, after *way* more than a
split second.

"He's a man," Reason said. "You look, all the men live a
decent amount. Except for the first, Raul." She pointed. "Him
you can't tell. See? Died in 1823."

Tom looked. Raul Cansino's year of birth was a question
mark. "But all the women." Mere had said it ran strong in her
family.

"Not all," Reason said. She'd come to the last name,
Esmeralda's mother. "Here's one: Milagros Luz Cansino, forty-
eight. She was practically an old lady." Reason was staring at
the plainly etched name. "But neither of her sisters made it
past twenty. This tomb is so well kept," she said, turning to
look at Tom. "Most of the other ones are overgrown and broken, hard to read. I haven't seen any others so recent either. I
thought the cemetery wasn't being used anymore."

"It isn't. Except for your family." Tom looked at Milagros
Cansino's dates.

"Is that my great-grandmother?"

Tom nodded. He was feeling stupid for not having figured
out Esmeralda's age based on her mother's dates. Though
Mere could have been a late baby.

"So she lived to be forty-eight. Esmeralda is forty-five.
Sarafina thirty. That's three who've made it to thirty. What
happened to the others? Do you know, Tom?"

Tom shook his head, trying to look innocent. He knew,
though he could hardly say so after Mere's request. It had to

do with magic. He wasn't from a long line like Reason. As far as he knew, his mother was the first, and she didn't understand what she was. It scared her. Tom had only been rescued by Esmeralda a year ago—there was still a *lot* he didn't know. But he did know that magic was dangerous, that it could, and usually did, kill you. Those with magic almost never lived long lives. If Reason was magic and didn't know *that*, Mere should tell her as soon as she could.

There was loud crack of thunder. They both jumped. Fat raindrops started to fall; within seconds they were both drenched.

# 10

# In The Asylum

My mother, Sarafina, was mad and my grandmother, Esmeralda, was evil. I wondered what that made me. Mad evil? Evil mad? Was that why the women in my family rarely made it past thirty?

I didn't feel evil or mad; I wanted to have a long, normal life.

The next morning, as soon as I was sure Esmeralda was gone, I went to see Sarafina. There'd been another letter under the door when I woke up. I couldn't bring myself to do more than glance at my name in her handwriting. I added it to the first two.

The walk to where they were keeping her, Kalder Park, took less than half as long as Tom had said. He probably didn't walk very often or very far. City folk.

It would've been even quicker if there hadn't been so many cars and trucks. Some of the roads were impossible to cross anywhere but at a pedestrian crossing, and the lights took forever to change.

When I was close, I stopped at a café and bought breakfast. Eggs and bacon and chips. Twelve dollars, it cost. I wondered if the eggs were made of gold or something. They didn't taste any different to normal eggs.

Across the road a sign had KALDER PARK written on it in big letters. I'd expected grey, looming buildings with bars on the windows and no greenery in sight. Instead there were hardly any buildings visible. It really was a park.

I finished my breakfast and crossed the road, walking among the trees and buildings trying to find the entrance. The park was next to a bay; as I walked, I watched the glitter of sunlight on the water and sailboats zigzagging across. If my mother weren't locked up here, I would never have guessed this was a hospital for the mentally ill.

In fact, one-half of the park was an art school. The buildings had the name of the school on them in big letters. Instead of loonies shambling about, students dressed in black sketched the bay with intense expressions or lay back in the grass with their mates, laughing and smoking cigarettes. They didn't seem too bothered about drifting over onto hospital grounds. Not that it was easy to tell where the one ended and the other began.

Some of the buildings were run-down looking, but the ivy-covered sandstone walls weren't depressing. The place was well worn, not neglected. And anyway, judging from the outside, the art school was in worse repair than the hospital.

I finally found reception in a small redbrick cottage. Inside, nothing remained of the home it had once been. The internal walls had been knocked down and now it was a waiting room, with chairs up against the walls, a wooden box full of kids' toys, a table overflowing with pamphlets, and a large curved white desk. The woman sitting behind it looked up from a computer screen and smiled as I walked in. There was no one else in the room.

"Can I help you?" she asked.

"I'd like to see my mother."

"Do you have an appointment?"

"Um, no," I said, feeling stupid. I should've asked Tom to describe the place and how it worked.

"Have you visited her here before?"

I shook my head.

"Didn't think so. Visiting hours don't start for another half hour."

"At eleven?"

She nodded. "Has your mother been here long?"

I shook my head again. Apparently they weren't used to fifteen-year-old girls just showing up and asking to see their mum.

"What's her name?"

"Sarafina Cansino."

"Why don't you take a seat and we'll see what we can do?"

I sat down. There was no one else waiting. I picked up one of the pamphlets: "Understanding Mental Illness" in large red letters above a picture of a woman holding her head and grimacing. As if being crazy was like having a headache. I put it down and stared out the window, seeing nothing.

It was Tuesday. I'd arrived at Esmeralda's on Sunday afternoon. I'd last seen my mother on Saturday. Only three days ago. How could that be? Everything had happened so quickly that I'd lost any sense of time. It seemed like ages since my coming to Sydney, but also like yesterday. My life before could have been a dream. Or I could be in the dream right now.

My stomach was in knots. As badly as I wanted to see Sarafina, I was also afraid. The last time had been in the Dubbo hospital. They'd pumped Sarafina's stomach, bandaged her wrists and throat.

I'd sat by her bed all night and into the morning, dozing in a chair. She'd mostly been unconscious and when she did come around for a few seconds, her eyes were unfocussed and watery. She didn't recognise me.

A policewoman and a social worker came and asked me if I was right to talk to them. I said I was, though I hadn't slept and my head felt strange and I was worried I'd start crying if I told them what'd happened.

They bought me breakfast and were kind, but I still cried when I answered their questions. When I went back to Sarafina's room, she was conscious.

She started screaming as soon as I walked in. She was strapped to the bed. As I walked closer, she only got louder. There were no words, just a raw, violent, piercing noise. It went straight through my head.

"Sarafina," I said, trying to sound soothing.

Sarafina screamed louder, words this time. "Get out! Get out! Get out! Get out! Get out!"

She strained forward, fighting to break the straps. Like she wanted to leap at me. Tear me to pieces. Her eyes were blood hot. They looked like they were going to pop right out of her head. Sarafina was wild and terrifying. She hardly even looked human.

"Get out! Get out! Get out! Get out! Get out!"

Nurses had come running, a doctor. They'd injected Sarafina

with something. Another nurse led me away, promising that I'd be able to see my mother again, later, when she'd calmed down. But I'd been flown to Sydney and my grandmother's house instead.

Sarafina had been mad before. But not like that. She had never, ever turned on me.

Sarafina talked to people who weren't there. She insisted we walk in straight lines, for days at a time. Sometimes she got confused, wasn't sure where or who she was. Then I would lead her back to the hotel room or caravan or campsite—wherever it was we were staying—and explain where we were and why and give Sarafina a mathematical or logic problem to solve. She always could. Solving the problem would bring her back.

Her episodes never lasted long, and until Dubbo she'd never been scary mad. I wasn't sure I could cope with my mother screaming at me again. Not like that.

Like she'd wanted to kill me.

"Reason Cansino?" asked a nurse.

"Yes."

"Are you hungry, love?"

I nodded, surprised by the question. The eggs and bacon had gone nowhere. I was still starving.

The nurse handed me a plate of Iced VoVos and shortbread. Not my favourites, but I was that hungry, I probably would have eaten frogs or brains or snails. The almonds I'd stolen from Tom's yesterday hadn't lasted long.

"Your mum'll be ready soon. She was asleep."

I tried to imagine Sarafina asleep this late in the day.

"Do you want to wait outside and eat your biscuits? It's closer to the visitors' room." The nurse pointed to a bench nearby. "Won't be long."

I sat on the bench, which overlooked the bay, munching on my bickies. A group of joggers ran by near the waterline. They were sweating so hard I could see drops of water flying off them. It was so hot. I thought they were completely mad. What was the point of running in circles, with no destination in mind? Especially on such a scorching day.

I had so many questions for Sarafina. Why was the house so different from how she had described it? Light and clean and beautiful. Did my mother know what the infinity key opened? Why hadn't she told me about our family? Did she know why all those women had died so young?

I pulled the ammonite out of my pocket, stared at it. Was it still lucky? I'd lost it countless times, but I'd always been able to find it again, even the time it fell out of my pocket and into the Roper River. I'd waded in, found it in the mud almost straightaway, like it was calling to me, then waded out again. Then Sarafina had pulled me into her arms and away from the riverbank as quick as she could. Two large crocs had been only metres away.

"She's ready, love," said the same nurse. "She wanted to wash and comb her hair before she saw you. Make herself nice, you know?"

I nodded and followed her. My stomach unknotted a little. Combed hair sounded like a good sign.

The nurse led me into the visitors' room, large and light, with lots of windows, which only highlighted its drabness. The lounge furniture was all brown, but each brown was faded to a different shade, none of it matched. The floor was covered in checked brown, beige and white linoleum, almost worn through in places. Seven people sat on the different couches and chairs, some wore robes, others pyjamas, all were clearly patients.

The nurse led me to a woman in a white terry-towelling robe, sitting in an overlarge chair on the verge of swallowing her. It took me a moment to realise that she was my mother. She was so still. She could have been carved out of wood or stone by one of the art students. She sat staring out the window. She didn't even seem to blink. Sarafina had never been a still person.

"Sarafina," I said. My mother did not turn to look at me.

Her hair did look newly combed, but it had a centre part. Sarafina always parted her hair on the left. Her hair was much shorter too. An uneven bob, just past her ears, instead of the shoulder-length cut I was used to. There was grey in it.

"Sarafina," I said again. I wondered if I should take her hand. It looked very small and thin. It was hard to tell through the bulky robe, but Sarafina looked thinner all over. Except her face, which was kind of puffy, bloated.

"Reason," she said. Her voice was flat, toneless.

I waited for Sarafina to say more. She didn't. I still hadn't seen her blink.

"Sarafina?"

"You look well," she said.

"Thank you," I said, though she hadn't looked at me and couldn't know how I looked. She looked terrible.

"Are you working for your grandmother now?" Sarafina asked in the same toneless voice.

"Am I? No. I mean, I . . . I haven't spoken to her." Well *hardly* spoken to her, I amended silently. "I haven't eaten any of her food. I know how to escape and I've gotten some supplies. And I—"

"That's good." Sarafina didn't sound pleased or displeased. There was no emotion in her voice.

I felt my eyes filling with tears. I clenched my hands. I wasn't going to cry. "You've got a bag," I began, "with three black marbles, two white marbles, and one red. You draw the first marble out, and—"

"You don't want to work for her."

"For Esmeralda?"

"Yes, Esmeralda. You don't want to work for her."

"No, of course not. I don't want to work for anyone."

"No," Sarafina said. "That's wise. Don't work for anyone. They'll only steal from you. You have to keep what's yours."

"Keep what's mine?"

Sarafina nodded. It was the first movement she'd made, but her eyes were still fixed on something outside the window, the sparkling water, maybe? I wasn't sure Sarafina was looking at anything. Her voice was completely flat. "But don't use it. Never use what you have."

"Use what, Sarafina?"

"Best you dig her up. Start with that."

"What?" I said, not quite managing to keep the frustration out of my voice. She was making no sense.

"You'll find her in the southeast corner. The cellar."

"Find who?"

"You'll have to shift the stones. It's not deep. Not difficult either. Just use your hands."

"You want me to—"

"It's not too bad," Sarafina said, as if she hadn't heard me. "Being insane. It's not too bad at all. There are worse things. It's pretty here." Then she was quiet again, her face completely closed. She didn't respond to anything more I said.

A nurse came and led Sarafina back to her room. I watched as she moved away slowly, not shuffling, just slow, as though she existed in a different, slower-paced world. Sarafina had never been a slow person.

The kind nurse asked me if I was okay.

I managed a nod. I didn't want to cry. I hadn't asked Sarafina any of my questions and had completely forgotten about the pin number for the bank card. I wondered if I'd ever be able to talk with her properly again.

"It's hard to see someone you love like that," the nurse said.

I nodded again.

"She's been doing quite well here. She's stopped trying to harm herself and she hasn't had any screaming fits. She's improved."

"She sounded so . . ." I paused. I wasn't sure what word I wanted. "Empty? She didn't sound like herself."

"Your mum is on a lot of medication. It takes time for the doctors to get the balance right so that she can be your mother again without wanting to harm herself."

"She never used to want to do that. We were happy." It sounded lame, even to me.

The nurse squeezed my hand, which only made me want to cry more.

"It will get better. It's good that you came to visit her. It will remind your mum of how things used to be."

I nodded, standing up. "I'll come visit again."

There was no question about it. I was going to rescue Sarafina. We would escape together. The hospital wasn't going to make her well, filling her with drugs that made her slow and strange. Sarafina just needed to find her old self. She would never be able to do that drugged to the gills.

I hadn't planned to run away with Sarafina because I had been thinking about the screaming, terrifying Sarafina. I had to concentrate on remembering the fun Sarafina, the one who had been my mother, my best friend.

I had imagined myself running away, just as my mother had run when she was even younger than me. Alone. Sarafina had escaped Esmeralda and made her own way in the world, even when she'd had a small baby to look after. I wanted to be as brave and resourceful as that.

I would be. And I would have someone to look after too: my mother.

## 11

## Going Underground

As soon as i got back to the house, I went down into the cellar, hoping to make sense of the only understandable thing Sarafina had said. The cool down there was a relief. I'd still have ages alone in the house, even if Esmeralda came home early from work. I had no idea when she'd gotten in last night. I'd fallen into a deep sleep thinking about all my dead relatives with their short, short lives.

The cellar was much easier to negotiate with lights blazing. This time I managed to avoid banging into the wine racks and stumbling on the uneven stones underfoot. In the southeast corner the stones were rougher, none of them bigger than a brick.

The racks of wine stopped about half a metre from the wall. Even for someone my size, it was a tight fit. I sat with my back to the wall and tried to get my hands around the biggest stone. It wasn't easy getting hold of it. The stone was wedged in tight. Using both hands, I heaved. The stone moved, making a groaning sound as it rubbed against the others, and then came flying out so fast I whacked myself in the nose. In my shock, I dropped it on my toe.

"Bugger! Bugger! Bugger!" My nose hurt like hell and was bleeding fast and heavy. "Bugger."

I took my T-shirt off, balled it up, and pressed it to my face. My hands were shaking and my nose throbbed with pain. What if I'd broken it?

*Not difficult,* Sarafina had said!

With my left hand pressing the T-shirt to my nose, I pulled out several of the smaller stones with my right. The only thing that held them in place had been the pressure of being jammed together. There was no grouting, no cement. With the large nose-crushing stone removed, all I had to do was lift the others out of the way.

Underneath the stones was a metal container about the size of a large shoe box. I was relieved—there *was* something in the southeast corner. Sarafina hadn't just been rambling. And it wasn't the trapdoor leading down to a chamber of horrors like I'd been imagining, where the "she" Sarafina had mentioned would turn out to be a zombie ready to eat me alive. The metal box wasn't big enough for a person, even an undead one.

I lifted the last remaining stones and tried to pull the box out. It was heavy, hardly budged at all. I felt around the lid to see if I could open it and found nothing.

Needing both hands to lift it out, I dropped the sodden T-shirt to my lap and felt my nose gingerly. The flow of blood had become a trickle, but I couldn't breathe out of it. Under my fingertips it felt grotesque and huge, swollen to several times its normal size. I wiped at the blood again with my T-shirt, realising that I should probably get some ice on it. The box first.

I tucked the bloody T-shirt into the top of my shorts, then stretched out my legs on either side of the metal box. As I heaved, my head throbbed. The effort of pulling made my nose hurt more. The box shifted some, making a loud scraping sound. Then it fell back, heavier than Uluru.

I pulled again, bending from the waist and bracing my feet against the brick wine racks. The box moved again. Blood from my nose and sweat from my face dripped into my mouth, but if I closed my lips, I couldn't breathe.

Finally the box came out, landing on the uneven ground with a tremendous echoing crash. The nearest wine bottles rattled loudly. For a moment I couldn't hear anything and wondered if I'd broken my eardrums as well as my nose. If Esmeralda had been home, no way she wouldn't have heard it. Probably Tom could hear it next door, not to mention the rest of the street. The damned thing had to be made of lead.

I let it sit while I rubbed my hands and shoulders and wiped more of the blood from my face. I was going to have a hot bath after this. With bubbles.

I looked at the box. Exactly where Sarafina had said it would be. What was in it? I closed my eyes and saw hundreds and hundreds of teeth all covered with the blood from my nose. But Sarafina had said "her," not "them." I had to dig *her* up. What was she?

The keyhole was tiny. I'd brought the infinity key just in case, but no way would it fit. I pulled the straightened bobby pin from my other pocket and jiggled it in the lock. The click was tiny, but I was relieved to hear it. Eardrums not broken, just my nose.

I pushed back the heavier-than-lead lid.

A cat. A very dead cat. Lying on its side with the yellow of its bones sticking out from the patches of remaining yellowish white fur. There were no eyes, no guts to fill its empty ribs. As I stared, my vision blurred. The cat turned its head, looked up at me through empty sockets. *Miaow.*

I screamed, wanting to throw the box away, leap up. Get out of there. I couldn't move.

Then it was perfectly still again, lying on its side, only one eye socket visible. Dead as dead as dead could be. I rubbed my eyes, only managing to rub in the dirty, bloody grime from my hands. The cat—Le Roi, I was sure—remained unmoving. Had I imagined the movement of her head? Her miaow?

I reached my hand into the box, terrified that she would bite me. Did you get diseases if a dead cat bit you? She didn't move. I touched her flank. Drier than the ground after a six-year-long drought. No trace of moisture. No trace of life.

Under the chin, the remaining fur was rusty with dried blood, as though her throat had been slashed with a sharp knife.

Just as Sarafina had told me.

I felt a surge of anger rush through me, hot and electric. I closed my eyes, breathed deeply, pushed the red energy of it away, blew it out with one big deep breath. How could Esmeralda have done that to a little kid's cat? It wasn't magic, it was insanity.

I was not going to stay in this house another night.

In the mirror my nose didn't look as bad as it felt. It was swollen and already starting to discolour, but it wasn't half as big as I'd thought, and the bleeding had finally stopped. My bra and T-shirt were blood- and snot-soaked messes, though my shorts hadn't caught any drops of red. I washed my face as best I could, then gingerly pushed cotton wool into my nostrils to absorb more of the blood. It hurt like buggery.

I felt light-headed. While I ran a bath, I ate one of the bags of chips and chocolate bars I'd bought on the way home from the hospital. I'd also bought nuts, dried and tinned fruit, cheese, muesli bars, and two large bottles of water. Not a lot, but it would have to do. My backpack also held the street directory, my compass and Leatherman, sunscreen, hat, and the rest of Sarafina's money.

When the bath was full, I tugged the cotton wool out of my nose, dropped the blood-soaked mess into the bin. I peered at my nose in the mirror again: I looked like a boxer after a fight. A bruise was coming up in the corner of my right eye. Brilliant.

I pushed aside the bubbles and sank into the tub, discovering that the big toe on my right foot had been hurt. That's right. I'd dropped the stupid rock on it. My shin stung too from where I'd grazed it yesterday. I was all cellar injuries.

Above me the skylights glowed in the harsh sunlight. I closed my eyes and let the hot water soak all the way through to my bones. Soon my face was sweating, salt running into my eyes. I didn't care.

I tried to remember the last time I'd had a bath. Long before Dubbo. It had been in a pub, a share bathroom. Dorrigo, maybe? The water had run out of the tap orange at first and, by the time it cleared, was more lukewarm than hot. The tub was dirty and the enamel worn through along the bottom, scratching my bum when I sat in it. This tub was smooth and clean and the water hot.

Lying there, I ran through everything else I would need. My sleeping bag, of course, tied to my backpack. I'd take two changes of clothing, plus my jacket and sloppy joe. If I headed south, I'd need them.

More money too. If I waited to leave till tonight, I could try to steal some from Esmeralda's purse or pinch some of her stuff to sell. I couldn't think of any other way to get more, not until I'd gotten myself a job somewhere.

I hoped that would be enough.

My biggest problem was Sarafina. How was I going to take her with me? I had imagined visiting her several more times, wheedling the nurses into letting me take her outside, and finally just walking away with her, taking the bus to Central, where we'd switch for a country train or an interstate bus out of Sydney.

If I went tonight, I'd have to leave Sarafina behind—come back for her later.

Could I do that? Leave her stuck there full of their slow-making drugs? I sank completely under the water though it made my nose sting. What if she died while I was away? Like all those other Cansino women, dead before they'd done anything? I wished I could ask Esmeralda what had killed them. Or Sarafina. Did she know?

I wished I knew more.

When I got out of the bath, I was so dizzy and hot I had to sit on the edge of the tub for a few minutes before the dots in front of my eyes disappeared. It was probably stupid to have run such a scalding bath, but I'd needed it.

When I could finally stand up, I filled a glass with cool water and sipped at it slowly. A little better. I put the fan on in my bedroom and opened the balcony doors, shutting them immediately when I realised the air outside was even hotter.

Well, if I did leave tonight, it would take Esmeralda by surprise. No one would expect anyone to exert themselves unnecessarily in such heat. All I really wanted was to rest. Though my nose wasn't bleeding anymore, it still throbbed.

I lay down on the bed. If I was going to do a runner, then a nap wouldn't hurt. I shut my eyes, taking some deep breaths, but my brain wouldn't let me sleep. It was too busy figuring out what I did and didn't need. Were Sarafina's binoculars worth carrying?

I *so* wished I knew more. Should I ask Tom more questions? I had the feeling he knew more than he'd let on at the cemetery. Had Esmeralda asked him to take me there? Should I put off going until I had that talk with her? I shuddered. The thought of talking to someone who would do that to a cat.

I got up and stuck the letters from Esmeralda in my backpack. Maybe there were answers in them. Likely they would be safe to read once I was far away from their author.

I got dressed, pulling on my not-too-dirty shorts and a clean bra and T-shirt, deciding it was way too hot for shoes, then headed downstairs. Maybe there was cash lying around. When I'd searched the house before, I'd been looking for escape routes, not money.

The key.

I could feel the infinity key in my pocket, digging into my thigh. Nasty thing. Hadn't opened the door to the cellar or poor Le Roi's coffin—might as well check if it opened the back door.

Before I put it in the lock, I knew. It slid in as if it belonged, though as it turned, it squeaked and protested. I pushed the heavy, creaking door open. When I stepped forward, it slammed shut behind me.

My jaw dropped.

# 12
# Through the Witch's Door

"Bloody hell."

I didn't know what I was looking at. It wasn't Esmeralda's backyard. The fig tree was gone. There were trees, but they had no leaves. They were brown and barren like after a bush-fire. But it wasn't hot. The summer had vanished.

White was everywhere. On the ground, clinging to the branches of the trees. I looked down at my feet. I was standing in white, and it was cold. The air was cold too. When I breathed, it hurt, and my nose started throbbing again.

Esmeralda's back verandah was gone. I was at the top of a few white steps, looking across at a row of buildings that shouldn't have been there.

It wasn't her backyard. It wasn't even daytime. The light was wrong. The sky was orangey-grey and I couldn't see the sun. Was it night? Then why were there no stars? No moon? Was it an eclipse? Had the sky been sucked away? Had the world ended as I stepped from kitchen to verandah?

The world had definitely been turned upside down. Nothing I could see or feel made any sense. Daytime and summer, both had vanished.

The buildings opposite looked like something out of an Escher drawing. There was a rickety iron staircase attached to the *outside* of each one. I wondered if there were stairs inside too. Or maybe they were on the outside because someone forgot about them? But they weren't even done right. The staircases started too high, even to jump up. Maybe this was a land of kangaroo people.

In front of the buildings were large white blobs. What on earth were they?

Soft wet drops hit my face and landed in my still-open mouth. Like rain, only softer. The air was full of white drops, like feathers or petals, floating through the air.

I walked down the steps, watching the gorgeous white dust dancing all around me. I caught some on my tongue and felt it dissolve. I shivered. It tasted like cold, wet air. I loved it.

"Snow," I said out loud, proud of myself for figuring it out. "It's snow."

I'd never seen that much snow before. In fact, outside of picture books, I'd never seen *any* snow before. Growing up, I'd met littlies who'd never seen *rain*. I tried to imagine what they'd think of this. They'd wet themselves!

I laughed and spun round and round with my arms stretched, feeling the snow against my bare arms and legs. It tickled. The brown, green, red houses, the railings, the strange staircases, a moustached face in stone, all flashed by, obscured by the falling snowflakes. I came to a stop, panting.

The big white blobs were *cars*, I was sure. But they were

covered in snow. I was looking at a street. A strange street, certainly, with such tall houses all crowded together, but definitely a street.

The snow, the cold, it was exhilarating. I couldn't help it—I had to run. I sprinted along the footpath, feeling the snow, deliciously cool and soft, splatter against my face, the crunchy dampness of it underneath my bare feet. It felt absolutely fabulous. No wonder people in books liked winter. If this was winter, I liked it too.

I turned to run back.

That was when I realised I didn't know where "back" was. Stretched out behind me was a row of houses, just like those on the other side of the street. They all looked the same with their iron railings and stone steps. I hadn't thought to notice which house I'd come out of.

So stupid.

I could hear Sarafina's voice in my head: *Always be alert, aware of your surroundings.* What had I seen? Red and brown houses. That was almost all of them. A moustached face in stone.

At that exact moment I realised I was shivering. I couldn't feel my nose anymore. My T-shirt and shorts were soaked. I had no shoes. Snow was cold. I was cold. Very cold.

The snow started coming down even harder.

# 13
# Rescue

This was Jay-Tee's third night waiting. Each colder than the one before. She hadn't even rescued Reason Cansino yet, and she already hated her.

"She'll come through in the dark," he'd said, which in winter wasn't very helpful given that it was dark practically all the time. On top of that, his dreams weren't always pinpoint accurate, but this time he wouldn't even consider the possibility that the Reason kid might arrive when the sun was up, or during a different week, or, God forbid, not at all.

So Jay-Tee sat in the dark, swaddled in a down coat, cashmere scarf, fur-lined mittens, boots, and hat (the fur wasn't visible, just in case animal liberationists decided to throw paint at her or something). And still her face was numb, and, weirdly, her knees—though not her calves or thighs—were icy. If she'd been able to move around, it wouldn't have been too bad, but just sitting here was turning her into a Popsicle.

The coffee in her thermos had long ago gone cold and she'd already finished all the chocolate chip cookies. She looked at her watch—strapped on over her glove so that her wrist didn't have to freeze every time she checked the time. Midnight. The sun wouldn't come up for ages yet. A few snowflakes drifted to the ground.

*Great,* thought Jay-Tee. Just what she needed, more snow. It'd fallen on and off all day, soft flakes, an inch or two sticking, making everything wet and slippery. Be just her luck if it turned into a blizzard. Nobody had predicted one, not that *that* meant anything. She got up and sat on the top step, out of the snow, pulling the heavy duffel bag stuffed with her useless coffee, as well as the coat and boots for Reason.

Jay-Tee looked across at the doorway, willing the stupid thing to open and the kid to step through. It had opened twice since she'd started her vigil, but both times it had been Esmeralda Cansino. Jay-Tee had been lucky—the witch hadn't noticed her.

She didn't want to think about what Esmeralda would do to her if she had. The witch wasn't keen on people knowing about her door. According to him, the witch was all about blood and sacrifice, mostly animals, but there'd been rumors of human babies. "And if a stray girl like you stumbled through the door . . ." He'd shrugged. "She might take the opportunity to move up a notch."

It was a pity the witch lived in the house on the other side of that door. Jay-Tee loved the idea of stepping out of this miserable winter and instantly into sunshine and warmth. Everything, he'd told her, was opposite on the other side of the door. When it was winter here, it was summer there. He'd promised that would happen soon if things went right. Jay-Tee snorted. She had not lived a life where many things went right.

The door opened.

A skinny Hispanic-looking girl with bare feet stepped through. Not at all what Jay-Tee had been expecting. The door slammed before Jay-Tee had a chance to see any of what was on the other side. She scooted farther back into the shadows and concentrated on not being seen.

Reason Cansino looked a few fries short of a Happy Meal, her mouth dropping all the way open, snowflakes landing in it. She looked delighted with herself, as if catching snowflakes was really hard.

She came down the steps slowly, staring at everything as if she'd never seen a street before. At the bottom she started twirling around and around. *Can't she feel the cold?* Jay-Tee thought, pulling her down coat tighter; watching Reason dance practically naked in the snow was making *her* feel colder.

Then the idiot went running down the block. Jay-Tee stood up, wondering whether she should run after her or not. Not that she *could* run, what with being wrapped up like a mummy with a huge duffel to haul along.

Up ahead through the snow Jay-Tee could just make out Reason stopping, doing some kind of dance, and then turning back. She'd crossed her arms across her chest now, finally feeling the cold. The snow was falling harder now and at a slight angle; the wind was starting up. Jay-Tee could feel the temperature dropping. Might be time for a rescue.

Jay-Tee walked down the steps and called out, "Hey, you! Hey, kid!"

Reason didn't seem to hear her. Jay-Tee moved closer. "Hey," she called. "Are you okay?"

Reason took a few steps. She was shivering. Up close Jay-Tee could see that she was one continuous goose bump. Her face was red, her nose blue.

"I have a coat," Jay-Tee said, pulling it out. Reason just looked confused. Jay-Tee wrapped the coat around her, reaching up to get it around Reason's shoulders—the girl had maybe two inches on Jay-Tee—and pulled her unresisting arms through the sleeves. "Put your hands in the pockets. They're warm."

This Reason managed, though her shivering had transformed into whole-body shudders. Jay-Tee could hear the chatter of the girl's teeth. She had to get her off the street.

Jay-Tee pulled the hood up over Reason's head. The snow was coming at more of an angle now. Jay-Tee didn't want to know what the windchill factor was—minus a zillion, it felt like. She hated it when the weather turned so fast.

"I got boots too," she told the girl. Reason nodded, but Jay-Tee wasn't sure she understood. They spoke English in Australia, she knew that, but maybe the girl was slow or something.

Jay-Tee pushed Reason back against the wall—the kid didn't try to resist—and lifted up one blue foot, drying it as best as she could with her mittens before pushing it into the fur-lined boot. She repeated the process with the other foot.

"It'll be better now. I'll get you home," Jay-Tee said, yelling into Reason's hood. "It's warm there. I think this is going to turn into a blizzard."

Again the girl nodded, but she said nothing. Maybe she couldn't speak with her teeth chattering so hard.

"This way," Jay-Tee yelled, slipping her arm through Reason's, making sure the girl kept her hands in her pockets. Half dragging, half pulling, she managed to get Reason moving in the right direction. *Should've brought a sled,* she thought.

"It's not far," she said out loud. "Honest."

The fire was going, hardly necessary considering the heat pouring from the steam pipes. *Must be at least ninety degrees in here.* He'd probably lit it. Jay-Tee could feel he wasn't around anymore. She was glad. She did not want to deal with him now. She was bone-tired. Dragging Reason six-and-a-half blocks had just about killed her.

Reason went straight to the fire, sinking down on the rug, hauling her hands out of her pockets and holding them to the flames.

"Not too close," Jay-Tee warned. "Don't want to freak them out. You know? First too much cold, then too much heat. Maybe you should just rub them."

Reason looked at her, blinked, and then starting rubbing her hands. So she did understand her.

"You should get out of those wet clothes. How 'bout I bring you a towel and some PJs and fix us some food? You want a hot drink? You hungry?"

Reason nodded.

"Okay. Keep wiggling your fingers and toes. Don't want any of them to drop off."

When she came back, Reason was still wriggling away like a kid in preschool. Jay-Tee bit back a laugh. She put the towels and pajamas down next to her. "Here you go. I'll be in the kitchen fixing some food. Holler if you need anything."

"Okay," Reason said.

*At least that's a two-syllable word,* thought Jay-Tee.

Jay-Tee handed Reason a mug of hot chocolate and two peanut butter and jelly sandwiches. (Other than cereal, sandwiches were all Jay-Tee ever made.) She hunkered down beside Reason in front of the fire. They ate and drank in silence for several minutes.

Jay-Tee glanced at Reason. Although she was wearing the coat over the pajamas, she'd stopped shaking. Her nose was no longer blue, but it was still swollen. She looked to have the beginnings of a black eye, too. *Aha,* thought Jay-Tee, *the wicked witch must be handy with her fists.* Why would she bother, though? She could do *much* worse things than hit a person.

Jay-Tee wondered for a moment if she had. There was so little energy or spark about Reason. Had Esmeralda already drunk her near dry? He wouldn't be happy about that.

Reason put down her mug, looked straight at Jay-Tee. "Where am I?"

"Eleventh Street."

"Eleventh Street? Is that in Newtown?"

"Newtown? Whatcha mean?" Though Jay-Tee figured that had to be someplace on the other side of the door.

"What suburb is this?"

"Suburb? This isn't the suburbs."

Reason looked even more confused. "I don't understand. Where are we? Eleventh Street where?"

"In the East Village," Jay-Tee said, trying hard for patience. He'd told her to be nice, make friends with Reason. He'd also warned her to tell Reason as little as possible. Jay-Tee was too smart not to do exactly what he said when he used *that* tone of voice. She wasn't going to tell Reason a thing. "You're in the East Village. You were in the East Village when I found you. Did you bump your head or something?"

Reason blinked. Her eyelashes were wet. "The East Village," she said slowly. "Um. Whereabouts is that?"

He had told her Reason didn't know anything, but she was Esmeralda Cansino's granddaughter, so Jay-Tee had found that hard to believe. And it had never occurred to Jay-Tee that there was anyone who *hadn't* heard of the East Village. This was the most famous city in the world. She guessed Reason was still in shock from the cold, because her confusion was real. She was definitely not faking; Jay-Tee would've felt it if she was.

"South of Midtown."

"Midtown?"

"East of the West Village." This was kind of fun.

Reason's face was blank. Seemed to Jay-Tee that it wasn't

just magic Reason didn't know about. She didn't know anything about anything. He was right; she was going to be *so* easy. "West of the East River," Jay-Tee prompted. "Above the Lower East Side?"

Reason's blankness didn't shift. Jay-Tee had to suppress a giggle. She decided it was time to cut the kid some slack. After all, she was also supposed to be making friends with Reason. She put her mug down and held out her hand. "I'm Jay-Tee."

"Reason." She gripped Jay-Tee's hand a bit too tightly, as though she was relieved to touch another human being, had been afraid maybe that Jay-Tee was a goblin or spirit or something like that.

"Weird name," Jay-Tee said, because it really was.

"My mum's mad."

"Your *mum?*" Reason sure did talk funny. "Don't you mean your *mom?* She called you that because she was mad at you?"

"My mother. I mean my mother's mad."

"Uh, whatever." Her accent was totally whack. "You don't sound Hispanic."

Reason looked puzzled. "Hispanic?"

"Where are your parents from? Down south? Do they talk Spanish?"

Reason shook her head. "Sarafina's from Sydney. She doesn't speak Spanish. I don't know where my dad's from. But Sarafina reckoned he was from somewhere up north, not south."

"Sydney, Australia?" Jay-Tee knew that, but she figured she should act surprised, not give anything away. She did *not* want him mad at her.

Reason nodded.

"Really not Hispanic?"

"No. My family's Australian," she said very definitely, "going back more than a century. On my dad's side way, way more."

"Then how come you're dark?"

"My dad's an Aborigine."

"He's a what?"

"An Aborigine," she repeated, as if Jay-Tee was just supposed to know what that meant.

"I heard you," Jay-Tee said, wondering again whether Reason really was nuts. Was she making this stuff up? It didn't feel like she was. "But what does that mean?"

Reason frowned, like she'd never had to explain it before. "He's one of the original people, from before the English came."

"Huh?"

"In the olden days, when white people first came here, there were already people—"

"Oh! I get it. You mean like Indians with spears and loin-cloths and babies on their backs? So Aborigines aren't white?"

Reason nodded slowly, and it felt like she was going to say something else before she finally said, "No, not white."

That explained her looks. Maybe her weird way of talking was how Aborigines talked.

"How long you been in town?"

"I don't . . . I just . . ."

The kid looked confused. He hadn't been pulling her leg. Esmeralda Cansino's grandchild didn't know about doors. How did that work out?

"I don't remember," Reason said at last. "I was at home—in Sydney. Then I was here."

She must have opened the door without knowing what would happen. "Maybe you were kidnapped and drugged. And they were going to do all sorts of unspeakable things to you, but you escaped. That would explain your face. They probably beat you up when they grabbed you."

Reason shook her head. "That was me. An accident."

*Yeah, right,* thought Jay-Tee, *an accident.*

"I was pulling up a rock and it kind of hit me in the face."

*Whatever.* "Here in the city?"

Reason nodded, then stopped. "Yes. In Sydney."

For a second she didn't look as confused. *She's faking,* Jay-Tee realized. But her confusion before had been real. Had she only just remembered? Was she not sure of what was real and what wasn't? But she knew about the door, about how she got here. Jay-Tee could feel it.

*She's going to give him more trouble than he thinks.* A large part of Jay-Tee was pleased. "You still could've been kidnapped and drugged after whacking yourself in the face."

"I guess."

"Why don't I call the cops?" asked Jay-Tee, just to see what she'd say.

Reason looked alarmed. "That's okay. Maybe I'll figure out what happened. I mean if . . ." She trailed off.

Jay-Tee smiled as widely and invitingly as she could. Despite being exhausted, it wasn't hard to smile; she'd just trapped Reason into as good as admitting that she knew how she'd gotten here. Why else wouldn't she want cops?

"You can stay here," she told her. "You sure look tired. It's late. Almost morning. Why don't I make up a bed for you and we'll figure this out when we've both had some sleep?"

"Almost morning? What time is it?"

Jay-Tee looked at her watch. "It's almost 1 AM."

"One AM?" Reason repeated, sounding confused again.

"Yup. Time we got some sleep."

Reason nodded, picking up her wet clothing. She seemed resigned to whatever Jay-Tee had to say, but Jay-Tee could feel her disbelief.

"That's okay," Jay-Tee said. "I can take those for you. I'll hang them up to dry."

She showed Reason to the second bedroom, hoping she wouldn't notice that the bed was already made up for her. "The bathroom's just next door and I'm in the other bedroom. Just knock if you need me."

Reason turned to Jay-Tee, her eyes all wet again. "Thank you," she said. "For everything. It was so cold. I could've . . .

Thank you." She blinked rapidly, then asked, "Do you remember where you found me? Could you take me back there?"

"Sure thing. If you think that'll help. We can go after breakfast. Sleep tight, Reason."

Jay-Tee put the fire out, scattering the remaining embers. She searched through the pockets of the shorts and pulled out a piece of wire, but no key. Well, that wasn't a big problem. Wasn't like there were many places Reason could hide it.

Or maybe she was like her grandmother and didn't *need* the key. That would suck.

# 14
## In Bizarroland

When I woke up, I didn't know where I was. I was completely awake, with no groggy feeling of being between sleep and awakeness, yet I didn't recognise anything. Not the PJs I was wearing, or the single bed with white sheets, or the doona fallen to the ground. It was hot, which was odd, because I remembered being cold.

I slid out of the bed, pulled open the curtains. The world outside was white and grey. The sun was up. At least it wasn't dark. It had been before, even in the afternoon. Somehow time had stopped working right. I pulled open the window and peered through the bars, trying to catch a glimpse of the sun, but there were too many buildings, the clouds too heavy. Was it morning? It didn't feel like morning. Why were there bars on the window?

If I needed to get out of this room in a hurry, the thick bars would leave no exit except the door. Besides, the bars were icy. I shivered and hugged myself, then shut the window.

I remembered being colder than I'd ever been in all my life. A cold so cold it could kill you. That really was snow outside the window, smothering everything, even the sound of passing cars. What was this place?

There was a knock on the door. I jumped.

"Reason? You awake?"

I recognised the voice. The girl from last night who wouldn't give me any straight answers. The girl who'd rescued me.

"Reason?"

"Yeah," I called out after I'd slipped back into bed and pulled the covers up to my chin.

"Can I come in?"

"Sure." Her accent was strange. I didn't remember noticing that last night. She sounded foreign. Not like any foreigner I'd ever met before, but then, I'd only met a few, all of them backpackers out bush.

She came in carrying a mountain of stuff. I could hardly see her face behind it. There was nowhere else, so she dumped all of it on the end of the bed. The room was almost empty. There weren't even pictures hanging on the blue walls. Besides the bed, there was a built-in wardrobe and a patterned rug in red and brown on the wooden floorboards. They weren't as shiny as the ones at Esmeralda's house. Nothing else. Not even a chair.

How did I get here? I had opened the door . . . then what? I shook my head. Thinking about it hurt.

I peered at the stuff. Clothing for me, I guessed, but the girl didn't say anything. She was shorter than I'd realised. Even shorter than me, with curly black hair, damp, as though she'd just had a shower. When she'd rescued me, I'd thought she was a grown-up. Now she looked the same age as me. What was her name again?

"Hi," I said cautiously, staying under the covers.

"Hi."

"Are those for me to wear?" It seemed like a lot. Did she think I was moving in with her?

She nodded. I wished I could remember her name. It hadn't been a real name, more like a nickname.

"Where are we?" I asked. "I didn't really get that straight last night." I was hoping she'd be a little more forthcoming than last night's stream of gibberish: streets that were numbers, villages that were named after their directions, a make-believe world invented by someone with no imagination.

"East Village."

I felt a surge of anger. *Never lose your temper,* Sarafina always told me. I closed my eyes, let the first twenty Fibs cascade through my mind, then opened them again, the anger gone. "And where's that?" I asked.

"East of the West Village," she said, as though this were obvious and I was a fool not to know it. She giggled and I had a strong urge to hit her. That or scream. She had rescued me, I reminded myself. I must not give in to my temper.

She rescued me from a snowstorm. My head hurt. How could there be snow? Jay, I suddenly remembered. Her name was Jay something.

"Jay," I began, "what—"

"Jay-Tee. No one calls me Jay. That's not my name. I'm Jay-Tee."

"Sorry," I said.

"That's okay. You were pretty hazy last night. How do you feel now?"

"Hazy."

"Any more ideas on what happened to you? Did you fall from the sky? Slip from the claws of a griffin?" She was grinning.

I didn't know what a griffin was, but it sounded like a made-up creature. Unless it was a real-life inhabitant of the East Village. I shook my head. "I don't think so." I had just opened a door . . . but that made no sense. That couldn't be what had really happened. I had to stay rational. Maybe Esmeralda had slipped me something, just as Sarafina had always warned me, and this was all an hallucination.

"You can have a shower if you want. If they shower where you come from. There's a couple of towels in with the clothes." She pointed at the mound of clothes on the bed.

"Thanks." I'd think about it later. When my head didn't hurt.

"Make sure you wear all of it, you know. You'll want at least three layers. As well as scarf, gloves, and hat." She picked up something red and green and woollen. I figured it had to be the hat. It was goofy looking, long and floppy like something a clown might wear. I hoped she was having a lend. "It's really cold. The windchill factor's off the charts. You especially want to cover your ears. They can fall off."

I wondered what a windchill factor was. It did not sound good. It was hard to imagine wearing all that stuff at once, especially as it was toasty warm in the bed. "Is it winter?"

She looked at me as though I was insane. Actually, she'd been looking at me that way pretty much the whole time. I wondered if I was. "Yes, Reason, it's winter. Snowstorms and freezing cold tend to indicate that."

"Not where I come from," I said softly so she couldn't hear, then louder, "How cold is it, exactly?"

"Twenty-two. But the wind chill makes it feel way colder than that."

I stared at her. How could it be twenty-two degrees? There was snow in piles everywhere outside, and it wasn't melting. It *had* to be below freezing out there. Twenty-two should be pleasant, almost *warm*. "You mean it's the *wind* that's making everything so cold?"

"Uh-huh. If it weren't blowing so icy, it wouldn't be nearly so bad. You can keep wearing the same coat." Jay-Tee looked at where I'd dropped it on the floor. "The boots you wore last night are out by the fire. They're dry now. They seemed to fit you pretty good, yeah?"

I nodded, though I couldn't remember if they'd fit or not. "Thanks."

"Then breakfast? You must be hungry."

I nodded again, though I hadn't realised I was until she asked. I wondered how long it had been since I'd eaten. The last I remembered it was January, with winter six months away.

When she left, I looked around for the clothes I'd been wearing. They weren't in the room. I went out into the living room. Jay-Tee wasn't there, but my clothes were hanging to dry in front of one of the heaters.

I took the opportunity to have a little look around. Two exits: the front door and a large window in the kitchen that led onto one of those weird metal outside staircases. The window was covered by a metal grate. I couldn't tell by looking whether it was locked or not.

Back in the living room, I found my shorts and T-shirt, the last clothes I remembered wearing. Somehow they'd made it with me from summer to winter, all the way here. Wherever "here" was.

"You still haven't showered?" Jay-Tee asked.

I jumped. "You scared me."

"Sorry," she said, though she didn't sound like she was. "Can you hurry up? I'm starving. Sooner you shower, the sooner we eat."

In the shower I scrubbed myself so clean I took layers of skin away. My toes and fingers still felt strange from the intense cold of last night, tingling as if a thousand tiny needles had been stuck into each one.

Jay-Tee's flat had bars on all the windows, even the tiny window in the bathroom. It was like a jail. The front door and the kitchen window were the only exits. Of course, knowing the escape routes was useless information until there was somewhere to escape *to*.

Where on earth was I and how had I gotten here?

The menu was almost big enough to cover the table and full of things I'd never heard of: kielbasa, pierogies, kasha, macaroni. My head spun with it all. I couldn't make sense of the menu, or the restaurant, or the East Village. I put the menu down and gripped the ammonite in my pocket, closing my eyes and letting its golden spiral unravel in my head, a cascade of Fibs, spreading out across the tables around us. Vainly trying to understand, trying to find something I recognised.

"Reason? You ready to order?"

"Huh?" I opened my eyes, the Fibs falling apart in my head. "Uh, sure. What're you having?"

She told me. I said I'd have the same, even though I had no clue what it was. I felt as if I was in a glass bubble. Everything was coming at me from a distance, light and sound distorted. I was like Sarafina, living in a slowed-down world while everyone around me went at their normal pace or faster, I guessed. Maybe someone had given me drugs and kidnapped me, taken me to this strange, cold city.

I sat and watched as people dashed in and out. Sat, ordered, then seconds later shovelled food into their mouths as though they thought someone might snatch it from them. Then out the door again. I could almost see streaks of light trailing behind them. Zoom, zoom, zoom. Was this how Sarafina saw the world? Was this even real?

"You're not eating." I looked up, confused. I hadn't even noticed the food arrive.

"I'm sorry. I guess I was distracted." We were having breakfast, but it didn't *feel* like breakfast time. "What time is it?"

"Twelve-thirty."

"In the afternoon?" It made no sense.

Jay-Tee nodded and gave me her *are-you-mad?* look again. Maybe I was. Nothing had made sense since I opened the back door at Esmeralda's house. My world had become undone. If I wasn't drugged, then I must be insane. Was someone in the real world trying to talk to me right now? Tom or Esmeralda? To them everything I was saying would be gibberish.

The heat inside the restaurant had made the windows steam up, but I suddenly felt cold. I'd gone mad like my mother.

"You should at least eat some of the kasha. The mushroom gravy's really good."

I dutifully spooned some of the stuff into my mouth. What kind of a name for food was "kasha"? It looked and tasted something like porridge, only not milky or sweet, and it was more grey than white. Why would my brain create something so boring? I'd thought I had a better imagination than this.

If, on the other hand, this was real, then I still had no idea where I was or how I'd got here, but I didn't want to go through another circular conversation with Jay-Tee trying to find out. Had Esmeralda drugged me and shipped me off to Antarctica? Did Antarctica even have this many people? And if it really was winter, where had the last six months gone?

My head ached. My nose had started to hurt again during the short journey from Jay-Tee's flat to the restaurant. Outside, it was unspeakably cold. I'd had no idea cold could be *that* cold. It was like living on the inside of a freezer. The five-minute journey had been almost unbearable. I still couldn't believe it was twenty-two degrees outside. Maybe I'd misheard Jay-Tee. Maybe she'd said *minus* twenty-two.

Though it wasn't snowing anymore, there'd been snow everywhere, piled up higher than the cars. On the sides of the road the snow had started to get dirty, turn grey. There were patches of yellow where dogs had peed.

We'd walked here along a wet path, cleared of snow, with something sparkly crunching under my feet. "Salt," Jay-Tee said when I asked. She didn't explain why, but perhaps it would help dissolve the snow? If so, it was about the first thing I'd seen that made sense.

There were lots of people, all of them huddled into huge winter coats—like the one hanging behind Esmeralda's back door. They walked as fast as they could despite being weighed down by their heavy coats. It figured. Who'd want to stay out in this misery a second longer than they had to? The glimpses of faces I saw were pinched and set, red and blotchy, their lips grey.

Out there in that unbearable cold, my nose hurt and my lungs burned every time I breathed. How could anyone live in this place?

I had been grateful when we'd come in from the street and I'd found the restaurant as perfectly heated as Jay-Tee's flat. A few minutes later I was sweating and had to shed the coat, gloves, hat, and then the jumper and long-sleeved T-shirt. I looked around. At every table sat at least one chair barely visible under a mound of clothing.

What was this place? The East Village. Eleventh Street.

The sky was grey, the people were grey, and the food was grey. The waitress hadn't smiled as she took our order. I watched the waitresses taking other orders. They didn't smile at anyone. No one had an accent like mine. Though they all sounded different from one another.

"You don't like it?"

Jay-Tee was looking at my food. "No, it's fine." I spooned some more of the grey stuff into my mouth, dutifully swallowed. I sipped orange juice and then some of the coffee, grateful for normal tastes, though the coffee was more watery than I was used to.

The last thing I remembered was walking through my grandmother's back door; then my memories jumped to standing in the snow, at night in winter, in this grey prison world.

The man at the table next to us unfurled his newspaper, rustling noisily, barely managing not to knock over the strange purple soup he was eating.

"Can you remember anything about last night?" asked Jay-Tee.

I shook my head, though I could. It just didn't make any sense.

"Do you think maybe you have amnesia? Should I take you to a doctor?"

*Amnesia,* that was the word for losing a big chunk of memory. But before I could agree, I thought of what the doctors at Kalder Park had done to Sarafina and shook my head. "No, really. I'm sure I don't need a doctor."

"Whatever you say."

Jay-Tee called for more coffee. I spread jam on a piece of toast and took a bite, chewing slowly. I remembered stumbling through the punishing cold barefoot. It had seemed wondrous at first. But not for long. I was unbelievably lucky that Jay-Tee had found me, that she was eager to help.

I'd woken up in the night (if *night* was really what it had been) shaking, convinced I was still out there in that incredible cold with no one to save me. I could have died. I'd fallen back to sleep almost instantly. One minute wide awake, the next my eyelids heavier than Uluru. I'd never felt so strange before.

Something prickled inside me, calling for my attention, but it hurt to go anywhere near it. I wasn't going to think about the boy who died. Drugs, I told myself. Or madness.

A peal of laughter, almost like a bell, rang out in the restaurant. I turned. A man was standing with his coat half off. Two women at the table were looking up at him and laughing uproariously.

"Take your coat all the way off!"

"Fix up your cape, Superman!"

The man was wearing a strange outfit. Red and blue. Skin-tight. I could see the exact shape of his bottom—I was glad I was sitting behind him. He still had on his winter hat and scarf. He looked ridiculous. I grinned too.

"And you sing?" asked one of the women in between gasps of laughter.

The man nodded. "C'mon," he said. "Twenty bucks an hour. Under the table."

I looked at Jay-Tee with a raised eyebrow. What was this place? Jay-Tee shrugged as though the whole thing was perfectly normal, not worth noticing. Their accents were more like hers.

I drank my juice. I noticed other people who, like Mr. Superman and his friends, weren't moving fast, who didn't resemble prison inmates. On the other side of the restaurant, near the windows, a man was feeding his baby daughter in a wooden high chair, making airplane noises as he propelled the spoon toward her mouth. She squealed happily. Some of the mush even made it into her mouth.

I turned back to my own mush, spooned a couple of mouth-fuls in, swallowed. Jay-Tee had finished her breakfast and was looking at me like she wanted to say something. I raised my eyebrows. Jay-Tee looked away, took a deep breath.

"Did you . . ." Jay-Tee said at last. "I was just wondering if you, maybe . . . Don't get mad, okay? You said you don't have amnesia, but you also say you don't remember anything. I fig-ure you might have, you know, run away from home. If you did, I wouldn't tell. I promise."

I stared at her. It wasn't what I'd been expecting her to say. I had been *going* to run away. My backpack had been all packed, ready. I'd gone downstairs looking for money. But then . . .

I looked at Jay-Tee, stunned, not sure what to say. I guessed that I *had* run away. At least, I'd wound up pretty far from Sydney *somehow*. But the result was the same: I wasn't trapped in Esmeralda's house anymore. I just hoped I wasn't trapped inside my own mind.

I just smiled.

"I thought so," Jay-Tee said, nodding. "Me too."

She made a writing gesture in the air and one of the waitresses came over with a piece of paper that said how much we had to pay.

Jay-Tee put her hand over the paper for a moment, concentrating. The air crackled, and I smelled something that wasn't food. Then there was money underneath her hand. I was sure it hadn't been there a second ago.

"What?" I began, but let the question trail away. The expression on Jay-Tee's face told me to stay quiet.

Jay-Tee stood up. "Want to go somewhere fun?"

"Sure," I said. "Where?"

"Top of the world." She winked at me. *We're mates now,* her wink seemed to say. Then she led me back out into the cold.

## 15
# Top of the World

We weren't out on the street battling the slushy footpath and pushing past other Michelin men bloated with winter clothing for very long before Jay-Tee led me into a building. It didn't look like hers, but I couldn't be a hundred percent sure until we were inside. The outsides of all the buildings were nearly identical. Large brown or grey or red bricks with iron stairs clinging to them—fire escapes, Jay-Tee told me, making me wonder how many fires they had in this village.

Once we were inside, though, this building was different. It had a huge foyer with a swirling floor of coloured marble tiles and an ornate plaster ceiling of interwoven doves carrying roses in their mouths.

A man in a black suit and red tie sat behind a large wooden desk, the top made of green leather fixed to the wood with 250 brass tacks. He was mesmerised by a computer screen, occasionally clicking the mouse.

"Playing solitaire," Jay-Tee said, making no effort to keep her voice down. The man didn't look up as we walked by. Jay-Tee giggled.

There was a bank of four lifts, all with their doors open. I'd only been in a lift once before, in the courthouse in Sydney. Three of these looked as though they'd just been wheeled off the production line, never ridden before, the gold and glass of their insides gleaming, the rich red of their carpets dazzling, like something you'd roll out for royalty.

Jay-Tee led me into the last one. It was nothing like the first three: threadbare carpet and no panelling—you could see all its workings. Jay-Tee hit the button for the top floor. The doors concertinaed shut with a shudder. I could see through the door. The other lifts seemed to be laughing at us for choosing their poor cousin.

The lift creaked and groaned but didn't move, as if it was considering Jay-Tee's request but had by no means agreed that it wanted to go up. It might stay where it was, or perhaps descend, or possibly spin round and round on the spot.

Jay-Tee pressed the button again, gently this time, and whispered something that sounded like, "Sorry."

The lift suddenly decided that up did, in fact, hold its interest, jerking into motion. We both lost our footing, and I stumbled into Jay-Tee. She giggled again.

I pushed my hood down and began to take off my gloves, watching the identical floors roll slowly by. Each had cream wallpaper dotted with roses, and gold doors, the numbers painted in black, and a red runner carpet—older than in the brand-new lifts, but far from threadbare—over floorboards. Jay-Tee watched me, her eyes narrowed, like a cat tracking a skink. When I returned her gaze, she blinked.

"It's one of the oldest elevators in the city," she said. "Kind of temperamental. Won't start for just anyone. Kind to runaways, though." Jay-Tee grinned. "It always starts for me."

I nodded. Everything tends to get crankier as it gets older. Especially people. I wanted to ask Jay-Tee who she'd run away from, opened my mouth to do so.

"Why'd you run away?" Jay-Tee asked instead.

I closed my mouth, opened it again. Had she read my mind? "Er," I said, not knowing how much to say. "My grandmother. Ran away from my grandmother. We don't get on," I finished pathetically.

"Get on what?" Jay-Tee stretched out the *a* sound in the word *what* until it hurt my ears. Her hands were on her hips. She looked annoyed.

"Huh?"

"You and your grandmother. What don't you get on?"

"We don't get on anything." Why was she acting so weird? "We don't like each other."

"Well, why didn't you say so?"

I *had* said so. Suddenly I felt unbelievably tired, eyes unwilling to stay open. I had to lean back against the lift wall. If I could've lain down, I would have slept for a month. "What about you?" I made myself ask.

"I ran away from my dad. He beat me."

"I'm sorry."

Jay-Tee shrugged. "I would've killed him if he touched me again. Better to run away."

I stared at her. Was she being serious? "What about your mum?"

"My *mom's* dead."

"Sorry."

Jay-Tee shrugged again. "She died when I was young. I never knew her. I don't remember what she looked like. Just photos."

"Brothers or sisters?" I asked, half expecting Jay-Tee to call me a stickybeak and demand that I stop with all the questions.

Jay-Tee shook her head. "Just me."

"Me too. Sarafina says it's the easiest and hardest thing in the world being the only child. All that attention."

"Who's Sarafina?"

"My mother," I said, careful not to say "mum" and set her off again. "How long since you ran away?" The tiredness was gone, leaving me as suddenly as it had come. Strange.

"A long time. No one's looking for me anymore. I'm free. Stick with me and you will be too."

The lift came to a shuddering halt that ate what I was going to say. I stumbled, but Jay-Tee, expecting it, just rolled up onto the tips of her toes. Then silence. Several seconds of silence. The lift sat, waiting. I reached for the open door button.

"I wouldn't," Jay-Tee said. "She needs to think a bit more."

*She?* I wanted to ask, but didn't. A loud groan rattled through the lift; the doors opened slowly and, from the sound, painfully.

Jay-Tee stepped out and I followed. We were in a red-carpeted

corridor with cream rose-dotted walls just like all the other floors
we'd passed. We walked by gold doors with numbers in black:
10E, 10D, 10C. I wondered which door we were looking for, but
Jay-Tee led me past them all and up two flights of stairs. She
stopped in front of a huge red door.

"Pull your hood up, put your gloves back on."

I did. Jay-Tee leaned forward and pulled my hat lower and
my scarf over my mouth.

"Ready?"

I nodded, though I didn't know what for.

Jay-Tee opened the door. Snow swirled around us, the wind
fast and cold. Jay-Tee pulled me after her, slamming the door
behind us.

"Top of the world!" she screamed, laughing.

We were up on the roof. I could see the whole city. Like I'd
thought, *definitely* a city. Why on earth had Jay-Tee called it a
village? Vast and high and crowded. Even more than Sydney.
As far as the eye could see: nothing shorter than six stories. In
the middle distance: tall, tall buildings everywhere, towering
far above, their heads lopped off by the heavy grey clouds. City,
city, city. This was what I had imagined that word meant: concrete and glass, grey and brown, towering buildings, some of
them crowned gold. People made small like ants. No plant life
at all.

I pushed through the snow and wind—there was no salt up
here, no ready-made paths—right up to the railing, sturdy and
taller than me, hung with hundreds of little icicles glittering

like diamonds. The street was a long way below, but not quite far enough to make ants of the people. I could distinguish the colour of their hats and coats from up here.

I wondered if the wind hadn't been so wild and loud if I could have heard their shouted conversations. How cold would it have to get before there were no people out? Seemed too cold for life *now*. But there they were below, in their layers and layers of clothing. Fifty-three of them on this side of the street and thirty-six on the other, all flat out like lizards drinking. Like the people in the restaurant, everyone in this place was in an insane hurry.

The street was clogged with cars, mostly yellow ones. They drove with their horns permanently blowing. Even over the wind I could hear the constant honking, though I couldn't see what they thought it would achieve. The cars were stopped because the lights were red. The blast of a horn couldn't change that. Maybe it just gave them something to do while they waited.

It really wasn't Sydney. No bridges, no long unbroken stretches of greenery, no greenery at all, definitely no flying foxes. They'd die in this cold. The wind roared in my ears. My eyes streamed water. I wondered if kidnappers had transported me to some arctic kingdom at the end of the world. Would I see penguins and polar bears if I got outside the city? Was this real at all?

Something hard hit my side. "Ow!" I turned.

Jay-Tee stood grinning at me—at least I imagined she was;

her mouth was hidden beneath her scarf—something round and white in her hands. She hurled it right at me. I ducked. It hit the railing behind me and exploded in a cloud of white, made the icicles tinkle.

"What the hell!?"

Jay-Tee bent, gathered up snow, forming it into a ball in her mittens. I bent and copied her actions. I was *so* going to get her.

Wasn't as easy as it looked, though. Gathering up the snow, I was hampered by the slipperiness of my thick gloves. And the wind kept blowing it out of my hands before I had a chance to pack it together. I mushed together the little I had. My snowball resembled an ice cube more than a ball. I grabbed more, feeling the satisfying crunch as it squished together. I rolled it in my hands into something more spherical. I grinned beneath my scarf and looked up just in time to get a Jay-Tee snowball in the eyes. Just a fraction lower and it would have smacked into my still-tender nose.

I screamed, blinking snow from my eyes, and hurled my very first snowball, too hard and fast—it zipped over Jay-Tee and exploded against the door. I ducked down and started on my second, faster this time, scooping up a palm full of snow, but with a wary eye out for more Jay-Tee projectiles. She loosed two more, but I ducked and they disappeared over my head. I made more, ducking and shifting away from Jay-Tee's efforts as I worked. Hard and round they were, about the size of cricket balls.

Jay-Tee was across the roof diagonally, nearest the door. She had quite a stash. I made as though I was still working on my weaponry, but as soon as she wasn't looking, I let them loose in rapid succession. Three missed, but the others got her on the head and chest.

"Yay! Gotcha, gotcha, gotcha!" I did a little victory dance, weaving out of the way of two more of Jay-Tee's snowballs.

Jay-Tee jumped up and yelled, "Truce!"

I threw my final effort, my biggest so far. Too big—it fell harmlessly half a metre in front of her.

"Okay, I said! Can you still feel your face, Reason?"

"Truce," I called out, trudging through the snow towards her; it crunched with every step. I could feel my face. It stung.

"You've never done that before, have you?" Jay-Tee asked, pulling me through the door.

"No," I shouted above the wind. But then the door closed and my yell echoed, suddenly loud, down the stairs. "No," I said quietly, still panting a little. "My very first snowballs."

"I could tell." Jay-Tee grinned. "Don't worry. You'll get lots of practice. It's more fun in a park. Especially when it's not quite as nasty cold. Winds are always worse higher up. Though in a park you've got to watch you're not scooping up more than just snow."

"Yuck," I said, remembering the yellow snow down on the street.

"Exactly. Throw *that* in someone's face and they're *not* going to be happy."

We both laughed and Jay-Tee held the door back into the hallway open for me. I rubbed my still-damp face. It tingled.

The corridor felt oppressively hot. I pulled my wet gloves off, wiping them uselessly on the equally wet surface of my coat. My fingers were pink and tingling, but they didn't feel like they were going to fall off. "How do you ever get used to this weather? Freezing outside, boiling inside."

"You just do. Snow is excellent. Not just snow fights, but snowmen and snow angels. I'll show you. You'll like it." She reached forward and pressed the button and almost instantly the doors of the old, recalcitrant lift opened. Jay-Tee grinned. "She likes you." Jay-Tee stepped in and pressed the button gently and respectfully.

"What else is fun for a couple of runaways to do?" I paused to let Jay-Tee know I was teasing, "In the East Village, east of the West Village but west of the East River?"

"Are you kidding? No school, no parents, no bossy brothers. There isn't anything we can't do!" The lift surged into life as if in agreement with Jay-Tee and willing to take us wherever we wanted to go.

I sighed happily, suddenly so tired I had to slump sideways to rest my head. I let all the anxious and confused thoughts float away. If this was madness, it was still better than where I'd been before. Esmeralda's house seemed such a long way away.

My eyes fell on a notice on the wall opposite me: City of New York. Department of Buildings. Elevator Inspections. Then in scribbled handwriting a list of dates and times and initials.

I was in New York City.

Magic was real.

# 16
# Feathers

Jay-Tee's skin prickled. She knew before putting the key in the lock that he wasn't home, but he'd been here. She opened the apartment door; the smell of him was everywhere: the air shimmered with it, taking away all the sharpness and corners and replacing them with wavering soft edges. Jay-Tee hated it when the apartment was like this.

Reason leaned heavily against her, a rag doll, not noticing a thing. One minute she'd been full of life, talking a mile a minute, and the next she was practically in a coma, slow moving, stupid again. Hardly able to keep her eyes open. Jay-Tee led Reason to her room, wondering if she'd need help getting into her PJs. He hadn't told Jay-Tee that she was going to have to be Reason's maid.

"You know, you should really try to stay awake. It's only three. You'll miss the last hours of daylight."

Reason made a noise that could've been anything and started struggling out of the down coat. She slipped to the floor and sat there on her ass, pulling at the coat with her head resting against the bed. Her eyes were half closed and her mouth half open. She hadn't taken her gloves off first.

Looked like one of them was caught in the sleeve, still on her hand. Reason kept pulling at the sleeve without moving it or the glove an inch. She probably hadn't remembered that the gloves were held on by buttons.

Jay-Tee sighed and bent down to help her, extracting the gloves, slipping the coat off, then pulling the sweater and long-sleeved T-shirt over her head before Reason could tangle herself in those too. Finally she slid Reason's boots off.

Reason still hadn't figured out where they were. Jay-Tee wondered how long it would take her. It still amazed her that the girl couldn't recognize New York City. It was like she was from Mars or something.

"How old are you?" Reason asked. Her voice seemed to come from somewhere a long way away.

"Eighteen," Jay-Tee lied. She didn't want Reason knowing they were the same age.

"I'm fifteen, just . . ." She trailed off. "Eighteen? Wow, that's so old." She giggled. "You could be dead already."

Jay-Tee felt her hands clench. She had to fight the urge to hit Reason. What did Reason know? A lot more than she'd been letting on. *Calm down,* she told herself. *Never lose your temper, especially not now.*

Reason grinned up at her dopily. Jay-Tee started to relax. The stupid kid didn't know what she was saying. She was just exhausted. Jay-Tee too. It had been a long, cold, bitter wait for Reason to appear and for Jay-Tee's life to stop sucking.

"Could we go dancing?" Reason asked. "I like dancing."

"Sure," Jay-Tee said. "It's the best thing about the city. Lots and lots of dancing." This wasn't a lie. There was nothing Jay-Tee loved more than dancing. "What night is it? Tuesday, right? Lantern's great Tuesday night. We could go there later, you know, when you wake up."

"Good," Reason said fuzzily. "Tuesday? Still? Huh. Can we have chocolate too? And pizza? I like pizza."

"Lots of pizza. Whenever you want."

He'd been in here. Jay-Tee could feel it. She wondered if Reason knew enough to take precautions. If she was even smart enough to check under the pillow. Jay-Tee doubted it. Especially not as crazy tired as the kid was now.

If Jay-Tee hadn't been sure he'd know, she might have cleared the room. It seemed unfair to be plucking Reason this way, her knowing absolutely nothing. Like taking candy from a baby. But if Jay-Tee made the room safer, even if he never knew she had, how would helping Reason help Jay-Tee? Not one little bit. She had to remember that. She was doing this for herself, not for him, Reason, or anyone else.

"It's fuzzy in here," Reason said in the same distant voice. She sounded like she was drunk. She'd gotten her jeans off and her pajama bottoms on, but the pajama top was on over her T-shirt, buttoned crooked. She was half in the bed, half out, looking all of ten years old.

Reason was such a goner.

"It's fuzzy in your *head*." Jay-Tee pushed Reason's leg into the bed, picked up the comforter from the floor, and covered her with it.

Reason nodded. "But fuzzy outside my head too." She sat up slowly, lifted the pillow, and blew a waterfall of feathers to the floor. "That's better," she murmured, putting her head on the pillow and falling fast asleep.

"Well, I'll be damned." Jay-Tee stared at the pile of black and purple feathers. "He's not going to like that."

# 17
## Searching

Tom hadn't been in New York City in two months. In the autumn, *their* autumn. He loved all the leaves changing colours: reds, browns, yellows, and oranges. So pretty that he hadn't minded how cold it was.

The first time Esmeralda had taken him through had been a year ago, when he'd first moved from the Shire to Newtown. She'd taken him through to see a snowstorm and he'd almost died. The snow was pretty, but not even *close* to pretty enough to make up for that cold. He'd felt it all the way down to his bones. It had actually hurt his teeth when he breathed.

He'd told Esmeralda he never wanted to go through in winter ever again. She'd laughed. Told him you could get used to it. Tom shook his head, knowing that there was no way he would ever get used to that and nothing that would convince him to step through the door into that bitter horror ever again.

*Nothing* didn't include Reason going missing in the snow and the cold. For her Tom had stepped through the door, even though he had absolutely no idea how he was going to find Ree in this lot. Howling winds that blew the snow around even when it wasn't actually snowing, everyone completely anonymous (including him) in many layers: hats, gloves, scarves, coats, jumpers. Sensing Reason through all of that, when there were millions of people around, well, it was close to impossible.

Mere had just told him to trust his senses, that he'd be able to feel for her. Under his breath he'd muttered, "Trust the Force, Luke." He was pretty sure she hadn't heard.

He trusted Mere's senses, though. She said Ree was still alive, was definitely here in Manhattan. Tom tried hard to believe her, but knowing that Reason had left the key in the lock, that she had no way back to Sydney, didn't fill him with hope.

He imagined Reason scratching at the door, trying to get back in, succumbing to the cold and freezing to death on the steps before they had even known she was missing.

He blinked the vision away. They hadn't found her frozen body when they'd come through and Mere said she was alive. He had to believe that and, impossible or not, he would do whatever he could to find her.

Cath had *not* been pleased to see him. Well, she had at first, for all of twenty seconds. Enough time for an embarrassing hug and kiss in front of her weird-looking boyfriend. She hadn't mentioned *him* in her e-mails. What on earth was that thing on his head? Kind of a dead-echidna, black-felt concoction. Tom couldn't see the stitching. *Probably glued,* he thought scornfully. Was that mascara he was wearing? They both stared at each other and Tom could tell the boyfriend didn't like him either. Good.

After that first twenty seconds Cath had realised she was

going to have to put Tom up, and that meant him sleeping on the couch, when her last guest had only left two days ago. Her two flatmates were starting to get well annoyed at the steady stream of Australian visitors.

Cath told Tom exactly how things stood. "They're not happy about Dillon being here all the time either, 'ken hell, there's only one loo. Hey," she said suddenly. "I haven't introduced you two! Tom, this is my boyfriend, Dillon. Dillon, my brother. You two should get on like a house on fire. Dillon makes his own clothes too."

*Dillon,* thought Tom, *what a stupid name.* He resisted the temptation to ask about the hat and nodded. Dillon returned the nod, every bit as unconvinced of the house-on-fireness of any possible friendship between them.

"I brought Tim Tams," Tom told her. Cath was a Tim Tam addict. "If it's such a pain, I could always stay with Mere in her flat. She offered." Which would be heaps more comfortable than this pile of dung. He was sitting on the couch in question and something hard was sticking into his bum.

The couch had no redeeming qualities. Uglier than sin, it was possible the thing had once been orange. Now it was yellowy grey, possibly the world's least attractive colour. The cushions were worn through in several places and the smell wafting from it was indescribable, though to be fair, Tom couldn't be sure the smell was coming from the couch. Could be from any of the other pieces of hideous furniture (who could have thought covering a chair in brown corduroy was ever a good idea?) or the walls or floor (both apparently *never* cleaned). Even the ceiling looked dodgy.

Tom had to admit, looking around, that the couch fitted *perfectly* with the rest of the flat's decor, even matching the walls in the kitchen. Ugh. If Dad knew Cath was living in a dump like this, he would not be happy. Tom thought about taking photos.

Cath looked scandalised. "Mere's already done so much for us. No way am I going to let you cramp her style. You know, Tom, you really could've given me some warning. I can't believe Dad didn't call to tell me."

Tom put on his most innocent expression. "It happened really fast. Mere had an extra ticket and before I knew it, I was in New York City." At least the last half wasn't a lie. He wished for the millionth time that he could tell Cath the truth. But he knew what Mere would say: *That's just part of being magic: Sometimes you have to lie.*

Tom looked around the flat with what he hoped looked like enthusiasm. "I've always wanted to see New York. And now I'm here. Cool, eh?"

"Okay, you can stay. But only for a week. When is Mere taking you back home?"

"Dunno."

"Hmmm," Cath said, with the put-out expression Tom knew well. "And you have to make yourself scarce as much as poss." She looked at him doubtfully. "What are you going to do with yourself? It's freezing outside. You can't go following me and my mates around. I've got classes."

"As if!" Tom rolled his eyes. Her friends were probably as poxy as the boyfriend. He'd never thought much of her Sydney mates. All they ever talked about were movies and books as pretentiously as possible. "What do you reckon I'm going to do? Find fabrics. Check out all the clothes. Issey Miyake, Comme des Garçons, Vivienne Westwood—"

"Closed," Cath's weirdo boyfriend said. He had the strangest accent Tom had ever heard, sounded like he was swallowing the words as he spoke. "Recession. It's gone."

"How do you know?" Cath asked. "Thought you were dead against name designers."

"Deb used to work there."

Cath nodded as if that explained things. Tom wanted to know who Deb was. Had she met Westwood? The old dame was known for making appearances at her stores. Did this Deb keep any of the old season catalogues or sample books? He wondered if she'd part with them, forgetting for a moment that he would probably never meet this Deb person.

Then he reminded himself that he was here to find Ree. Suddenly he felt exhausted, wanting nothing more than to sleep, even on the smelly, ugly couch.

That was the crappiest thing about coming through the door: jet lag was even worse without the jet. It didn't seem right. But Mere said your body was even more confused about the time and the season when it took just seconds to go from middle of the day to middle of the night, from summer to winter. You had to expect a freak-out. More than one.

In New York City right now it was 2 PM on Tuesday afternoon, but when he'd stepped through the door with Esmeralda four hours earlier, it had been *Wednesday*. Right now in Sydney it was six in the morning. It did his head in when he tried to think about it. His body too.

Tom forced himself to push past the fatigue, listened to Cath telling him which things in the fridge he could touch and which he couldn't (nothing but Cath's horrible vegan health-food stuff), which towels he could use (only the ones from her room), and which bathroom products. "Don't touch anything with the word *Kiehl's* on it. Those are Andrew's and he 'ken spews if anyone else uses them."

"Don't touch the Kiehl's. Check."

A phone rang. Cath and the boyfriend looked around, patting their pockets, searching through their bags before Tom realised it was the mobile Mere had given him and fished it out of his coat, an apologetic look on his face.

Unsurprisingly, it was Mere. He turned to Cath. "Mere. She wants to know if you'll have dinner with me and her tonight."

Cath shook her head. "Got a class till ten. Maybe tomorrow?"

Tom arranged it with Mere and then hung up.

Cath handed Tom a set of keys, showed him how to lock up. Twice. Making him do it in front of her to make sure he followed, which Tom did not enjoy, especially with the smirking boyfriend looking on, and then, mercifully, Cath and her sad wannabe-from-the-eighties boyfriend pointed Tom in the direction of the Issey Miyake store and went off to do whatever it was poseur film students did. Tom wondered how many years it would take off his life if he turned Cath's boyfriend into a frog.

So here Tom was, rugged up to the point of strangulation, looking for Reason. He walked north up Second Avenue, disappointed by the lack of clothing stores and by the lack of cool in the overcoats people wore. Lots of doona coats, which looked super-warm but were about as stylish as Cath's boyfriend's stupid hat. Tom swore he could see the feathers leaking out of them.

To check out interesting clothes, Tom would've headed southwest, in the direction of the Issey Miyake store—he wondered if he'd find any clothes by the new Belgian, Dutch, and Moroccan designers he'd been reading so much about—but Mere had said to stay in the East Village for the first week. Her theory was that the bitter cold meant Reason wouldn't have strayed far from the door.

Where on earth *would* Ree go? What would she do? If she was alive—and Mere had promised she was—someone *must* have found her. She couldn't survive long in a T-shirt, shorts, and no shoes, with no money or food. What if the person who found her was hurting her? Or something worse? Mere had already rung heaps of hospitals. Nothing.

Or maybe Reason had finally figured out how her magic worked. Tom shuddered, thinking of the years you could burn through just keeping yourself warm. They *had* to find her.

She'd been planning to run away; they knew that. Her backpack was jammed full of running-away necessities: food, money, water, extra clothes, and his dad's street directory.

When Mere had told him, Tom's cheeks had burned; he'd felt acid in his stomach. He was hurt. He knew it was dumb feeling that way. Reason wasn't running away from *him,* but if she'd liked him even half as much as he liked her, she'd still be in Sydney.

Reason was running away from Mere.

Why? Tom had asked Esmeralda, because it made no sense to him. Reason seemed smart; why hadn't she realised Mere would look out for her? She'd been looking out for Tom and his mother for well over a year and they weren't even related. Ree definitely wasn't better off lost here in the cold.

Mere had explained that she and her daughter, Sarafina, had been estranged for years. Sarafina had been so freaked out by the magic thing she'd done a runner when she was twelve (Tom tried to imagine himself running away at twelve: there was no way—he'd had braces on his teeth and had been barely able to cross the street on his own). She'd convinced herself magic didn't exist and raised Reason to believe it was crap and Esmeralda was the devil incarnate.

Esmeralda hadn't told Tom about them because she was ashamed of how badly she'd handled things with her daughter. The mess between them was one of the reasons she'd done so much to help Tom and his family. Which left Tom in the odd position of being grateful things had been so bad for Esmeralda way back when.

New York City was not at its best on a freezing, grey, January afternoon. Tom had learned that spring and autumn were best. Now people only hurried past, their coats buttoned up tight, their heads down. Tom couldn't help wondering whether one of them was Reason. Under all that winter clothing, how could he tell?

Tom's head was down too. He'd walked four blocks straight into a headwind. Even through all his clothing, the silver chain Mere had given him hung cold around his neck. His head ached and his eyes stung. He wondered idly if your eyes could freeze. Lots of liquid in eyes. What would happen if they froze? Would they stop seeing? Or only see whatever they'd been looking at when they froze?

Time to get off the street. Tom was hungry anyway, more than ready for bacon and eggs. (It was breakfast time in Sydney and Tom's stomach was definitely still on Sydney time.) Dumb idea to keep searching when he was about to pass out from lack of nourishment.

Tom walked into the next restaurant he passed, through the double doors, and, obeying the sign telling him to seat himself, sat at one of the tables furthest away from the steamed-up windows and doors. He almost sighed as he sat down, already feeling himself beginning to unthaw. The restaurant was hot and steamy and glorious. Tom leaned back against the wall, peeling off his gloves and hat, loosening his scarf and resting his hands on the table.

That's when he knew.

He could feel it: Reason had been here. At this very table.

# 18
# Nightmare

The scream was loud enough to wake the dead. It scared Jay-Tee halfway there. She dropped her glass of milk, splattering white liquid all over the green and black tiles of the kitchen floor. Mercifully the glass didn't break. Jay-Tee didn't pause to clean it up; she bolted straight into Reason's room.

Reason stood upright in the middle of the bed, screaming her lungs out, tears rolling down her cheeks. There were creases from her pillow on her face. "Nooooo!"

"Reason?" Jay-Tee said, shaping her words to slip easily into Reason's mind, pulling at her pajama top gently. "Shhh, Reason. You don't need to yell. I can hear you."

The terrified expression slid from Reason's face, replaced by the openmouthed look of deep sleep. The scream died; the tears stopped.

"What's happening, Reason? What do you see?"

"Door's locked," Reason mumbled, hardly able to open her mouth to let the words out. "It's a big door." Her eyes weren't closed the whole way; a slit of white showed. It made Jay-Tee's skin crawl.

"Open it, Reason. Find the key and open it."

Reason shook her head slowly; her lips wobbled, the muscles slack with sleep. "Key's hidden."

*Clever girl,* thought Jay-Tee. "Where's it hidden, Reason? Is it near?"

Reason moved her head back and forth, up and down, as if she were looking for it, but the rest of her body stayed unmoving. Her eyes were still mostly closed, glinting white. Like a zombie.

"Near. Not near," she muttered, continuing her blind looking. "Somewhere. I think it's with the dead boy."

"Dead boy?" Jay-Tee leaned closer, as if somehow that would make Reason tell her more.

"Dead boy." Reason whimpered. "I didn't mean to. It's not my fault." She began to cry again, but silently, as if she didn't know the tears were dripping from her eyes, down her face, onto her pajamas.

"Think about the key, Reason. You know where it is. *Think.*"

Reason crumpled, almost knocking Jay-Tee over. Her eyes opened all the way. She looked up at Jay-Tee and blinked, half asleep. "Huh?"

"You're safe," Jay-Tee said, because that's what her father used to say to her when she woke from a bad dream. At least he had before he'd become a complete asshole and she'd spent most of her time wishing he was dead. "You're safe."

"Jay-Tee?"

"That's right. I'm Jay-Tee. You ran away and now we're looking out for each other." *At least* I'm *looking out for* me, she thought. *You'd be better off if you kept on running.*

Reason nodded and sat up, rubbing her eyes. "My face is wet."

"You were crying. You had a nightmare. But you're okay now. It was just a dream."

"A dream . . ." Reason's forehead wrinkled as though she were trying to remember. "What time is it?"

Jay-Tee almost laughed. She'd been expecting Reason to ask where she was again. "Just before eight. You were asleep for almost five hours." Jay-Tee hadn't been able to go anywhere while Reason slept and slept, trapped being the babysitter.

"Five hours?" Reason said unbelievingly.

"Yup. It's dark now."

Reason wiped more of the tears from her face and yawned. "Night?" She sounded like she'd expected it to be morning.

"Night."

Reason smiled. "But I feel like breakfast."

"It's dinnertime. But no problem, there are places around here that do breakfast all day. If that's what you want."

Reason yawned again.

"Can you remember your dream?" Jay-Tee wondered if Reason remembered about the feathers under her pillow but couldn't think of an innocent-sounding way to ask.

Reason shook her head slowly. "Just that it was scary."

"Maybe you'll remember later."

Reason shuddered. "Not sure I want to."

"Dreams tell you stuff about yourself," Jay-Tee said, hoping she didn't sound too earnest. "They're pretty cool. Could be it might help you remember how you got here, you know?"

"I guess."

"Are you hungry?"

Reason smiled a little, some of the sleepiness disappearing. "Always."

"Want to go get some pizza?"

Reason rejected the idea of a single slice out of hand. She wanted a whole large pizza—which she was willing to share with Jay-Tee—and she wanted it to have anchovies, pineapple, and "beetroot" on it.

Freddie glared at Reason when she gave him the order. "Beetroot? What's that?"

Reason smiled back at him. "Beetroot. You know? It's purple and sweet, comes out of a tin—"

"She means beets, Freddie," Jay-Tee guessed, conscious that the next customers, a group of college students, were staring at them.

Freddie looked horrified. "Out of a can?" He shook his head. "Anchovies, yes. Beets and pineapple, no. They don't belong on a pizza. *Especially* not with anchovies." He looked at Reason again as if she were demented. "You want peppers?"

Reason started to ask what they were. "They're sweet," Jay-Tee said. "You'll like them. How about mushrooms? You do know what those are, don't you?"

Reason laughed. "Of course. Okay."

"One large pizza: anchovies, peppers, mushrooms. That right?" Freddie asked.

Jay-Tee nodded, put her hand on the counter, and looked

him in the eyes. As usual, she connected. "Keep the change, Freddie," she told him. "Next time I'll bring a friend who understands about pizza."

"You do that, Jay-Tee," he said, looking down at the counter and smiling.

She turned to lead Reason to one of the white plastic tables. They sat down on the squeaky plastic chairs.

"Where did the money come from?"

"What do you mean?" Jay-Tee asked. "It was in my hand."

"Oh."

Jay-Tee knew that Reason hadn't bought it. "You don't put pineapple or beets on a pizza," she said to change the subject. "That's just weird."

"Not at home it isn't."

"You're not at home."

Reason sighed. "No, I'm not."

"You'll like it," Jay-Tee said quickly. She didn't want the kid getting all depressed and whiny on her. "This is the best pizza joint in the world. You're about to eat the best pizza you've ever tasted. You'll see."

When the door stayed closed for any stretch of time, the place was warm and humid, the smell of pizza coating everything, including the inside of her mouth. Unfortunately, Jay-Tee wasn't the only one who thought it was the best pizza in town, and every few minutes the door opened and shut, letting in great gusts of cold wind. Jay-Tee pulled her coat up higher. "Doesn't it smell great in here?"

"It does." Reason smiled. "All toasty warm. It's just that anchovies are so good with pineapple and beetroot. It's all salty and fishy and sweet. I love that."

"I'm sure." Jay-Tee wondered if that was normal food in Australia. Maybe they also ate chicken ice cream or liver with licorice. Yuck.

When the pizza arrived, Reason tore into it, eating two slices for every one of Jay-Tee's.

"Got your appetite back, huh?"

"Food is wonderful," Reason said in between mouthfuls. "I was still kind of confused when we ate. . . ." She paused. "I guess that was morning, right?"

"It was breakfast, anyway. Told you the pizza here was good, didn't I?"

"It's great. Plenty of anchovies. Crust's a bit thin, though."

Jay-Tee rolled her eyes. "You want the last piece?"

"Ta."

*Ta?* thought Jay-Tee. *What the hell does that mean?*

Reason picked up the slice and bit in. "Even cold it's good."

"Leftover pizza's the best," Jay-Tee said. Reason seemed to have recovered from her nightmare. She was much more alert, looking around the pizza place curiously, watching two guys having a spat over an unreturned phone call. "Can you remember any more of your dream? The one that made you scream?"

"I screamed?"

"Uh-huh. You were yelling and crying. You seemed really scared. Do you remember what it was about? I mean, I know you said you don't have amnesia, but you are kind of . . . confused. Maybe your dream was trying to tell you something."

Reason ate the last bit of pizza and wiped her hands on a napkin. She shook her head. "I just remember that it felt horrible. Did I say anything?"

"I think you said, 'No.' But it was mostly just yelling, not words. You don't remember anything?"

"I remember being frightened. Nothing else." She grimaced.

Jay-Tee wondered again who her dead boy was. What had Reason done? And what did it have to do with the key?

"How did you run away?" Reason asked. She spoke into a rare moment of silence: the door was shut, the music was in between songs, customers at the tables were busy eating, and those at the counter had already given their orders. Reason's question hung in the air. Jay-Tee glanced around, caught Freddie's eye. Everyone was looking at them.

"Want to get dessert?" she asked quietly after the door had opened, letting in cold and the noise of the street, and talk and music had started up again.

"Sure."

"There's a place just across the street."

Jay-Tee ordered and led them up the back past the glass counters filled with every kind of dessert, picking a table nowhere near anyone else. The place wasn't nearly as crowded as the pizza joint, but to make extra sure of their privacy, she sat them under a speaker blaring Frank Sinatra.

"Who are all the photos of?"

"Broadway stars who've eaten here. Famous ones."

Reason didn't look very impressed. She probably didn't know what Broadway was. "This used to be a mafia hangout."

"Really?" Now Reason's eyes were big. At least she'd heard of the mafia. She looked down at the floor like she thought there might still be bloodstains.

"A long time ago. Mostly just locals and tourists now."

"Jay-Tee . . . what day is it?"

"Tuesday."

"Still?"

"Uh, yeah, still. You showed up last night. Monday night. Why? What day did you think it was?"

"Wednesday. It should be Wednesday." Reason sighed. "Of course, it should be summer."

Jay-Tee smiled. It *was* summer, back where Reason had come from.

The waitress set their cannoli down on the table. "Enjoy, girls," she said.

"Thanks," Reason replied, taking a bite. "It's really good. Creamy. I love sweet things."

The waitress smiled indulgently, as if they were still babies. "Don't we all," she said, and headed back behind the long counter. Hanging with Reason was turning Jay-Tee into a kid by association. Reason had to be the youngest fifteen-year-old she'd ever met. Jay-Tee was going to have to make her grow up. Or at least she would if they were going to be living together for more than a few days. Not that *that* was going to happen. Not if things went how he wanted them to, which they would. They always did. It wasn't like Jay-Tee could stop him.

"So," Reason said when her cannoli was history, "how'd you run away?"

"I just left."

"Me too." Reason giggled. "Not quite as dramatic as I'd planned. I just opened the door . . ." She stopped. Jay-Tee didn't have to guess why.

"For me too," Jay-Tee said. "It was much easier than I thought."

Reason scraped her fork across the bottom of her plate, trying for the last dregs of custard. She looked like she wanted more. Reason sure could eat.

"You seem to be doing great," she said, licking the fork. "Your own place and everything."

Jay-Tee took a deep breath and took the opening given her. "Well, the apartment isn't mine, exactly. There's this guy. . . ."

Reason's eyes widened.

"No, no, it's not what you think. He's a . . ." Jay-Tee paused, not wanting to lay it on too thick, and crossed her fingers under the table. "He's a nice guy. He looks out for me, makes sure I don't get into trouble. Lets me live in his apartment. I just have to do him favors every so often. Nothing terrible. Run a few errands. It's easy."

"Like what?" Reason didn't sound suspicious so much as

curious. She had to be the most gullible person Jay-Tee had ever met.

"Like shopping. That kind of thing. It's not a big deal. He rescued me, kind of like I rescued you. Saved me from having to live on the streets. I owe him, big time. And he doesn't come around that often. At most I see him once a week. Mostly not even. Anyways, I thought I should let you know. 'Cause you'll see him and you should be nice to him. He's the one letting you stay with me."

"He knows about me?" Reason sounded surprised.

"Of course—I had to ask if it was okay. Your staying, I mean." Jay-Tee wondered if her nose was growing. She almost had to hold back from checking. Lying didn't normally bother her, but this was different. Even though it went against her own interests, part of Jay-Tee wished she could warn Reason. She could casually mention feathers or the color purple. Reason had known enough to get them out from under her pillow. Hell, she'd known enough to hide the key. Maybe she didn't *need* a warning.

Jay-Tee looked at her closely. There was something more alert about Reason since she'd woken from her nightmare. She hadn't once asked where she was. Maybe she'd finally figured it out.

Then Reason smiled and her smarts disappeared. All Jay-Tee could see were Reason's wide, big eyes and the trusting expression on her face. *Hell,* she thought. Why wasn't Reason like Jay-Tee? Why couldn't Reason just know when people were lying?

They got back to the apartment late. He was there this time, just like she knew he would be. There'd be no dancing tonight.

After the cannoli they'd wandered around. The wind had died down and it wasn't nearly so cold. Jay-Tee was delaying. Seeing him was never her favorite thing, but she especially didn't want to face him with Reason by her side. Instead she'd given Reason a tour, pointed out more of her favorite places to eat, described what it was like out on the streets when it wasn't freezing.

They'd walked past stores, restaurants, cafés. Reason was quieter than she had been, asked hardly any questions, but she seemed to be absorbing everything she saw. Jay-Tee wondered again if she knew where she was now.

They passed an old man selling hot roasted chestnuts and warmed their hands over the grill. The old man was delighted and amazed that Reason had never even heard of chestnuts before. He insisted that they take a bunch wrapped in newspaper for free as long as Reason ate one in front of him and told him what she thought. "Don't burn your lips, girl," he warned her. Unsurprisingly, she said she loved them. Reason was a very polite girl who, Jay-Tee was beginning to realize, was all about food.

Jay-Tee told Reason stories about the city when it was warm, of music everywhere, people dancing on the pavement, of summers that were so hot the roads melted, but Reason obviously found the stories hard to believe when icicles hung from the leafless trees and everyone who passed was gray-faced, grim, and moved with almost no rhythm.

Jay-Tee switched tack and started filling Reason's ears with all the cool things about winter. Not just chestnuts. She told her they'd go uptown, skate at Rockefeller Center or in the park, go see some basketball in the Garden, that they'd go dancing every night. She filled her head with all the cool stuff about this city, all the things a person could do even when it was colder than a dead man's breath.

He was sitting in front of the fire, shoes off, a smug grin on his face. He looked like he owned the place. Which, of course, he did. His presence, as usual, made the apartment seem tiny. The walls seemed to be pushing in on them, leaving barely enough space to move, stealing the breath from Jay-Tee's lungs.

When they'd gotten their coats and the rest of their winter bulk off, he stood and smiled at them, showing almost all his white teeth. His lips seemed even redder than usual. *Just like a wolf,* thought Jay-Tee.

He held out his hand and Reason shook it, smiling.

"I'm Jason Blake," he told her. Jay-Tee had wondered what name he'd use.

"Reason Cansino. Though I guess you know that." The idiot girl turned to Jay-Tee, smiling as if meeting him was a good thing. "Jay-Tee said she told you about me."

He nodded. "All good things. Said you needed a place to stay. It makes me feel better to know that she has someone her own age around."

"Not *exactly* the same age," Reason said, and Jay-Tee could've pinched her.

"Well, I'm sure even when you're fifteen, a few months doesn't make that much difference."

Reason stared at Jay-Tee, who said nothing, silently cursing him. He was grinning. She was sure he knew she'd fibbed about her age.

"You're really doing both of us a favor, Reason, staying here. I worry about her living alone."

Jay-Tee thought she was going to throw up. He was talking like he was her kindly grandfather. Surely even Reason wouldn't buy that crap. Jay-Tee glanced at him out of the corner of her eye—he looked more like a snake than a wolf, really. Though she had no doubt he would, that he *had,* torn people to pieces when he needed to. A snake *and* a wolf.

"You girls eaten?" he asked, flashing his bleached white teeth some more. He was very sparing with his magic.

They nodded.

"I'd like to take you both out to dinner. Someplace special. Do you like fancy restaurants, Reason?"

"I don't know. I've never been to one." She looked pleased at the idea of it. Thinking about the food, Jay-Tee didn't doubt.

He clapped, grinning. "Excellent—what a treat is in store for you. I'll reserve a table for tomorrow night. Somewhere very special. Eight o'clock. I'll pick you up at twenty of."

*Great,* thought Jay-Tee, shuddering at the prospect of seeing him again in less than twenty-four hours.

"Thank you," Reason said. "I'll look forward to it." She

seemed sincere. Though Jay-Tee couldn't read her decently with his magic hanging so heavy in the apartment. Well, if Reason liked him that much, Jay-Tee would be happy to hand her over to him. *Anything to keep him farther away from me.*

He stood up. "I'll leave you two girls now. It's late and I'm sure you're both ready for bed."

He slipped on his shoes and picked up his coat. "Lovely to meet you, Reason."

"Thank you, Mr. Blake."

"Jason."

Reason lowered her head. "Sorry. Jason."

"Good night, Jay-Tee."

Jay-Tee nodded without saying anything, relief at his swift departure washing over her.

He put his hand on the doorknob and then half turned. "Reason?" he said, as if something trivial had occurred to him, but he couldn't help sharing. "I was wondering if you'd do me a favor?"

"A favor?" Reason asked, smiling sweetly.

"Yes. Would you be able to help me out?"

"Well," Reason said, "I'm sure I could, but it would depend on the favor."

"Nothing difficult. Just an errand."

"What kind of an errand?"

He smiled, more wolflike than ever. "Perhaps some other time. What happened to your face, Reason?"

Her hand went to her nose. "Nothing. I slipped."

"Really?" His smile widened. "Good night, Reason."

# 19
# Into Magic

When i woke up, i was still in New York City.

New York City. That's what I'd learned yesterday and once I'd learned it—New York City—those words were suddenly everywhere, not just on the plaque in the lift, but on people's caps, in window displays, on the sides of trucks, all over the newspaper that was wrapped around the chestnuts I'd eaten last night—the *New York Times*—the same newspaper that sat in piles on Esmeralda's bed. Once seen, once understood, those three words multiplied until they were almost all I could see.

Lying there, I was thinking something else that made my head hurt. Something I'd been trying not to think since I'd stepped through the door. I wasn't mad after all, and I hadn't lost my memory. Part of me had known that all along. I sat up, recognising the plain room straightaway. Not crazy, not disoriented. I knew where I was and how I'd gotten here.

Magic is real.

That was the thought. . . . It made my head hurt.

Magic is real. I am in New York City and it is Wednesday when it should be Thursday, morning when it should be night, freezing when it should be boiling, and magic is real.

I opened the door in Sydney in summer, stepped out to New York City in winter, the opposite season on the opposite side of the world. One moment and everything had changed.

If magic was real, then Esmeralda really was a witch. Witch as in magic, not witch as in bitch. Just like that Jason Blake last night. He had actually *smelled* like Esmeralda.

If magic was real, then Sarafina was a liar.

If magic was real, then everything I had ever learned was wrong. The world wasn't explicable. Wasn't rational. Wasn't any of the things Sarafina had said it was. Smoke and mirrors did not cause me to travel thousands of kilometres in one step. I was not hallucinating.

Sarafina had lied to me. Not just once, but every single day of my life.

*That's* why Sarafina had gone mad. She hadn't just lied to me, she'd lied to herself. Run away from the house of magic and spent years convincing herself it was nothing but tricks. *My mother is evil,* Sarafina had told herself, *not magic.*

Then, somehow, it had all fallen apart. *That's* why she was in Kalder Park. Because she had been telling herself lies for years, had begun to believe them, and finally her head had exploded.

Lying here thinking about it all was making my head explode too.

If Sarafina was lying, did that make Esmeralda a good person after all? I thought of the thirty-three teeth, of the dried-up cat. I shuddered. The stories Sarafina had told me—those were true, I was sure. Except that Esmeralda's magic *did* make things happen; doors opened out on places they shouldn't. From Sydney to New York City in a single step.

Had Sarafina started the lies to protect me? From what? Was *magic* why all my relatives died so young?

Or had Sarafina's lies been to protect me from myself? Because if magic was real, then I was a murderer. I had wished that boy dead and less than a second later he had died. I had done it. Part of me had always known *that* too.

My head was crowded with thoughts and I didn't want to think any of them, but I had to, didn't I? Being too scared to think (*magic is real*) had made me hope I was crazy, had stopped me from facing what was plain as the no-longer-white snow out the window.

Magic is real. Magic has *always* been real.

After breakfast I asked Jay-Tee to take me to the street where she'd first found me. For less than a second she looked at me strangely.

"I was hoping it might jog my memory. Sarafina says if you retrace your steps, it can help you find stuff. I thought it might help."

"Sure," she said. "No problem." I wondered if I'd imagined her look.

The wind was back up again, making walking hard work. I watched my breath turn into mist, then, when my lips started to sting, I pulled my scarf up. It was too cold to talk, though my head was bubbling over with questions.

I wanted to know about Jason Blake. The way he had talked just before he left . . . well, he was *not* a nice man. He had shark's eyes and when he smiled, it made the hairs on my arms stand on end. He was too much like Esmeralda. What was he doing to Jay-Tee?

He'd wanted me to say yes, I knew. Sarafina had always taught me to be sparing with my yeses because *you never know what the question really is.*

I thought about some of her other lessons, the meditation, turning feathers upside down. She'd been teaching me to protect myself. She'd denied magic existed and then taught me how to shield myself from it. I longed to talk to her, to ask her why.

It was almost too cold to breathe.

When Jay-Tee finally said we'd reached the street, my heart sank. It looked like every other street we'd walked along. Every one had buildings with staircases on the outside—fire escapes. Every house in New York City, it seemed, was tall, and all were jam-packed together, no gaps between. They lived like sardines, without any green in sight. Depressing.

But it wasn't all horrible. I thought of Jay-Tee's boasting last night about the wonders of winter, the ice sculptures and roaring fires. Seeing the trees glittering with ice *had* been incredible. Especially now that I could admit that it was real. And the chestnuts, hot and nutty and sweet. It was so cool just buying them on the street like that. I loved the chestnuts. All the food I'd had in this city had been amazing: the pizza (even

without beetroot or pineapple), that canoolly dessert stuff—
even the kasha had grown on me. I decided it was worth spend-
ing an evening with creepy Jason Blake to see what fancy New
York food was like.

It had snowed again overnight. Eighteen inches, Jay-Tee
said; she held up her hand to demonstrate how high, around
half a metre. Snow was banked up on the sides of the road, in
the tiny little fenced-off gardens. I pulled the scarf up over my
nose. It was warm and wet from my breath, but within seconds
it was cold and wet.

"Recognise anything?" Jay-Tee asked, standing close. She
rubbed her mittens together. "This is the exact spot where I
found you."

"Not sure. Think I need to look at all the doors. Maybe I
can spot where I came out onto the street."

"Does it look familiar?" Jay-Tee asked.

"Not sure," I said, because I really wasn't.

"Let's start at the beginning of the block," Jay-Tee suggested, her teeth chattering. "So you don't miss one?"

I nodded, though the one thing I was sure of was that I'd
come out of a building in the middle of the street.

All the doors were big and wooden. They had door knockers
that were brass hands or faces; one was a skull with its eyes
painted red. I didn't recognise any of them. Many of them had
locks big enough for the infinity key. I touched each one, but
not one felt right.

I stared at the spaces above each door too. That's where I

was pretty sure I'd seen the painted man with the moustache, above the door like a guardian angel. Lots of the houses had the usual kind of angels painted or carved above them. Cats too, and stained glass. I knew my door didn't have stained glass. At least, I thought I knew. I wasn't even sure the moustache man was above my door. Maybe I'd seen him later when I'd run along the street.

What would Sarafina think of me? A lifetime of being taught to be observant, and instead I'd stood there catching snowflakes in my mouth.

All the buildings looked virtually the same, with only the tiniest variations, like the clothes in Esmeralda's wardrobe. I wished I still had the infinity key, then I could try it on each door. But somehow I had the feeling that I would know when I came to the right one.

None of these was it.

At the end of the block, Jay-Tee suggested we try the other side. Just because she'd found me on this side of the street didn't mean that I hadn't somehow gotten turned around. By the time she'd shown up, Jay-Tee reminded me, I'd been so cold I couldn't think straight. I nodded.

I examined each door carefully. No moustached man, no lock that felt right. Jay-Tee didn't say anything, just trailed behind me, trying to stay warm. I wasn't sure how long I could stay outside. My nose was starting to throb again.

What was I going to do if I couldn't find my way back? I was a long way from Esmeralda. Which was what I'd wanted. But now I wanted to know who I was, what I was, what I'd done.

Besides, was I really far away from her? It was Esmeralda's door, after all. She came here, I knew from the winter coat hanging on her door, from the United States of America coins in its pockets, from the copies of the *New York Times*. Was I any safer from her now than I had been in her house?

I wished there was some way I could talk to her without putting myself in her power. I wanted to ask so many questions. I wanted to read those letters. I wanted to know what magic was. I thought again of the teeth, the dead cat. Maybe it was Sarafina I needed to talk to, not Esmeralda. The witch, I was sure, would eat me alive. The real Esmeralda, hidden from view, was just like Jason Blake. They even smelled the same.

How could I get home? If I found the door, it wasn't going to open without the key. How would I get back through? Wait until Esmeralda showed up and let me through? Too scary to contemplate. Catch a plane? I had no passport and if I tried to get one, they'd notify Esmeralda for sure.

I stepped back from the last house—in my pocket through my gloves I could feel my ammonite, neither warm nor comforting. I looked up at the grey sky. I couldn't find the sun. It was impossible to tell what time of day it was. Every time Jay-Tee said it was night, I thought it should be day; when she said it was dinnertime, I was ready for breakfast.

I shivered. Jay-Tee looked as cold as I felt.

## 20

# With Bubbles

That night—Wednesday night, I reminded myself, not Thursday—Jason Blake came to pick us up in a long, black limousine. When we got in, he was sitting with his back to the driver, dressed in a black suit as if we were going to a funeral. He gestured for us to sit opposite him and handed us glasses of champagne.

I took a sip and the bubbles got up my nose, making me giggle, just like I'd read in books. I'd never had champagne before. It tasted lemony, light, dissolving on my tongue like sherbet. It was the first alcohol I'd ever liked, not to mention the first cold thing I'd enjoyed since stepping through the door.

A screen blocked off the front of the limousine—we couldn't see or hear the driver, nor he us. It made me feel like I was in some high-tech car that drove itself. It was enormous. The back was more like a lounge room than a car. The seats were made of soft leather and there were cushions and footrests. There was even a television.

The limousine seemed to be designed for drinking champagne, with special holders that fit the skinny champagne glasses perfectly and behind a panel a tiny fridge to keep the bottle cold. I wondered if there was a hidden toilet too, which instantly made me want to pee.

Jay-Tee had loaned me a black dress that held my legs together so tight they felt glued. She'd insisted that you couldn't wear jeans to this kind of restaurant. The shoes were high and when I walked in them, I wobbled. They pinched my toes. Jay-Tee said not to worry, we'd be sitting down most of the time.

Her dress was black too, with red around the hem. Actually, I hadn't seen a dress in her wardrobe that *wasn't* black. The shoes she wore were even higher than mine and made of metal. They made a loud clicking sound every step she took. She'd put makeup on herself and then on me. When I protested, she said it was to hide my black eye. It made my skin feel weird, tight and itchy. When I looked in the mirror, I saw a doll's face: lips and cheeks red and glossy. I didn't recognise myself. Jay-Tee said I looked great.

"Will this be fun?" I'd asked her.

She squeezed my hand. "Afterwards we'll go dancing."

"In these?" I gestured at the ridiculous shoes on our feet.

Jay-Tee had laughed.

We hadn't talked about Jason Blake all day. Every time I started to ask, Jay-Tee changed the subject. I was a little relieved. I was almost afraid of what she might say, of what I'd gotten myself into.

Jay-Tee had lied to me about her age, about what a nice man Jason Blake was. What else had she lied about? I wasn't quite sure why, but something made me trust her despite the lies. I had a feeling she would tell me what was going on, just not quite yet.

"To new friendships!" Jason Blake raised his glass and we all clinked together and then sipped our champagne. My head was spinning out of control, lost like a feather in a willi-willi. "Don't forget to look out the window, Reason. We're almost at Midtown; you *have* to see Times Square in the flesh."

Jay-Tee snorted. "I bet she's never even *heard* of Times Square."

I hadn't, but I wasn't going to admit it. I moved closer to the window, which radiated cold like a block of ice, wiped the mist of my breath away, and peered out at the jumble of lights: reds, greens, blues, and yellows. We drove past a giant television screen that was the entire side of a huge glass building, showing a white-sand beach with palm trees and a red car without a roof driving along. Snowflakes drifted slowly past the screen, and for a moment the sand looked like snow.

There were hundreds of fast-moving people outside on the footpaths, crossing the roads as if they, not cars, ruled. Too many of them. Too crowded together to count. I'd never imagined there *could* be this many people in one place. How did they manage to walk in such a huge mob? It made my skin feel even tighter. I was glad to be safe behind the glass of the car window. What if someone tripped and fell? Would they be trampled? At least their many layers of winter clothing would give them some protection.

Up above, the buildings glittered with electricity, colours, words, and faces, the biggest billboards I'd ever seen. An electronic fairyland. Across one building a ribbon of red words scrolled by. I caught a stream of numbers, but I couldn't see a pattern, then names I didn't recognise, something about troops somewhere. Everywhere I looked lights flashed off and on, broke up, fell in cascades down the sides of buildings, were reflected in all the glass that towered over the roads.

"Your mouth's hanging open, Reason!" Jay-Tee laughed.

I closed my mouth.

"Incredible, isn't it?" Jason said.

I nodded. "I've never seen anything like this."

Jay-Tee laughed louder. She was already on her second or third glass of champagne. I'd forgotten to drink mine. "She says that a lot. Everything's a first for Reason."

"Lucky Reason," Jason said, smiling at me. I could've sworn his teeth were glinting. I was grateful for all the space between us. If he leaned any closer, I wouldn't be able to stop myself from flinching. He was not a nice man. I glanced at Jay-Tee. I was positive she didn't think so either.

Every table had a crisp white cloth and was set with shining silver cutlery and plates so white they gleamed brighter than Jason Blake's teeth. Waiters in white and black darted between the tables, ferrying jugs of water and platters of food. The room was vast and the tables set far apart. At every one we passed sat men in suits and women in dresses, their necks

and ears sparkling with jewels. Jay-Tee had been right: in jeans
and a T-shirt I'd've stuck out like a fir tree in the desert.

Including the three of us, there were fifty-seven diners.
Fib (10). A good omen, I told myself.

In the room's centre was a large black-and-silver sculpture
of a naked man and woman embracing. At their feet was a
stream of water that trickled over black and white rocks. One
wall of the restaurant was a giant window, looking out over the
brilliantly coloured electric city.

A woman led us to our table, her long red dress swishing
around her ankles, and a waiter appeared to hold out our
chairs as we sat down. He shook out the cloth napkins and
placed them on our laps as if he were our mother. I was
relieved that he didn't tuck them in like a bib.

Our table was by the giant window, all the colours and
lights I'd glimpsed from the car laid out in front of me like a
carpet. We were on the forty-seventh floor, the street and the
people so far below they weren't even ants, they were invisible.

The light fall of snowflakes blurred the colours, making
them even more dazzling. I shivered, though not from cold.
The restaurant was so perfectly warm I was able to sit in my
sleeveless dress and not wish for a cardie.

"Would you care to have something to drink, miss?"

"Champagne, please," I said, and Jay-Tee giggled. Jason
ordered a bottle for all of us. The name sounded something
like "Crude." It sounded wrong. Champagne should have a
name that sparkled or tinkled. A name with bubbles in it.

I stared out the window, trying to read the brilliant signs through the snow. Everything was too blurry, like fresh paint with water spilled over it. Colours bled into one another. Primaries became secondaries, became tertiaries. Suddenly there were purples, pinks, and browns. Some of the lights were circled by tiny rainbows. The snow was falling a little harder, blurring everything even more. Freezing out there, but perfect in here. I wondered why the window wasn't all steamed up.

"If the snow keeps up any longer," said Blake, following my gaze out the window, "it'll shut the city down."

The waiter returned with the bottle of champagne and a silver bucket filled with ice. He displayed the bottle for Jason, who peered at the label and nodded. This time the champagne tasted like cream, and the bubbles were smaller than the head of a pin, flying up through the liquid in streams, bursting through to float in the air above the glass and into my nose. The strange sensation of breathing in tiny bubbles was almost better than the creaminess of it coating my tongue.

Ever since I'd come through the door, I'd felt as though I was living in a bubble. A thick layer of transparent material between me and the world. I'd felt gummed up, slowed down behind my bubble while every one around me powered along. Drinking this glittering drink sent the bubbles pouring inside me, somehow destroying the one that held me trapped. They made me feel part of the world again. They made the world beautiful.

"Another toast," Jason said. The champagne had softened

him, making him seem less predatory. Now he seemed just like Esmeralda: softness and smiles on the outside, sharp shiny teeth on the inside. "To helping one another."

I raised my glass but did not repeat his words and made sure it only touched Jay-Tee's glass, not his. Jason looked directly at me, half smiling. I turned back to the snow and the lights.

The waiter returned with three tiny glasses on tiny plates with tiny spoons. They were filled with a frothy, creamy substance topped with tiny orange bubbles. I wondered if everything we ate and drank tonight was going to be tiny and made of bubbles.

"Salmon reduction with roe," the waiter said. "Enjoy."

"But we didn't order anything," I said once the waiter was gone. I knew enough to not embarrass myself in front of *everyone*.

Jay-Tee grinned and I wished I'd kept my mouth shut, but I just wanted to know.

"You don't order here," Jason explained. "It's called a tasting menu. They'll bring us a small amount of everything that's good. That way you get ten courses instead of only three."

"Ten?" It sounded like a lot, but then I looked down at my minuscule glass. Ten servings of that wouldn't go far. I decided not to volunteer the information that I'd never been to a restaurant that served *three* courses before. I wasn't exactly sure what a course was, but I figured it meant a helping. I'd only ever been to cafés, fish-and-chip shops, and, rarely, Chinese restaurants.

Sarafina wasn't interested in food. She didn't even call it food; most of the time she called it "fuel." If it was up to her, we'd just eat fruit and nuts all the time. Me, I was *very* interested in food. "But what if you don't like something they bring you?" I asked.

"Tell them," Jason said. "They'll bring you something else."

I wondered if he was kidding or not. He and Jay-Tee picked up their little spoons and dipped them in. I did the same. It was fish soup. I spooned some of the orange bubbles into my mouth. They popped between my teeth, exploding with an intense fishiness. Very strange, like nothing I'd tasted before. I thought I liked them, but I wasn't sure.

Jason picked up the glass and drank down the last bit of soup. Jay-Tee and I did the same. There were two last orange bubbles. I popped them between my tongue and my teeth. Salty fishiness. They were good, I decided.

"Do you like it?" Jason asked.

I didn't say yes, just in case. "It's delicious."

"Yeah," Jay-Tee said, "the roe tastes like fishy Pop Rocks."

He laughed. "Barbarian."

Jay-Tee shrugged. "It's what it tastes like."

Jason refilled our glasses and, when the waiter came to clear the plates, ordered another bottle. I'd already lost count of how many glasses I'd had. I could feel the little bubbles moving along my veins. I sparkled.

"What kind of food is this?" I asked after the waiter had placed a plate of something that was composed of layers of white, then brown, then red, then green, sitting in a pool of creamy sauce with red and green swirls in it. I'd been watching the snowstorm and missed the waiter's description, not that it would've helped much. I wasn't used to food that looked like art.

"Modern American," Jason said. "Although the chef trained in France and Italy, so they're a big influence."

"Huh," I said, because his answer hadn't explained a thing. "Modern American" wasn't a glamorous enough name for this fairytale food. Of course, I'd never eaten food from France or Italy either. It had never occurred to me that every country in the world had different food.

"I meant what I said, Reason, about helping one another," Jason said, after he'd tried the layered thing and made an *mmmm* sound. "I've been helping Jay-Tee a lot and I'd like to do the same for you."

He glanced at Jay-Tee and she nodded. She kept her head down, wouldn't let me catch her eye. Was that true? And if it was, *how* did he help her?

"It seems to me," he continued, "that there's a lot you don't know." He gave the words *a lot* extra emphasis. I couldn't disagree. "I can help you with that. Explain things to you, as I suspect neither your mother nor your grandmother ever has."

## 21
## Knowledge

That was one of his tricks, of course: when it's least expected, tell the truth. Reason's mouth fell open, showing the whole world her tonsils. Again. *She's lucky it isn't summer and we aren't outdoors, or she'd have a mouth full of flies,* Jay-Tee thought.

Ever since Reason came here, she'd been confused. She wasn't prepared for anything that had happened to her. She didn't know how to tell when someone was lying to her. Reason didn't have any idea that Jay-Tee'd taken her to the wrong street that morning. Kept staring at every house, every door on Thirteenth Street between Avenues A and B, hoping it was the one. Unsurprisingly, given that Esmeralda's door was on Seventh Street between B and C, she hadn't found it.

And now Reason was drop-jawed and staring even more, this time because he'd told the truth. She'd paused in her rapid food and champagne consumption and stared at him, mouth *still* open. She looked almost sick.

"I can tell you what you want to know, Reason. But I want something from you in return. It has to be reciprocal. You do for me, and I'll tell you about yourself. Your grandmother, she would take everything and give you nothing."

*Not unlike him, really,* thought Jay-Tee. *What a choice.*

Reason gulped down the rest of her glass. He poured her more. She gulped at that too. The waiter whipped away their dirty plates, and within seconds they were replaced with wobbly towers of rice and greens and who knew what else. None of them was listening as the waiter explained.

"You stepped through a door in Sydney," he said once the waiter was out of earshot. "And you found yourself in New York City. You didn't expect that to happen, did you?"

Reason shook her head, finally closing her mouth. "No."

"But you know *why.* You know it's magic. You've been kept in the dark all your life and yet you've figured out that much."

Reason's gaze had finally dropped to her plate. "Magic is real," she said, half under her breath. Jay-Tee wondered if she was going to start crying. Her face had that pinched look of someone trying to hold back tears.

"It is. But you don't know much more than that, do you?"

"No, I don't," she said, her voice still faint.

"I can tell you." He leaned closer, directing all his energy at her. "I can tell you who you are. I can tell you what magic is. What you can do with it. I can teach you and help you. The same way I have Jay-Tee."

*Lucky me,* thought Jay-Tee, taking a sip from her glass. Reason didn't look at her.

"You need a teacher. Without my help you could hurt yourself or worse." He was managing to look sympathetic, concerned. She imagined that he was. Reason dead was no good to him.

Reason blanched. "How do you know?" she asked, finding her normal voice at last. "How do you know who I am? Who my mother is? My grandmother?"

"I am your grandfather."

Jay-Tee felt her own jaw drop. They were both staring at him now. He'd never told her *that* little snippet before. He and the witch Esmeralda had done the nasty? Or was he lying?

Jay-Tee looked at him closely, trying to feel whether it was true or not. He raised an eyebrow and she pulled back. She should have known better than to try. Reason looked like she was just about ready to keel over. Talk about information overload.

"My . . ." She dribbled to a halt. Jay-Tee couldn't imagine how *she'd* feel if it turned out he was *her* granddad. Ugh.

"Your grandfather," he said, staring back at Reason. "Father of your mother."

"And you're magic too?" Reason asked, her voice small. "Like Esmeralda?"

He nodded. "Like your mother too."

"She never mentioned you." Her voice had grown a little louder but was still somehow thin.

"Interesting." He smiled. "But there are many things she never mentioned, aren't there?"

Reason shook her head, but not so much to say *no;* more in confusion. "Do you even know Sarafina?" she asked. "I have a father. I've never seen him."

"Sarafina and I have met." He smiled broadly and Jay-Tee felt sick. He was enjoying this too much. It wasn't like he would tell Reason anything that would help her. This was all about helping him.

"Why . . ." Reason stopped and said instead, "Do you know why they all die? Why the women in my family all die so young?"

"I do. I also know why your mother is insane."

Reason's eyes widened. "Tell me."

Jay-Tee could have told her *that*. She needed to ask the right questions.

"Say yes, Reason. And then I'll tell you everything you want to know. Give me what I want."

"What do you want?"

He picked up his glass, rolled it in his hands, watching the bubbles spinning. He brought it slowly to his mouth and, instead of sipping, drained the full glass in one slow, steady drink.

*That's what he wants,* thought Jay-Tee. *He wants to drink you dry.*

"I want to take a little of what you have. A little of your magic."

"My magic?"

"Yes. You can give it to me. A little at a time. You'll hardly feel a thing. Will she, Jay-Tee?"

Reason looked sharply at Jay-Tee, who forced herself to meet Reason's eyes and say, "No," even though it was a lie. Jay-Tee felt what he did to her. She missed what he took. She did everything she could to get it back. That was why she had wanted him to take from Reason: to stop him taking from her.

It had seemed a good idea, back before she'd gotten to know
Reason.

"How does it work?"

"Tell her, Jay-Tee."

Jay-Tee swallowed, drank more of the champagne. Her head
was spinning at about a hundred miles an hour. She figured
she was probably drunk. "I've got to go to the bathroom," she
said, knowing he'd be pissed at her. When he asked questions,
you were supposed to answer. She could practically smell the
acid gathering in his mouth.

When she stood up, she didn't wobble, which was quite an
accomplishment with the heels she was wearing. She strutted
in a reasonable approximation of a straight line toward where
she hoped the bathrooms would be. The loud click of her metal
heels against the floor caused many of the other diners to turn
their heads and watch her progress.

Someone was walking behind her. Jay-Tee carefully turned
her head. Reason wobbled along behind her. *Damn,* thought
Jay-Tee. *Now he's really going to be mad.*

The bathroom was all marble and gold. Very classy. There
was a separate room with chairs and mirrors for fixing your
makeup. When Jay-Tee had peed and washed her hands, she
went in and sat down, waiting for Reason to be done.

She redid her lipstick. It took a while because her hands
were shaking. Her cheeks were flushed and her eyes shiny, but
they weren't bloodshot. Jay-Tee figured that would come in the

morning. Her head would probably ache too. Especially if he decided to exact revenge on her.

Reason was taking her time. Jay-Tee could feel herself starting to sweat. She should probably go back to the table, face him without talking to Reason first, but Jay-Tee figured she owed her. Which was crazy. Reason couldn't hurt her the way he could.

A tall woman with dreadlocks down to the small of her back came in, sat down, nodded at Jay-Tee, and began to redo her makeup, starting with concealer under her eyes. She'd looked great to start with, and Jay-Tee couldn't imagine she'd look noticeably different afterward.

Reason sat on Jay-Tee's other side. She wasn't at all flushed. All the color had gone from her face, making the black eye Jay-Tee had carefully painted over stand out. Her skin was flat, sallow, like the color of a paper bag. The shock had drained all the champagne away.

Jay-Tee's need to help her grew, which was crazed. The longer they stayed in here, the madder he'd be—at *both* of them. How would that help Reason?

"You okay?" she asked, but Reason didn't say anything.

"Want me to fix your lips? Put some more blush on?"

Reason nodded.

"But we shouldn't stay too long. He won't like it." She glanced at the woman, now curling her eyelashes, and wondered when she would leave.

Jay-Tee got the blush and lipstick out of her purse, shifted around on her chair and leaned forward, started putting the lipstick on, but her hands were shaking. She kept slipping, going beyond the line of Reason's lips.

"Sorry," she muttered, grabbing a tissue and rubbing it off.

"Here," Reason said, taking them from her. "I think I know how to do it."

She did her cheeks and then her lips, much more evenly than Jay-Tee would have managed. She had half a mind to ask Reason to redo hers. But how much longer would that take? Jay-Tee could almost see him sitting there, his eyes growing colder and his lips thinner.

The dreadlocked woman finished with her makeup, nodded at them both, and finally left.

"How does he take your magic?" Reason asked at once.

Jay-Tee put the makeup back in her purse. Well, he'd said he wanted her to tell Reason; might as well do it here. "He asks me if he can, and when I say yes, he puts his hand on me. Like this." Jay-Tee leaned forward and lightly touched the back of Reason's hand. "And then there's this weird sensation of heat, kind of like it's burning, but not that bad, and when I want it to stop, I say so. And it stops right away."

"It's up to you? You make it start and stop?"

"Yes."

"Does it hurt?" Reason leaned closer, as if she was trying to see the truth in Jay-Tee's eyes.

"No." *Not exactly.*

"How do you feel after? Like something's gone?"

Jay-Tee hesitated, decided to tell the truth. "Yes. I feel tired. The more he takes, the worse it is."

"Does it mean you can't do magic? 'Cause he's taken it from you?"

"I can do magic. You've seen it." Jay-Tee smiled, thinking about everything she'd done right under Reason's nose. "He hasn't taken all of it. I wouldn't let him," she said with more confidence than she felt. "It's not that bad. Honest."

Reason's nose wrinkled. Jay-Tee figured the word *honest* didn't carry much weight coming out of her mouth.

"Can *you* answer my questions? Is there stuff Blake knows that you don't?"

"Lots. I didn't know he was your grandfather."

"Do you think he really is? Do you think that's true?" Reason sounded distressed.

Jay-Tee understood why. She couldn't help feeling relieved all over again that he wasn't any relative of hers. Her dad was mad foul, but not even on the same scale as *him*.

"Don't know, Reason. I don't know anything about your family. Except that your grandmother's heavy-duty scary. I guess that means they'd be a perfect match." Jay-Tee smiled, but her joke was too true to be funny.

Reason said nothing, thinking it all through. Her learning curve had been steep tonight. But they couldn't just sit here like this. He'd be getting madder and madder by the second. "We should get back."

"Are you frightened of him?"

Jay-Tee looked down. "Sometimes." *Most of the time.*

"What has he done for you? Why do you let him take it?"

A blond woman in an ugly brown-and-green dress came in.

"Tell you later," Jay-Tee said, although she wasn't sure she could. She stood up, lowering her voice. "It's not all bad, I promise. I'd've run away from him if it was. He leaves me alone most of the time."

Reason didn't reply.

He didn't say a word as they picked the napkins up off the backs of their chairs and sat down. Jay-Tee started to raise the champagne to her lips but was too nervous and put the glass back down, bracing herself for the acid to start dripping from his lips.

"Yes," Reason said before he could open his mouth, staring straight at him, putting her hand palm down on the table as Jay-Tee had shown her. "Yes, take some now."

He reached across and laid his hand on hers. It made Jay-Tee sick to watch but also relieved it wasn't her. Even so, she flashed back to the feeling of skin contracting, the slowly increasing burning sensation crawling up her arm. Like ants, poison devil ants.

Would it make Reason want to hurl? Make her head suddenly ache right where the spine and skull met? Would Reason's body scream at her that this wasn't right? Color appeared in a spot the size of a nickel on both her cheekbones, clashing with the blush. Jay-Tee thanked God it wasn't her and then felt like a bitch because it *was* Reason and that was her fault.

"No," said Reason. "Stop."

He took his hand away. He wasn't buzzing like he did when he drank from her, and Reason wasn't shaking. But Jay-Tee knew that even such a short time was enough for him to get a taste and for Reason to get an inkling of what it felt like to be drained. She'd been wise stopping it so soon.

The waiter brought yet another dish. A dessert this time, Jay-Tee was relieved to see. This would end soon. She'd be able to get away from him. She wondered how the three of them looked to the waiters: rich old white guy with his two Chicana girls, one with a suspicious hint of a black eye. None of them was going to know Reason was a . . . whatever it was she'd said she was. But appearances didn't tell you everything, she thought. This was much, much creepier than it looked.

"Now tell me," Reason said, "about magic."

Jay-Tee leaned back in her chair, twirling her champagne glass, all ready to hear how he was going to weasel out of telling Reason anything.

"After a mere ten seconds? Hardly fair. I should keep my explanation as abbreviated as your scant offering." He ate some of the dessert. "It's very good, girls. You should at least try it."

Jay-Tee had lost her appetite watching him take from Reason, but Reason would be starving. "You should eat it," she told her. "Food helps. You'll feel better."

Reason smiled halfheartedly, spooned some of the wobbly

creamy stuff into her mouth, then proceeded to inhale the rest of it. Jay-Tee switched their plates, feeling slightly better for having done *something* to help her. "Have mine."

"Thanks." She finished it as quickly as the first.

"What exactly do you want to know, Reason?" he asked. The smile on his face was genuine. He was enjoying this.

"What *don't* I want to know!" Reason said, sounding fed up, almost angry. It was the first time Jay-Tee had heard her use such a sharp tone of voice. As she spoke, her voice grew sharper, a red haze grew around her eyes. Jay-Tee could feel the hair standing up on her arms. Reason was losing her temper. The questions bubbled out of her like lava. "What is it? How does it work? How do I use it? Why am *I* magic? Why do you want it?"

As Reason continued to fire her questions at him, Jay-Tee leaned across to put her hand on Reason's arm. *"Tranquila,"* she whispered softly, like her father would whisper when she was little and losing it. *"Cálmate."* She could feel Reason simmering down, regaining control. She squeezed Reason's hand for a second, glad to have helped her but sad to remember what her dad used to be like before he turned into a monster she wished dead.

"Why do you want to take mine?" Reason asked in a less-agitated voice. "Or Jay-Tee's, for that matter? How does the door work? Does it have to do with maths?"

*Math,* Jay-Tee mentally corrected her. Unless there was more than one math? What a horrible thought.

"Why do they all die so young? Do I—"

He held up his hand. "Enough. I can't answer all of those

questions. You are magic, Reason, because it's in your genes. It's hereditary; it runs stronger in some families than others. You're from a long line. Jay-Tee's the product of two magic-wielders who were, as far as they knew, the only ones in their families. Many appear out of nowhere, with no relatives like them and no idea what they are."

Jay-Tee had a sudden, clear image of her parents together, flowers floating in the air, teaching her about magic, about how to protect herself. But her mother had died before Jay-Tee was old enough to talk. She touched the leather bracelet on her wrist.

"There are very few families like yours, Reason. I come from another. You have to remember that it's genetic. Like being tall. It's not something you can choose. It's in our genes. More women than men express it. Like left-handedness in men. But much, much rarer." He took another sip. "And yes, it does have to do with math."

Jay-Tee smiled, wanting to say to Reason, *See? Math, not* maths.

"Many of us are as gifted with numbers as we are with magic."

Jay-Tee snorted. "Not *all* of us."

"No, not all. It's a particularly strong talent in your family, Reason. Other magic users have other talents. Magic comes from people. It's generated by people. It's stronger and more plentiful in cities than in small towns."

"Or out in the bush," Reason said, more thinking out loud than asking a question.

He nodded. "That's why you were raised in the country. Much harder to find you there."

"And much easier to be found here? In a city? Especially one this big?" She glanced out the window at Times Square.

He nodded again.

"So she can find me here?" There was fear in her voice.

"But there are magics that help with hiding. I've been using them. And while you're with Jay-Tee, her magic shields yours. It's your magic that Esmeralda is tracking."

"She's tracking me?" Reason's eyes were wide. Jay-Tee couldn't believe she hadn't thought of that before.

"Of course."

"And—"

He held up his hand. "I believe that was more than enough payment, Reason, for such a paltry amount. Jay-Tee will most likely tell you more," he finished, the acid finally evident in his voice.

# 22
# Maelstrom

The limousine ride back from the restaurant was quiet and tense. No champagne, no bubbles, and no stupid toasts. Reason wasn't in the dark anymore. Jay-Tee was still unsure what to make of it. He hadn't given her any warning before his little performance tonight. She'd had no idea he was going to be *honest*.

But what had he told Reason that didn't help *him* more than her? Jay-Tee could fix that. She could think of some things he wouldn't want Reason to know.

But then she sighed. He'd know. He'd question her, and he'd know and make everything worse for her again. There had to be a way to warn Reason *and* keep him from hurting her because of it. Jay-Tee could let herself get angry, like Reason almost had at dinner. Let it explode in his face. Jay-Tee doubted she had more than five years left anyway. Why not just take him out now?

She glanced across at him and then at Reason sitting beside her, staring out the window, not saying anything. She could see no resemblance between them. Was it true? Was he really her grandfather?

He had the driver let them out in front of their building. "I'll see you both in a few days," he said. Neither of them responded. Jay-Tee wished a few meant many or, even better, never.

"I can't sit still in the apartment," Reason told her in the elevator. "I feel like I'm going to scream." Her skin was like parchment, making her black eye intense even under the makeup. She looked worse than when she'd first come through the door almost frozen to death.

"We'll go somewhere you can scream as much as you want. Out dancing. Remember? I promised. We'll just change into better clothes. Get rid of the wobble shoes." Reason didn't smile.

Neither of them said much getting changed, going out to the street. Jay-Tee wondered whether she should apologize but didn't know how. And anyway, it wasn't her fault. He would have gotten to Reason without her. But, Jay-Tee reminded herself, she'd helped. A lot.

She hailed a cab and they both piled in. Jay-Tee gave him the address and Reason stared out the window, her hood pulled over her head.

"How do you feel?" Jay-Tee asked her.

"Not exactly ace."

Under any other circumstances Jay-Tee would've teased her about the weird words she used. Not right now.

"You feel tired?"

"Yeah. Like he took energy, not magic."

"They're connected," Jay-Tee said. "But we'll get it back for you. He didn't take much. Magic flows in as well as out."

Reason looked at Jay-Tee with an expression that made her wonder if she hated her now.

The driver had the heating cranked up to the max. He was sweating like a pig. The taxi stank of him and a burning smell coming from the heater. Summer was a lot better: You could walk everywhere and forget about taxis.

They got out in the meatpacking district. The cobblestones were slick with ice. "Careful," Jay-Tee warned Reason, holding her gloved hand and pulling her along to the entrance to Inferno. Reason almost fell twice. She had absolutely no idea how to walk on ice and it wasn't exactly a good moment to start teaching her.

Jay-Tee wrenched the door open, still dragging Reason. The walls were shaking with the beat, the heavy bass pounding up through her feet. Jay-Tee smiled at Peter, the bouncer.

"Hey, Jay-Tee," he said. "Going to shake the place down?"

"Depends on how you mean."

Peter laughed. "Got your voodoo all tuned up? I told you I'm not losing my job 'cause of you."

Jay-Tee rolled her eyes. "Come on, Peter, you know you're just about the only person it *doesn't* work on."

Peter snorted. "You be careful with that one," he told Reason. "She's trouble."

They both walked by, shedding their coats, jackets, scarves, gloves, hats, sweaters, burying the coat-check girl under them. She gave Jay-Tee the ticket with a glazed smile. They were down to jeans and T-shirts. It wasn't warm yet, but it would be.

Through the next door and in the club proper, a blast of heat and music to go with the beat hit them. Jay-Tee started dancing. Dragged Reason behind her along the path she could feel between bodies, because Jay-Tee knew crowds, knew when they'd move, when they'd stay still, when they'd sway. This crowd was dancing, bobbing in and out, up and down, forming lots of little eddies, like a river. She danced Reason along it, out into the thick of the dance floor, which was really the whole club. Even the bartenders were half dancing. Hundreds of bodies all around them. The walls slick with sweat.

Jay-Tee closed her eyes and let herself unravel, falling into the dance maelstrom. A split second before she fell all the way, she slid her eyes over Reason. She was there already, little Reason, as lost as Jay-Tee was about to be. Jay-Tee smiled. This was her real magic. This was what she loved best.

Jay-Tee came back with two large bottles of water, handed one of them to Reason, grinning.

"Bet you never thought you were going to be hot again! Dripping with sweat," Jay-Tee said into Reason's ear.

Reason returned the grin. "Nup. You were right. My energy's back. Does that mean the magic is too?"

Jay-Tee started to nod and then stopped. "I don't really know. Not exactly. I do know that when I dance in a crowd, I feel it flow into me. It's created by all these people. I can connect to it and end up bigger than I am. You felt that too, right?" Jay-Tee had never talked about this with anyone before. The words felt strange coming out of her mouth.

"Yeah." They leaned over the railing of the balcony, staring at the crowd surging below them. Jay-Tee couldn't wait to fall back into it. From up here it looked like the ocean in a storm, everything in motion, cresting waves of bodies turning and twisting in the tempest. The walls were shaking.

Reason unscrewed the lid of her bottle and took a large swig. "Did you actually pay for these? Or for us to get in?"

Jay-Tee laughed.

"You never pay for anything, do you? Just wave your hand and they see money."

"Doesn't work on everyone. Pete, you know, the bouncer up front?"

Reason nodded.

"He just lets me in 'cause he likes me. I tried it on him and he burst out laughing." Jay-Tee shook her head at the memory.

"Is it real? The money, I mean."

"Yeah, it becomes real."

"How?"

"My magic's got to do with the connections between people." Jay-Tee had never explained it to anyone before. Wasn't exactly sure how to. "That's what a crowd is—not just a bunch of people together, but the connections between them. And I use that, the energy of it; I pull the money out of that."

Reason nodded, but Jay-Tee wasn't really sure she understood.

"Is that how my magic works?"

"Yours is more bound up in numbers than people."

"What can I do with it?"

Jay-Tee shrugged. "I don't know. You should know. I mean . . ." She paused. "It's something you'll figure out. Everyone's magic is different."

Reason considered this. "Blake's credit card," she said finally. "Was that real?"

"Oh, sure, *he's* rich. He always uses real money." Her voice changed to his precise, measured tones: "He would never expend magic on anything so *trivial*." She returned to her normal voice. "He's all about hoarding his."

"And taking other people's?"

"Yeah, that's the truth. Let's dive back in. Get some more of our own."

Reason nodded. "We could run away, you know, from him." They were at the top of the ladder from the balcony, about to climb back down to the dance floor.

"Where would we go?" Jay-Tee asked, trying to keep the hope out of her voice.

"Australia. Through the door." Reason didn't quite know how they'd manage that without the key. "I know where to hide back home. Out bush. We'd be safe."

"Your grandmother caught you before."

"Only 'cause Sarafina went nuts. If it was just you and me, we'd be fine."

"Dance now," Jay-Tee said, feeling the pulse calling her, imagining a life out in the wilds of Australia: kangaroos and crocodiles. She wondered if kangaroos danced. "Think about escaping later."

They climbed down the ladder and slid back into the crowd, twisting and shaking through eddies and rivulets of magic and energy and people.

# 23
# Closer

Tom felt self-conscious talking to Mere on the mobile in the middle of the restaurant. He kept his voice low, even though the reception wasn't great.

"She's been here," he said again, slightly louder. "Yes." He gave Mere the address. "See you soon. Bye."

Tom was cold, tired, and hungry. For the last two hours he'd wandered around the surrounding blocks, going into restaurants and shops, touching things, sitting down at as many of the tables as he could, and getting lots of strange looks for failing to buy or order anything. It had been cold, but now it was cold and dark. Not a trace of Reason anywhere except here, back at this exact table again. Faint, but here.

A tall blond waitress with a gloomy expression came over and dumped a large glass of ice water on the table, handing him an oversized menu. Some of the water sloshed onto the table.

Tom picked up the menu and was startled by the strong feeling of Reason. He almost dropped it. She'd held this very menu. She *was* alive. Tom hadn't realised that some part of him believed his own visions of her frozen to death in the snow. Apparently Mere's reassurances hadn't been enough.

"You want coffee?" the waitress asked in a tone of complete uninterest. She had an accent he didn't recognise. Definitely not American. German, maybe? Tom immediately abandoned his plans of playing detective and asking her if she'd seen Reason. Not only did the waitress not care about his consumption of coffee, she had the air of someone for whom life itself meant nothing. Tom decided she must be the saddest waitress in the world.

"No, thank you. Just bacon and eggs." A man at the next table was sipping at his coffee, glancing at Tom over his newspaper. He was wearing a pinstripe suit, but the stripes were thin bands of purple over charcoal, and the lapels were just a tad wider than usual. Tom couldn't help admiring the tie, purple with tiny gold flecks, which would've been disastrous with any other suit. He couldn't be sure without touching, but the suit looked to be a very fine wool. Merino, maybe.

"How you want the eggs?" the waitress asked, looking at her pad, not at Tom.

"Fried, please."

"How you want them fried?"

"Er," Tom said, trying to think what she meant. "In butter?"

Wrong answer. The waitress slid her eyes from the pad to regard him mournfully, as if his stupidity only further proved that the world was worth nothing.

"Over easy? Sunny-side up?"

"Sunny-side up," Tom said, because it sounded warm and cheerful.

"What toast you want? Challah, brown, rye, white, seven

grain, pumpernickel, whole wheat?" she asked. The words all ran together. She had asked this question many times before.

"Challah," Tom said, never having heard of it, but she'd said it first.

"You want hash browns, home fries, or kasha?"

"Hash browns," Tom said, sticking to the principle of ordering whatever was said first.

"You want something to drink?"

"Orange juice," Tom said before she could start another list.

"Small, medium, or large?"

Tom sighed, realising there were no requests he could make that wouldn't generate further choices. "Large, please."

The waitress took the Reason-saturated menu from his hands before he could think to ask if he could hang on to it and walked away. Tom's palms were sweating. He took a sip of the water, then peeled his jumper off, relieved to have gotten through the ordeal of ordering relatively unscathed. If Americans could make bacon and eggs that difficult, it boggled his mind thinking what it must be like trying to order in a fancy restaurant.

"Too many choices?" the woman on the other side of him asked, though she didn't look at him and didn't seem to expect an answer. She had a big notebook open that she had momentarily paused from scribbling in. Her clothes were all the same uniform black. An intense black, as if she had dyed them all in the same vat just that morning. Their light-eating blackness made it impossible to see where jacket ended and trousers started. "They're trying to distract us with all the choices so we don't realise that when it comes to the *important* things, there are no choices. None at all. Hmmm." She picked up her pen and resumed writing at an even more frantic rate.

*Okay,* thought Tom. *Whatever you say.* He glanced at the man on his other side and wondered if it would be okay to ask him who designed the suit and tie. Apparently, like at home, it was okay for strangers to talk to each other. But what if it was only okay for the lunatic ones?

He put his hands back on the table, wishing Mere would hurry up and get here. Ree, faint and fading. He had an image of her at the top of Filomena, gazing at the view of Sydney, exclaiming about the smell of flying foxes. His eyes prickled with tears. Tom blinked them away. He *was* going to see her again. Soon.

Maybe he should get started on her cargo pants ahead of time? That way he could give them to her as a welcome-home present. He was sure Ree wouldn't mind if he picked the fabric for her. A sturdy cotton. Brown or olive green'd be best, definitely not black. Tom had a vision of the pants, bulky with all their pockets, lying on her bed waiting for her.

If only the waitress hadn't taken the menu away. What were the odds of the same menu she'd touched being given to him, sitting here at her table? He wondered how to tell how long it was since Reason had been here. He hoped Mere would know.

A different waitress put his orange juice down on the table.

She didn't smile either. He looked around. Not a smile any-where. Well, not on the faces of the waitresses. Each one was the saddest woman in the world. Tom imagined a snarling, vicious ogre of a boss.

Mere came in, looking glamorous and perfectly coiffed as usual. The jersey fabric of her charcoal-grey-with-black-piping suit moved with her, blending its shape to hers, so that both Mere and the fabric looked their best.

Tom had made that suit. He'd slept on top of the jersey and the piping for a week before cutting it. The longer he was in con-tact with fabric, the more imbued with him it became. When he made clothes for people like Jessica Chan, the magic gradually dropped away. But Mere's magic reinforced his. He doubted that suit would ever fit badly, no matter how Mere's body changed.

But the suit was unable to hide the fatigue on her face. She was more tired than he had ever seen her. Tom wondered if the shadows under his own eyes were that dark. Probably. Both wrecked by the jet lag. *Door* lag.

She kissed his cheek and sat down opposite just as his eggs arrived. The smell filled his nostrils. Tom was starving.

The man at the next table stood seconds after Mere sat, folding his newspaper and pulling on his overcoat: ankle length, camel mohair. Quite gorgeous. He nodded to Tom, who nodded back and wished he had the nerve to ask about his clothes. The overcoat was incredible. Perfect lines.

Mere peeled off her gloves and touched the table. "Yes," she said, smiling, looking relieved. Maybe she hadn't quite believed her own pronouncements about Ree either. "You're absolutely right." She reached across to squeeze his hand. "Well done, Tom. This is the first trace I've felt since we came through the door."

Tom couldn't help feeling proud, absorbing her praise as if it were sunshine.

"It feels recent too. Probably today. What do you think? Does it feel that way to you?"

"I'm not sure," Tom said, enjoying Mere consulting him as if he knew as much about these things as she did. "The menu felt stronger." He shook his head. "I can't tell."

"Not to worry. We'll find her. I'm sure of it. Now eat your eggs before they congeal."

Tom dug in. They were every bit as good as they smelled. Challah turned out to be a weird sweet bread that melted in your mouth, and hash browns were potatoes cut in strips, pressed together, and fried. Sunny-side up, as far as he could tell, meant that they were normal fried eggs. He gobbled it all, grateful not to have made any wrong choices.

Mere ordered coffee, which came almost instantly. She took a sip and grimaced. "Oh, well. How're your eggs?"

Tom made a thumbs up gesture.

The woman at the next table spoke, once again not looking up. "Eggs are produced by emaciated, diseased prisoners. They eat their own feces, their own young. All of *that* is in eggs. Better to . . . Yes." She seized her pen, returned to scribbling her latest profound thoughts.

Tom and Mere exchanged a look. Mere pulled a face, grinning. The expression only emphasised her fatigue. "How are you settling in at your sister's?" she asked.

Tom half expected a diatribe from the mad lady about how sisters were poisoning society, but she was too busy scribbling. He nodded at Mere, still eating. He'd love to tell Cath what was really going on, but both his dad and Mere had insisted that was not a good idea.

"There's a way," Mere said, glancing at the mad lady and keeping her voice low, "something I haven't shown you yet. It might help us learn more, get an idea of where she went."

Tom's eyes widened. He swallowed rapidly. "There is? Can we do it here? What would we use? Will it be okay? I've already done magic this week."

"Yes. It will be fine. We can do it right now. There are a few small magics that we can do without objects. It's more advanced."

"Really?" Tom asked. Up until now Mere'd taught him the only safe magics were ones worked through something inanimate, preferably an already charged object. Like the door or the silver chain she'd given him. There was still so much he had to learn about magic.

"Put your hand on the table."

"Which one?"

"Either hand. It doesn't matter."

Tom looked around nervously. The restaurant wasn't completely full, but it was busy. Waitresses moving back and forth and a few guys in white whose sole job seemed to be clearing the tables and topping up people's water glasses. It seemed too public a place for magic.

"It's fine, Tom. No one will see. There's nothing *to* see."

"Okay." He put his right hand on the table.

"Do you feel her?"

He nodded. The trace was stronger with Mere here.

Mere looked directly into Tom's eyes, holding his gaze. "I'm going to put my hand on yours. Is that okay?"

"Yes," Tom said. "Of course."

Mere nodded. "Will you share your magic with me?"

"Yes." Tom knew that two magic-wielders could work together but that they rarely did. Working magic with someone required lots of trust. He shivered. He hadn't realised Mere trusted him *that* much.

Mere touched him. Tom felt a faint burning sensation. His stomach contracted, and for a moment he thought he might chunder. He concentrated on seeing the true shapes of the room and of the people around him. His vision floated with triangles, circles, squares, but none of them were quite true. He felt heat radiating up his arm, across his shoulders. It felt wrong somehow. The little magics he'd done before now had never felt wrong. He looked at Mere for reassurance—her eyes seemed brighter, but far away. Spots started to appear in front of his eyes.

She took her hand from his. He had no idea how long it had been. He was dizzy, suddenly knackered, wishing he could sleep there and then. Great, the magic had set off his jet lag again.

"Eat," Mere told him. She leaned further back in her chair,

her expression still distant. Worse hit than him. He hadn't realised sharing magic would be so awful.

Tom took a mouthful of toast. It hadn't gone cold. He chewed and the dots from his eyes receded. He kept eating until there wasn't a speck of food on the plate. He was still intensely hungry. He signalled to a waitress. "Same thing again, please. And a muffin. Blueberry," he said quickly before she could offer him any choices.

"Toasted?"

"Yes."

"Butter?"

"Yes," he said, utterly defeated.

She nodded, taking his dirty plate away.

The muffin came quickly and Tom bolted it down so fast he barely tasted it. Mere seemed to be returning from wherever she had gone. He imagined the magic-working had been a lot harder for her than for him. "Did it work?"

Mere nodded. "You did good, Tom."

He felt himself blush.

"Reason was here today. Definitely. We're close. She hasn't left the East Village." Mere smiled, her eyes lit up, and for a moment there was no trace of fatigue on her face.

Tom returned the smile, though it made him tired.

"We'll find her." She nodded at him as if to say it was a promise. "How do you feel?" Mere asked, her voice soft with concern.

# 24
# At Inferno

If it were up to Jay-Tee, we'd keep dancing until they calculated pi to the last digit. My legs were shaking, I was dripping with sweat, my water bottle was empty, and if I didn't sit down, I was going to die.

Jay-Tee was lost inside the dancing. In an ecstatic trance, like the dervishes Sarafina once told me about. Her eyes focused on something no one but she could see, body moving so fast she almost seemed to blur. Too fast for me.

I tried to signal to her that I was going to sit down, but she was too far gone. I made my way out through the crowd. When Jay-Tee had pulled me along, it had been like sliding through silk. Without her it was a sea of elbows and feet and mumbled mutual apologies no one could hear. It was a relief to get into the bathroom and refill my bottle.

I climbed the sweat-slick metal ladder to the tables on the balcony overlooking the dance floor, sat down at the only empty one with my water bottle, and took in gulps of hot, humid, sticky air.

I'd never danced that crazy for that long. I was knackered yet buzzing, surges of energy running through me faster and stronger than the blood in my veins. When I closed my eyes, I saw tangles of Fibs and the spirals they created. They pulsed and disintegrated in time with the thudding beat. If I'd lain down in my bed, sleep would've been impossible.

I leaned my forearms on the railing, but they slid off. The railing was dripping with sweat too. I wiped it dry with my T-shirt, then leaned forward again, looking at my right hand where he'd touched me. I was surprised to see no sign of it. There should have been something. It still tingled with a foul kind of pins and needles. I was glad I'd never said yes to Esmeralda, never let *her* touch me like that. I never would, and I was going to do everything I could to make sure that Jason Blake never touched me again either.

I sipped my water and watched the crowd, more than 780 of them (783 at this precise moment, but in less than a second the number changed, people arriving, leaving, buying drinks, coming and going from the bathroom), seething and undulating like a snake. Like lots of snakes. I traced the patterns, changing and shifting as fast as windblown sand. What was the connection between numbers and people and magic?

I could see Jay-Tee in the heart of it, a faint glow around her. A group of dancing admirers surrounded her, trying to mirror her movements, but she was too fast, too agile, too far into the dance for them. I wondered if she even knew they were there. Was it Jay-Tee's magic that had given me energy and strength out there? Or was it mine?

What could I do with my magic? Easy for Jay-Tee to say that I'd find out; she already knew all about hers. We were the same age, but I knew nothing.

*Almost nothing,* I thought, remembering. What could I do besides kill people?

I hadn't meant to kill him, but my intentions didn't make any difference, did they? He was still dead. A nasty, creepy boy who might have grown up to be a nasty, creepy man but might not have. And he was dead because I was magic but hadn't known it and had lost my temper. *Never* lose your temper, Sarafina had always said. I wished she had told me why.

I shook my head, trying to push those thoughts away. Magic didn't only kill. Jay-Tee used it to make money. Could I do that? Why did Jason Blake not want to expend any of his? Why was he intent on sucking up other people's? If magic was infinite, then that made no sense. Why—

"Amazing, isn't it?" a guy asked, sitting down beside me, yelling into my ear.

I nodded, turned to look at him. He was gorgeous. The best-looking guy I'd ever seen. Huge brown eyes. Tight curly hair cut close to his scalp. Skin a slightly darker shade than Jay-Tee's and gleaming with sweat. He'd been out there dancing too. I wondered for a moment if he was magic. Was this a love spell? After one look I wanted him and I'd never *wanted* anyone before. It had to be some kind of magic.

He smiled, wide and beautiful. It reached his eyes and revealed his even white teeth. All except an upper front one, which was crooked. Instantly I decided it was my favourite. I hoped that he would lean close to me again.

"You like dancing?" he asked, his mouth close to my ear. The intimacy made my skin grow hotter than it already was.

I nodded again. My cheek muscles were hurting. I tried to tone down my smile, but when I looked at him, it sprang back into action. I could think of nothing to say.

"But you got to rest too, right?"

I nodded. He would be wondering if I was mute fairly soon.

"No use blowing a gasket out there."

This time I shook my head. Such variety.

"Do you come here a lot?" he asked, then grimaced. "That was a dumb-ass thing to say. I'm not trying to pick you up. I saw you dancing out there with Julieta."

"Julieta?" I asked.

"Jay-Tee. My sister. I'm Danny."

I stared at him, and suddenly I could see it. He was much taller, his face more angular, his eyes bigger, with longer eye-lashes (I just bet *that* killed Jay-Tee), but he really was her brother. Same mouth, same shape of the eyes, some of the same expressions. I should've seen it straightaway. Just like Jay-Tee.

I froze. He really could be magic, then, like her.

He held out his hand, but I hesitated. What if he wanted my magic? His smile was open, nothing like Jason Blake's. I risked it, saying *no* over and over in my head as we shook hands.

"She didn't tell me she had a brother." He didn't hear me. I leaned closer and said, "She didn't mention having a brother." She'd told me she didn't have any brothers or sisters. Another lie.

"I'm not surprised. She ran away."

"Do you know why she ran away?" There, another whole sentence from me.

He nodded. "I think so. It had to do with Dad. What did she tell you?"

I opened my mouth and then closed it.

"That's okay," he said. "I'm not asking you to betray her or anything. Just tell her I want to see her, talk to her." He looked down at where Jay-Tee was still lost in her dancing. "She's always loved it. Dancing. This is exactly her kind of place. BPMs in the stratosphere and way too many people."

I wondered what BPMs were.

"Ever since she was little," Danny continued, "she's loved crowds. I figured eventually I'd find her in a place like this." He turned back to me. I thought I'd dissolve under his gaze. "If I give you my number, will you give it to her?"

"Sure," I said without thinking. Then I remembered about magic and numbers. Would passing it to Jay-Tee do something to her? Hurt her? Or lead Danny to her?

"Do you have a pen?"

I shook my head.

"Will you wait here? I can get one from the bar. Friend of mine works there."

"That's okay," I told him. His eyes were back on the dance floor, following Jay-Tee. "Just tell me. I'll remember."

His eyes narrowed a little, but still gorgeous. Was I losing my judgment because he was so pretty? *Had* he magicked me? My stomach felt like there were butterflies inside. "You sure you can remember it?"

"I'm good at numbers."

"Ten digits good?"

I nodded, and he told me.

"Got that?"

"Huh! If you leave off the 917, that's Fib (33)." But was that a good or a bad thing? Fibonacci maths had always seemed magical to me; now I was sure it really was.

Was Danny trying to work a spell over his sister? At least I could talk to Jay-Tee, find out what she thought, before I told her what the number was. Would a spoken number be more or less powerful than a number on a piece of paper? Would it affect me just by memorising it? I didn't feel any different, any *more* different.

"Huh?" Danny said. "Fib (33)?"

"It's the thirty-third number in the Fibonacci series." I repeated the number in his ear to make sure I'd heard it right.

He nodded. "You've got a great memory, girl. What's your name?"

"Reason."

"Lisa?"

I put my mouth closer to his ear, tingling all over. "Reason," I said slowly.

"Your name is Reason? As in 'reasonable'?"

I nodded. "That's the one."

"Strange name for such a pretty girl." But he wasn't looking at me; his eyes were on the dance floor, on his sister.

"Everyone says that."

"That you're pretty?" He glanced at me and grinned. "I bet they do. Don't let it go to your head."

I blushed as completely as if I were Tom. "I meant that they say my name is strange." Then I felt like even more of a spaz. He knew that; he was just teasing.

"Is she all right?" he asked. "Julieta? She got somewhere okay to live? She's eating enough?"

I nodded, wanting to tell him about Jason Blake but not wanting to dob Jay-Tee in. She'd lied to me—a lot—but she still felt like a friend. I didn't have many of those. Just her and Tom.

"Will you tell her I'm looking for her? That I'm worried. That things aren't like how they were before? That she'll be safe at home now?"

I nodded again. He reached out and squeezed my hand just like Jay-Tee had, but too briefly. He looked out over the crowd at her. She was dancing her way slowly out through the swirls and whorls. No elbows in the face or trampled toes for her.

Danny stood up, leaned into my ear. "I'm going to talk to her, but if she runs away again, you'll tell her what I said? Give her my number?"

"I promise I'll tell her." My hand was in my pocket and I felt the ammonite, strong and warm. Every time I'd ever lost it, I'd found it again. No, not found, *known* where it was. Ammonites curled outwards in a golden spiral, more Fibonaccis. My stone was magic, I was suddenly sure.

"Wait," I said. "Take this." I handed it to Danny and he looked at it and then at me as if I were mad. "It'll give you luck," I said. It sounded lame, but I couldn't think of anything else. He was still looking at me strangely but put it in his pocket. I could feel it there, warm and strong. I would know where he was now. If he did try to kidnap Jay-Tee or hurt her, I'd find him.

I didn't really believe he would. Danny seemed concerned. He'd only spoken to me to get a message to Jay-Tee. Of course that could be a bad thing, too. But it hadn't felt like that. Not like Jason Blake.

I watched him climb down to the dance floor, head towards Jay-Tee, the ammonite glowing in his pocket. Jay-Tee was heading for the bathroom, Danny not far behind her. How'd he managed to follow her so easily through the crowd? He was tall, but she was tiny and disappeared easily in the dancing throng.

Magic, most likely. *Bugger.* I stood up. But even if he was magic, that didn't necessarily mean he was bad, did it? I was magic and so was Jay-Tee. I worked my way along the railing, pushing past people as politely as I could, keeping my eyes on the two of them below still moving through the crowd. Then they went under the balcony and I lost them, but not my ammonite. I could feel it, in Danny's pocket, there outside the women's dunny.

I reached the ladder, stood there, not knowing whether I should go down or watch out for them from up here. Then I saw Jay-Tee waving to me from the entrance. How did she get there? Crowd magic, I guessed.

Danny was still waiting outside the dunny. I clambered down, made my way to her by skirting the edges of the dance floor as fast as I could, being trodden on and whacked with elbows. I did not have Jay-Tee's kind of magic.

She grabbed my arm, her fingernails digging in, hissed that we had to go, and dragged me through the door. We retrieved our gear from the coat-check girl, piling into it as fast as we could. My fingers stumbled on the buttons. Jay-Tee pushed my hands aside and did them for me. Danny and my stone were still inside, waiting for Jay-Tee to reappear.

Then we were out onto the street, blinking in daylight. My eyes stung with the shock of it. Morning. How long had we been dancing? It was still freezing cold, but the sky was clear and blue and the sun had finally come out. I tried to remember the last time I'd seen the sun. Sydney. Three days ago? Four? I'd lost count, or rather, I'd lost my sense of night and day.

Everywhere men were unpacking huge trucks, having no difficulty at all rushing back and forth across the icy surface of the uneven road. Me, I was just about to go arse over tit with every step. The workday had started and here I was just wanting to fall into bed and sleep forever. I wondered if I'd ever be sorted about what time of day it was again.

Jay-Tee led me into one of the taxis waiting outside Inferno, gave the driver an address, sank back into the seat, and closed her eyes.

"What—" I began.

"We're going to get breakfast," Jay-Tee said, cutting me off, her eyes squeezed shut. She sounded furious, like she'd hit me if I asked any questions. "I'm hungry. We're going to eat."

As the taxi drove away, the ammonite got fainter and fainter until I couldn't feel it all.

# 25
# Friends

They were halfway through breakfast before Jay-Tee found herself able to breathe evenly. Reason was stuffing herself with pierogies, kielbasa, and kasha, not saying a word, but Jay-Tee could almost hear the questions she wanted to ask. Jay-Tee was sick of answering Reason's questions.

She wished she could get away from her. Forget about Reason and him and all the rest of it and go somewhere far away. But she'd never been outside New York City. Hell, she hadn't even been to all five boroughs. Staten Island was as big a mystery to Jay-Tee as Sydney was. Reason had said they could escape through the door, hide in the country in Australia. Yeah, right, like he'd let them, like they could get past the witch.

Jay-Tee raised a piece of bacon to her mouth, but halfway there she felt the angry acid in her stomach and put the bacon down. She'd messed up her breakfast, broken the yolks of the eggs so they'd spread out over everything. Now they were turning into a cold yellow sludge that coated it all. She'd been starving and now she wasn't sure she could ever eat again. She wished her dad to hell for about the hundredth time.

Reason had almost finished her food and was looking at

her, eyes wide and curious. Jay-Tee couldn't see her keeping her mouth shut much longer. She sighed, trying to let go of her anger. She was *not* going to lose her temper. Ever.

"At the club . . ." Jay-Tee began, because there was no getting away; she had to tell Reason something. "There was this guy. My dad sent him."

"Your brother, Danny," Reason said, continuing to eat as if she'd said nothing unusual.

Jay-Tee stared at her. How on earth did she know about Danny? What else did she know?

"He talked to me," Reason said, grinning, clearly enjoying being one up, "before he went looking for you. What are BPMs?"

"Beats per minute," Jay-Tee said reflexively. "He what?" she spat the words out. She had to get a grip. That asshole! How *dare* he? He was trying to turn Reason against her. "I don't believe it. What did you tell him? You didn't tell him where we lived, did you?" The thought terrified Jay-Tee.

"No. What do you reckon? That I'd dob you in to the first person who asked? I didn't tell him a thing."

"Sorry," Jay-Tee said, wondering what *dob* meant. She wished Reason would learn to talk normal.

"No worries. Is he magic?"

"What?" What a stupid question. Of course he wasn't magic. Didn't Reason know anything? Couldn't she just tell? But then Jay-Tee realized that no, she couldn't. "No, no, of course not," she said. "Why would you think that?"

"Huh," Reason said, sounding relieved. "I just thought . . ." She trailed off, smiling. "Never mind."

"What did he say to you?" Jay-Tee asked. Her stomach had knotted again. "I can't *believe* he talked to you. Tell me what he said. What did he say about me?"

"He said that things had changed at home, that it was safe for you now. That he loves you and misses you. He wanted to know if you were okay, getting enough to eat, living somewhere not too foul. He was concerned. And he gave me his phone number."

"Damn." Jay-Tee dropped her fork onto her plate and put her hands in her hair.

"He's really not magic?" Reason asked.

"What? No. Why do you keep going on about that? He's not magic. Okay? He got the basketball-playing genes. I got the magic ones."

"Oh," she said. "Not the left-handed gene?"

Jay-Tee couldn't help laughing. "Actually, he's left-handed, too."

Reason smiled. She reached across and squeezed Jay-Tee's hand, who had an immediate memory of doing the same for Reason when she was boiling with anger. *We're friends,* she thought, surprising herself. She and Reason had somehow become friends.

"Danny seemed okay to me."

"He is," Jay-Tee said, feeling somehow calmer. Her stomach was starting to unknot. "But he doesn't know about Dad—"

"He told me he thought you ran away *because* of your dad. So he must know something."

"He said that?" She stared at Reason.

Reason nodded, looking down at her completely empty plate. Her stomach rumbled, the sound ridiculously loud considering the amount of food she'd just stuffed in her face. But Reason'd been drained and then danced all night. She had to be ravenous.

"Damn," Jay-Tee said. Her hunger was starting to return. She ate a mouthful of cold, slimy-with-egg bacon. "What else did he say?"

"Not much. That he reckoned you were going to show up at Inferno sooner or later 'cause it was your kind of place. That he's been looking for you everywhere. He seems like a really nice guy."

"He's cool. It's just that he was away when things got bad. He had no idea."

"Away?"

"Boarding school. Got a scholarship on account of the basketball genes."

"Why didn't you tell him?"

How could she have told him? Why would he have believed her? Their dad had always been so gentle. Jay-Tee shook her head. "Did Danny say *anything* about Dad?"

"Just that he thought that's why you ran away." Reason smiled at her again. Jay-Tee guessed that was supposed to be reassuring. "He seemed to be on *your* side. Not your dad's. You should call him."

Jay-Tee glared at her, had to fight down an urge to storm out of the restaurant. "Right. And have him lead that bastard straight to me. I don't think so."

"Danny wouldn't do that. He said things have changed."

"Yeah, well, I doubt they'll be changed enough."

"If you call him," Reason said, "you'll find out, won't you? It can't be that bad."

"What would you know?" Jay-Tee demanded, her anger returned and aimed full blast at Reason. "You don't know anything about my family."

"Nope, I don't," she replied. "Though you seem to know heaps about mine."

Jay-Tee closed her mouth, feeling like total scum. None of this was Reason's fault.

Reason waved at a waitress, ordered mashed potatoes and gravy as well as macaroni and cheese. "You want something else?"

Jay-Tee nodded. "Same as her," she told the waitress. "Sorry," she said when the waitress was gone.

"'S'okay. You're right, I don't know anything about your situation."

"Not that. I mean sorry for everything. For helping him, you know? I just wanted him to stop doing it to me." She looked at a point below Reason's chin.

"Don't worry. I'd've done the same thing if I was you."

Jay-Tee doubted that.

"We just have to get out of this," Reason continued. "Get

away from Blake and away from your dad and from my grand-mother too."

Jay-Tee looked at her. "Yeah, right. Easy as pie."

"Pi's not easy, but there's two of us. And we're *both* magic. There's got to be something we can do. Let's start by calling your brother."

Jay-Tee opened her mouth to speak. Reason didn't understand: she *couldn't* call her brother.

Reason put her hand up. "You know why you and Blake were able to get me so easy? Because I didn't know *anything*. Because I was an innocent kid who'd just walked in out of the bush."

Jay-Tee felt even more ashamed. Reason was right. She could have told her what was happening, but what had she done instead? Told her the East Village was east of the West Village.

"We have to find out everything we can. Find out what's changed with your family. Maybe your brother will tell us something that can help us. Maybe he'll know somewhere we can go. It's just a phone call. He's not magic, right? So how can a phone call hurt?"

Jay-Tee looked up. "I'm so sorry." What a stupid word *sorry* was. It didn't come close to describing what it was like to be as full of shame and guilt as she was. She could've helped Reason, warned her. But instead . . .

"I know you are. You'll call him?"

She nodded slowly. "But we'll call from a public phone, okay? One far from here."

"Sure," Reason said. The rest of the food arrived and they plowed in.

As they ate, Jay-Tee watched Reason. She'd never seen her look like this before. Not confused, not bewildered; certain, determined. As if she really could do something to get them out of the mess they were in, get them away from him, from Reason's grandmother, from her dad. At that moment, Jay-Tee believed it too.

They took a cab all the way uptown into Washington Heights until Jay-Tee found a cluster of phones that felt far enough away. She'd been thinking Australia, but 188th Street would have to do.

She passed her hand over the cabdriver's, letting the magic flow through her mother's leather bracelet, watching the money appear. They jumped out, huddling in the inadequate shelter around the phone. Even colder up here; Jay-Tee would've sworn the wind was a thousand times stronger.

She picked up the receiver and wiped the mouthpiece on her coat.

"That doesn't make any difference," Reason said. "Any bacteria's still going to be there." Jay-Tee just bet that was something her mom had said.

"Yeah, but their wet icky saliva's gone."

"Onto your sleeve."

"Better than on my mouth. So what's the number?" It was freezing. Jay-Tee just wanted to do this and be gone. God only knew how they were going to find another cab up here. There wasn't exactly the normal sea of yellow. Compared to downtown, there were hardly any cars at all. She should have thought of that. Maybe Tribeca would've been far enough away.

"It's 917—"

"Huh," Jay-Tee said, "sounds like a cell phone. Why didn't you say so?" A cell phone meant it was Danny's number, less chance of her dad answering.

"'Cause I didn't *know* it was a mobile." Reason rolled her eyes.

"Mobile," Jay-Tee muttered. She had forgotten in the midst of Reason's current take-charge mood that she didn't know jack about shit. She'd sure gotten a lot more feisty since Jason had laid it all on her tonight, or rather, *last* night.

How long was it since they'd slept? Jay-Tee could definitely use some sleep soon. A lot. "Okay, give me the rest."

She reeled off the number. "See? Fib (33)."

"What? You're keeping count?"

Reason looked puzzled. "I always keep count."

Jay-Tee dialed, then held the receiver between them. They both listened as it rang. She hoped it would just keep ringing, or go to voice mail, or something. A deep male voice answered, sounding just like her dad. She slammed the phone down.

"What are you doing?" Reason asked. "What did you do that for? That was Danny."

"Really? He sounded just like Dad. He's only seventeen. Eighteen." She corrected herself, realizing he'd just had his birthday. "When did he start sounding like Dad?"

"Call him back. It's freezing," Reason said, bouncing back and forth on her feet. "I swear my nose is going to fall off. The sooner you do this, the sooner it'll be done."

"You sound like a grandma."

"Just call him, *Julieta*."

Jay-Tee glared at Reason, then decided it was too cold to call her out for using her given name and fed more coins in, entering the digits as Reason recited them.

"Hello," said Danny. Jay-Tee froze again at the sound of his voice, but she didn't hang up again. "Hello?" he said again.

"Hi, Danny," Reason said, butting in. Jay-Tee would've loved to slap her. "It's Reason and Jay-Tee."

"Yeah, it's me," Jay-Tee said. She imagined she sounded as hesitant as she felt.

"Julieta? Reason?"

"Yeah, it's me. Reason's just listening."

"I'm so glad." His voice sounded choked, like he might cry. Jay-Tee felt her throat constricting too. She forced herself to breathe. "It's really you?"

"Yeah."

"Will you meet me? I have to see you. Things have changed—"

"How?" she said, her voice scraping in her throat. "How have they changed?"

"I wanted to tell you in—"

"Tell me. Now. I won't meet you unless you tell me. I can't see Dad again. You understand? I just can't."

"You don't have to see Dad."

"How can you promise that? What if he follows you?"

There was a silence at the other end of the line, then she heard her brother taking a deep breath. "He can't follow me, Julieta. He's dead."

Jay-Tee hung up the phone. She felt sick. She could feel the mess in her stomach moving. "We have to go," she said, amazed that the words came out. "It's cold. I have to sleep."

Reason looked like she was going to say something, but Jay-Tee's glare shut her up.

Jay-Tee stepped out onto the road, hardly able to see. She felt hot and cold and her nerve endings stung as if her skin had been reduced to a single layer. There was nothing to protect her. A black gypsy cab appeared at once. Now, *that* was magic.

Jay-Tee called her brother again from the apartment, doing as much as she could through her fatigue to shield the conversation from *him* but wasn't too confident of her success. His snares lay all over the apartment.

They arranged to meet at 1 PM for lunch just around the corner. Reason had insisted they meet somewhere close. It was nine-thirty in the morning and Jay-Tee could see that Reason was as close to keeling over from lack of sleep as she was. She hoped four hours would be enough to keep them going.

When Jay-Tee's head hit the pillow, she closed her eyes and slipped into oblivion, not thinking of her dead father, dreaming of nothing.

# 26
# Snot

"Twenty-four hours?" Tom couldn't keep the astonishment out of his voice. "What time is it?"

"More like twenty-six," said Cath's male flatmate, the one who worried about his bathroom products. Based on that, Tom had been expecting interesting clothes, but he was wearing a yellow T-shirt with crooked seams and badly cut jeans. Seemed odd to Tom to care about your skin, but not what you put over it.

"You know," daggy jeans continued, "this chair sucks for watching TV. What you've been sleeping on for *twenty-six* hours—it's a *couch,* not a bed."

"You know," Cath said, imitating her flatmate's tone, "my brother's been sick. He really needed to sleep."

"Yeah, well, you and all your friends and boyfriends and relatives aren't the only ones who live here." The guy's eyes were bugging out and one of the veins on his neck had suddenly become visible. "Is your brother going to pay rent? Put in for the utilities?"

" 'Ken hell, Andrew! Give him a break. He just woke up. Let's talk about this later."

The flatmate stood up, shot a poisonous glance at Cath,

didn't bother to look at Tom, and stomped out, slamming the door of his bedroom, which made more of a squeak than a bang. Tom imagined the lack of a satisfyingly loud slam would make him even more ropeable.

"What time *is* it?"

Cath looked at her watch. "Eight at night."

"Bugger. Twenty-six hours! Sorry," Tom said, sitting up and rubbing his eyes. "I didn't mean to sleep that long."

"Not your fault. You needed it. You looked bloody awful when you got in. I'm just glad you woke up. Mere said I wasn't to worry, but honest, you looked *dead*." She shuddered.

"Sorry."

"Stop saying that! Anyway, this is just a reminder that I've got to find somewhere else to live. Andrew's such a dropkick." She sighed. "You look heaps better. How do you feel?"

"Not too foul. Good, even, I think. Definitely hungry."

"I'll get you a couple of muffins and then after you wash, we can go out and get something more substantial. If you're up to it?"

Tom nodded vigorously to indicate that he was more than up to it.

Cath went into the kitchen and returned with two terrifyingly healthy-looking muffins. Whole grain, he imagined, shuddering inside. He picked one up. It weighed more than a cricket ball. Oh, well, he told himself, at least it was food.

"So, what's really going on?" Cath asked. She'd made a concession to Tom's desire to eat normal food and taken him to a pizzeria. While he hoed into a huge pizza with the lot on it (only here they said "with everything"), she ate a salad without dressing, the only thing she deemed safe in such a place.

"Why are you really here?" she continued. "I talked to Dad on the phone and he sounded really weird. Is everything okay with Mum?"

"She's not doing great. But Cath, she hasn't been doing great since we were kids."

"Nothing new?"

Tom shook his head, wishing that he could tell Cath the truth. Dad knew and he wasn't magic; why couldn't Cath? Tom hated secrets, especially from Cath. Except for things that had to do with magic, he told her *everything*. Always had. "Nah. Nothing new. Dad gets down, but I reckon he's doing better than he has in ages. He's finally figured out she's never coming home."

"Then what's going on?" Cath was leaning forward, giving him her high-voltage interrogation stare. Probably the main reason he told her everything in the first place. Tom couldn't lie when she hit him with it. "Mere said you'd been sick. When? Why didn't you lot tell me? And why the hell would she bring you to New York in the depths of winter if you'd been sick? 'Ken hell, Tom! It makes no sense at all. And how come on your one day out you didn't come home with fabric samples and sketches of clothes or any of the things the Tom Yarbro I know would do? And why have you been looking so worried? Hmmm?"

"Been sick, you know . . ."

"What kind of sick?"

"Flu," Tom said, because it was the only thing he could think of. He wasn't sick very often; for the life of him he couldn't remember the last time.

"Dad said it was glandular fever."

"Same thing," Tom said, hoping it was. He'd never heard of glandular fever. "*Feels* like flu."

"Tom, you're a piss-weak liar. And Dad's just as crap. You're going to tell me what's going on. Come on, when have I ever kept a secret from you?"

"How about Poncey the Eighties Boyfriend?" Tom asked, relieved to have a response.

"Who?"

"What's-his-name? Dillon."

"Oh."

"How come you didn't mention *him* in any of your e-mails, eh?" Tom tried to turn her interrogation look back on her, but she was oblivious. Cath had actual eyebrows, whereas his were as pale as his skin and, though thick, pretty much invisible. Tom bet the success of Cath's stare lay with her eyebrows. He could raise each of his independent of the other, but as no one could actually see them, it wasn't very effective. One day he would dye them, his hair too, put an end to being an indistinguishable blur of white and pink. Not till he finished high school, though.

"Only just met him," Cath said, not meeting his eyes. A sure sign that she wasn't telling the truth. "Don't know how serious it is, you know? I wouldn't actually call him my boyfriend yet."

"But you did when you introduced us! How long have you been going out?"

"Well, I guess it's been, um, three months."

"Three months! And you reckon *I* keep secrets! That's your longest relationship ever."

"Nuh, Steve was longer. We were going out for almost five months."

"Ugh, Steve the tattooed wonder." Tom screwed up his face. "He was disgusting."

"He wasn't *that* bad."

"Yeah, he was. I caught him picking his nose and then scraping the snot off underneath our kitchen table."

"Yuck. He didn't!"

"He did," Tom said, not flinching under her stare, because it was the absolute truth. The memory was trapped in his brain for all time, though he'd be thrilled to forget. It had been a *lot* of snot, in a scary variety of colours.

"Okay," Cath said, "he was kind of gross, but I was only fifteen."

"I'm fifteen," Tom said with all the dignity he could muster, "and I don't wipe my snot on other people's furniture, and I wouldn't go out with anyone who did."

"Oh, yeah, Mr. Sophistication, when have you ever gone out with anyone?"

"Well, I haven't, exactly, not technically, but I have kissed a girl."

"Woo-hoo! My baby brother's kissed a girl!" She said it loud enough that the people at the next table turned around to look at them. One of the girls smiled.

Tom could feel his face get hot; he mock-punched Cath's shoulder, not nearly as hard as he'd've liked. Sometimes he hated his skin. Cath never blushed. How come he got *all* the dodgy genes? "There'll be time for girls later when I'm a world-famous fashion designer."

"Kind of a long time to wait for a second kiss, don't you reckon?" Tom punched her again. "Lay off," she said, punching him back. "Come on, then, who was the lucky girl?"

"I'll tell you if it happens again. Promise."

"Nup, you got to tell me now." The laser beam stare revved up.

"Jessica Chan. She kissed me 'cause she loved the dress I made her so much."

"Tongues?"

Tom's skin got hot again. He knew it was scarlet: the colour he'd meant Jessica's dress to be. Cath giggled. "Okay. Tommy, I'll ask no more. So will you tell me what else's going on?"

Tom shook his head slowly. "Can't. I'm not allowed." Cath leaned closer. "Cath! I can't. If it were up to me, I'd tell you— you know that, right?"

"Yeah, I do. Will you try to persuade Dad and Mere to let me in on the big secret?"

Tom nodded. "I promise."

"Thanks. I mean, I know it has to do with Mum and why Mere's been so amazing helping us out and I know—"

"Cath! Can we talk about something else?"

She sighed. "Wanna go see a movie, then?"

"Yeah, I would. That's exactly what I feel like." Cath was religious about not talking during movies. He'd be safe for a while. "One with good clothes."

"Sure."

Tom sat through the movie, an old one from the fifties. He felt too weird to really follow the story-line, but there were lots of big-skirted New Look clothes swishing in and out of rooms. He'd've bet money they were by Bill Thomas, not Edith Head.

He wished he could talk to Cath about Ree, about how scared he was they weren't going to find her. He desperately wanted to tell her about magic, about how terrifying it was.

He looked at his sister, her mouth slightly open, staring at the screen, the moving images reflected in her eyes. She was dead lucky she hadn't inherited the curse. Tom did not want to die young. He did not want to go mad. Every time he visited his mother, he saw what he could become. Tom shuddered.

Cath giggled and then shocked Tom by speaking. "Her dress isn't that bad, is it?"

"Puce, darling," Tom said in his most Oxford Street tones, "with ruffles and a gold trim, I mean to say." The only other person in the cinema hissed at them to *shhh.* They both giggled and shut up.

After midnight, Tom crawled into the sleeping bag on the couch and dreamed that he had to make Mere a suit out of an Italian parchment linen that could not be cut or sewn.

# 27
## Out the Door

Even before i opened my eyelids, I could feel Jason Blake staring at me. My stomach went cold. Had he put his hands on me while I slept? Had I said yes as I lay dreaming? I still felt bone tired but not as exhausted as I had before I slept. I didn't think he'd taken any more. I hoped not.

"I know you're awake," he said.

I opened my eyes, sat up, and looked at him as if he wasn't freaking me out at all. Was he really my grandfather? "You don't knock in New York City? What are you doing in my room?"

"Actually," said Blake, "given that I own this apartment, I'd say this bedroom was mine."

I couldn't think of an answer. I sat there with a smile on my face not much more convincing than his, willing him to go away. I wondered how long Jay-Tee had been with him. How could she stand it? Her father must've been a monster.

"I thought I might take you girls out for lunch. Seems to me we need to discuss our new arrangement in more detail. Things were left rather unsettled last night." He turned to the door. "I'll give you half an hour to get dressed. Casual is fine."

He gave me one last glance; his smile seemed to say he was

doing me a favour, that I should be pleased by the prospect of another meal with Jason Blake, then he closed the door behind him.

I closed my eyes again. I could feel it, very faintly, but there—my ammonite in Danny's pocket. Though it was only twelve-thirty, he was already at the restaurant waiting for us. Good. My impulse was just to go. But there were bars on the window and Jay-Tee was in the other room.

I was not going to panic. I'd been in this situation before. I'd been trapped before and I'd always escaped. Yes, that had been with Sarafina, and we'd been running from police and investigators who, as far as I'd known, weren't magic. But this was not entirely new; I could do this.

And this time I knew *I* was magic; that had to help, surely? Except that I had no idea how to use that magic to get through the bars or how to call to Jay-Tee without Blake knowing. I *still* knew next to nothing. Why had he suddenly decided to take us out to lunch? He'd said he'd see us in a few days. Obviously, he knew *something* was up. Why else would he be here? I hoped he didn't know what it was *exactly*.

I got dressed fast, not bothering with a shower, shoving scarf, hat, and gloves into the big pockets of the coat. I wished I had talked in more detail about escape last night, discussed what to do if Blake showed up again, but we'd both been too tired even before Jay-Tee had learned about her father.

I saw the layout of the flat in my mind. Two exits: front door in the living room, fire escape in the kitchen, which was on the other side of a large window that had a metal grate

across it. Both had to be unlatched and opened, then me and
Jay-Tee'd have to climb out the window and onto the fire
escape, which was mostly likely slippery with ice. How to do all
that and not attract Blake's attention? Not possible.

The front door with all its chains and bolts wasn't much
better. What were the odds of Blake deciding to go to the
dunny? Pretty much zero.

It would probably be best to simply go with Blake down to
the street and *then* make our break. I tried to imagine giving
him the slip on the icy streets and failed. I had no idea how
fast Jay-Tee could run, but I wasn't fast, especially not on ice
and snow. I could barely *walk* on that stuff.

I had nothing I could use as a weapon. And besides, he was
at least thirty centimetres taller than me, not to mention double my weight and way stronger.

They were sitting in the living room. Jay-Tee's coat lay across
her knees. When I walked in, she was looking down at the floor,
and Blake was staring intently at her. She looked up and gave me a
sad smile. The silence was so heavy, it was as if all sound had been
sucked away. You'd've thought no one had ever spoken before.

Blake didn't smile. He stood up and beckoned to me as if I
were his dog.

"No," I heard myself say. "Jay-Tee and I do not care to lunch
with you today." I had no idea where those words came from. I
sounded like someone from the olden days.

Jason Blake's eyebrows went up. He looked genuinely

surprised. "Then I haven't made myself clear. Lunch is not optional. If you both wish to stay in this apartment under my protection, then you will come to lunch with me."

"We don't." It was remarkable how strong my voice sounded. Jay-Tee's skin looked yellow; her eyes were wide open, staring at me. "We don't want your apartment or your protection or your lunch. Jay-Tee?" I smiled at her, held out my hand. "Let's go."

Blake was standing in front of the door. He didn't move as Jay-Tee and I walked toward it. I had to remind myself to breathe. *What could he actually do to us?* I asked myself. *Lots of things. Bad things.*

"If you leave," he said, still blocking the door, "she will find you. Once you go through that door, there's nothing hiding you. She'll find you straightaway. I can feel her. She's not far."

I stopped. There were barely ten centimetres between us. Jay-Tee's hand was trembling in mine.

"I'll risk it," I told him, my voice still steady despite the thought of Esmeralda sending a spurt of chill terror through my body. "Get out of my way."

"You will not leave," Blake said, in the same tone of voice he might have used to say it was still cold outside. The expression on his face, though, had changed. "It's not safe for either of you. Your grandmother is an evil woman."

"This is not a choice between you and Esmeralda. I'm choosing *neither* of you."

"You don't seem to understand, Reason—that's not an option. You're young, ignorant, and unprotected. *Someone* will prey on you. Your only option is to find someone who will give you something in exchange. As I have. Esmeralda will give you nothing. I'm not letting you make the wrong choice. I care what happens to you and Jay-Tee."

I couldn't help laughing. "Oh, please." I'd heard cops say the same thing. None of them knew me or wanted to. Finding me was their job, how they got their pay so they could eat. Blake cared about us in the same way—because we were a source of magic. He was a wolf and we were his food; that's what I saw in his eyes, that's why he wasn't going to let us go.

I tried to push past him and he grabbed me, one arm wrapping around tight, crushing my arms to my sides, the other pressing into my throat. I gasped for air, kicked back with my feet as hard as I could, getting him in the shins. He didn't react, just squeezed my throat harder. I was furious and scared. He didn't *have* to use magic against us—brute force would do. I kicked even harder.

Jay-Tee screamed and ran at him. He swung me around to hit her hard, and she went flying to the ground, falling heavily and just lying there. "You bloody bastard!" I yelled. If she was hurt, I would kill him.

Something was growing in me, something hot and liquid, under my skin, way down deep; something uncoiled slow, then surged up fast like bubbles through champagne, going to burst through my skin.

Blake dropped me as if I were on fire. I was.

"Don't," he said.

I was staring at him, but I didn't see him, I saw the veins

inside his body, the steady beat of his heart propelling the red liquid out and along those veins. I thought about it slowing. Like I'd done to that boy back in Coonabarabran when I was ten years old, who'd called me a *boong*, who'd tried to touch me.

That day, my anger had gotten bigger and bigger. A scream growing inside me. The rage was like a wave, a tsunami. My eyes exploded in red light; that was all I'd been able to see. When I opened them, the boy was on the floor, dead. Later they told me he'd had a blood clot, but somehow I'd always known it was my fault. It had felt like this. It had felt good.

"Don't," Blake said from even further away. Could I really kill him too?

I almost felt like I was flying. I thought about his heart shrinking, the veins contracting, the heart stopping.

His face was purple.

"Don't," said someone who wasn't Jason Blake. It was Jay-Tee. Dimly, I knew that. "Stop, Reason. Don't."

I felt incredible; I hadn't felt this wonderful in such a long, long time. Something sharp cracked across my face. The blow made me stumble. "What?" I asked. The glorious feeling started to recede.

"Don't, Reason. You can't do that!" Jay-Tee was yelling now. "It will kill you."

It had already stopped; the wonderfulness was draining away. I was unsteady now, overwhelmingly tired. Jay-Tee grabbed my hand and dragged me through the door, slamming it behind her.

## 28
## Eau de Reason

"You can't ever lose your temper," Jay-Tee said, dragging her into the elevator. She wasn't sure how much Reason was understanding. "You just can't. Your mother *never* told you that? Reason?"

She nodded, but her eyes still weren't fully focused. Jay-Tee was starting to wonder just who the dead boy in Reason's nightmare had been. Someone she'd killed? With Reason's temper and no one to warn her not to lose it, it was a wonder she hadn't taken out half of Australia.

"Reason? Talk to me. Say something!" Jay-Tee grabbed her by the shoulders and shook hard, terrified she was losing her.

"Stop it! I can hear you. I'm here." She rubbed her left shoulder. "Is Blake following us?"

Jay-Tee nodded. "Probably. He was coming around when I pulled you out of there. You know, you only got to him because he wasn't expecting anyone to do what you did. Which was stupid given that you almost did him at the restaurant."

Reason was drifting off. Jay-Tee slapped her again.

"Owww!" She put her hand to her cheek and glared at Jay-Tee.

"You *have* to pay attention. He's coming after us. He's

pissed. You're wiped out 'cause of that really, really dumb display upstairs. He said Esmeralda's nearby, which could be a lie, but it could be true, and—"

The doors to the elevator opened. They both stepped outside. Jay-Tee glanced out through the glass doors. It looked cold and gray. Everyone who hurried by was bundled up good and tight.

"Give me your gloves," Jay-Tee said, pushing the door open, stepping through.

Reason looked at her. "Where's your coat?"

"Back in the apartment."

"Oh. Bugger." Reason handed Jay-Tee hat, gloves, and scarf. "This coat's huge; we could both huddle into it." She lost her footing on a patch of ice. Jay-Tee steadied her.

"We're only going a block," Jay-Tee said. "We'll buy me a coat after the restaurant. Are you going to be okay? You're still wobbly."

Reason nodded, but her skin was more yellow than brown. Jay-Tee was unconvinced. She hoped Danny would know somewhere they could hide, but she couldn't imagine anywhere they would be safe from *him*.

From Tom's first step inside the restaurant the feeling of Reason was so strong he felt like he was breathing in her essence. He'd decided to have breakfast—a late breakfast: he still seemed to need millions of hours sleep—at the same restaurant where he'd sensed Reason, hoping he'd find another trace.

Tom looked around at every table. She wasn't at any of them. In the bathroom, maybe? Or had she just left? He half turned to check outside when he realised that the eau de Reason was coming from the far corner. The closer Tom got, the more intense it felt.

He went as close as he could, pretending that he was staring at the black-and-white mural on the wall. It was coming from a bloke drinking coffee, nervously glancing up at the doors every few seconds. The guy was practically glowing. He'd been with Reason, that was for sure, and for quite a while, too. She must be staying with him.

Tom sat down at the nearest empty table. It wasn't that close, but he could still watch the bloke. A sad-faced waitress brought him water and a menu. Tom looked over the top of the menu. The guy was tapping his fingers, gulping down coffee, and continuing to gaze expectantly at the doors.

Tom pulled the mobile out of his pocket and called Mere. She was close by, she said, and was headed over. He pocketed it, feeling relieved. Without Mere he had no idea how to approach the guy, what to say.

The table hid his trousers or jeans, but his T-shirt wasn't much to look at, which was a pity 'cause he'd look great in tailored clothing. The coat scrunched up next to him was one of those foul doona coats, completely barren of beautiful lines.

Tom wondered what his connection to Reason was and had a sudden horrible thought. The guy wasn't hideously old or anything. Actually, he was kind of good-looking. And Reason was gorgeous. And the feel of her was *all over him*. Tom took a large gulp of his water, hoping it would wash the awful thought away.

A waitress came up to the table, standing tall and blond and intimidating, looking down at him with infinite sadness. Tom turned back to his menu in a panic, looking for something clear-cut that would require no endless follow-up questions. While the waitress stood there regarding him as if he were yet another cross for her to bear, he frantically searched.

"What you want?"

"Ah, turkey sandwich," Tom blurted.

"What bread you want? Challah, brown, rye—"

"Challah," Tom said quickly.

"You want salad or soup with that?"

Tom sighed. "Soup?"

"Chicken noodle, borscht, lentil, vegetable—"

"Chicken noodle," Tom said. At least he'd discovered the trick of cutting her off early. The waitress departed, menu in hand.

Tom grinned, feeling well pleased with himself.

"Tom?" a startled voice asked. He looked up. It was Reason.

# 29
# Away from the Witch

When i walked in past the second set of doors, the first person I saw was Tom. I stopped in my tracks. Jay-Tee ran into me. "Tom?" I said out loud. How could Tom be here?

"Keep going, Reason. I'm frozen."

Tom stood up. "Reason?"

"What are you doing here?" I asked.

"Looking for you."

"But how?" I stopped, conscious of Jay-Tee beside me. "This is Jay-Tee. Tom's a friend from Sydney."

Then I saw Danny further back, smiling, waving at us. Jay-Tee returned the wave. I did too, grinning like an idiot. He was even prettier in daylight.

"And here's Mere too," Tom said, sounding happy.

"What?" I turned to the other door, not quite believing that I'd heard him right, but there she was, walking towards us. Tom had betrayed me. Jay-Tee turned to look as well.

"The witch," she said. "We got to run." She grabbed my hand, dragging me out onto the street. Tom cried out behind us. I was so tired my bones ached. I didn't know if I could run.

"Run where?" I asked as I stumbled along behind her. Jay-Tee was sure-footed, agilely weaving her way through the crowd. "Know anywhere warm we can hide?"

Jay-Tee nodded, still moving fast. She dropped my hand. "Follow me," she called, then bolted down the street.

I ran after her as fast as I could, slipping and sliding, almost going arse over tit, knocking into people, apologising, trying not to break stride. It was torture lifting my heavy legs. Within seconds Jay-Tee was half a block ahead, sprinting across the road. I was terrified she was going to leave me behind.

"Goddamn," came Danny's voice, suddenly behind me. Strong hands brought me to a halt. "What the hell's going on? Why is Jay-Tee running away from me? I thought she wanted to see me."

"She does. We're not running from you. We're running from my grandmother."

Danny let go of me, looking at me like I was insane. "Your grandmother? You know, I think I can deal with a grandmother."

"You don't understand. I don't know where Jay-Tee's running to. We can't let her get away."

We both looked up ahead to where Jay-Tee was fast disappearing. "We got to catch her." The air was cold and hurt my lungs. All I wanted was to lie down and sleep.

"Reason!" someone yelled from behind me. Tom.

"Bugger." I started running again, slipping and falling almost immediately. Danny hauled me up as if I weighed no more than a kitten. "Crap," he said, looking up ahead and then back at me. "She's almost out of sight!" He slung me over his shoulder in a fireman carry before I could answer and then started running hard after Jay-Tee.

"No way!" I yelled, but I was shouting at the people behind me. Danny didn't respond.

I couldn't see or hear much of anything. My stomach felt like it was being sawed in half by Danny's shoulder. It hurt even more when I tried to raise my head to see better. I wanted to figure out where we were going. I could see flashes of shop fronts and people's legs and shoes flying by on one side. On the other, mounds of dirty snow and parked cars.

I could tell when we were crossing the road more from the sound of horns honking than from anything I could see. Even if I'd been upright, I'd've had no clue where I was. I hadn't exactly managed to get oriented during my few days in this city.

My vision was blurring, my eyelids fluttering, struggling to stay open. I was exhausted, beyond exhausted. It was as if something had been sucked out of me, the thing that kept my blood pumping, my neurons snapping. My magic gone.

It was hard staying awake even bouncing up and down, with Danny's shoulder cutting me in half. I had to force myself to think. I'd seen Tom. What did that mean? What was Tom doing here? Was he waiting for Esmeralda? Had he *known* I was going to be at the restaurant? How?

My head pounded. The cold air hurt my eyes, made tears streak down my cheeks. The salt stung. But when I closed them, I could feel myself drifting into sleep. Staying awake felt important.

I turned to Fibonacci. I could feel my ammonite in Danny's pocket. On the backs of my eyelids I saw it clearly: a tightly wrapped spiral, the impression of a seashell, long ago broken down into sand. I traced the growing spirals, the area of each section equal to that of the previous two. The spiral grew, bigger than my ammonite, bigger than me, big as a car, big as the block we were running along. A neatly turning spiral. I jumped into it as though into a whirlpool. Spinning and floating.

Below me, Danny ran faster and steadier.

# 30
# Worse Things

Jay-Tee was running rather than thinking. In school she had always been the fastest girl. She could keep going for ages too. She liked it, but not as much as dancing. When she'd run at school, there were coaches yelling at her: knees up, elbows in. Running now she could still hear their shouted instructions. When she danced, she just danced. No one told her how to do it better, faster, longer. She just knew.

As she ran, her mind was with the crowd, seeing the gaps, the clearest paths, how to duck and weave, thread her way through, avoiding slick ice, people's toes, discarded trash. She was glad it wasn't that cold, no snow, and the wind blew from behind her, making her run faster and easier.

She'd stay warm as long as she was running. She shot a look back. Danny ran with Reason slung over his shoulder. Jay-Tee felt a wave of homesickness for her brother and for her dad, for how it had been before he'd turned into a monster. Part of her was dying to stop and hug Danny, but how on earth was she going to explain everything that was going on?

Seventh Street. She cut left. Jay-Tee knew where she was going now. The door. If Reason had the key . . . hidden, she'd said in her dream. If she'd hidden it on her person or, more cleverly, near the door, they could go through, grab Reason's stuff, and keep going.

Maybe they could even figure a way to shut the door against Esmeralda. Reason knew how to hide in Australia, out in the country with the kangaroos. Jay-Tee liked the idea of living with kangaroos.

Tom pulled on the rest of his winter gear in the street, trailing behind Esmeralda, still stumbling over his explanations. "Hurry, Tom," she said. "She's not that far ahead."

"Right," he said, pulling his glove on and then off again when he realised it was the wrong hand. He could see Reason up ahead, slipping and sliding. He took off. Within seconds the man from the restaurant had sprinted past him. "Crap!"

Tom ran harder, determined to stop him from doing anything to Reason. He'd seen the fear on her face. But he kept slipping. Up ahead Reason was having an even harder time with the salt and ice. The guy caught up to her, grabbed her, leaning close, yelling in her face. It looked like he was shaking her.

"Reason!" screamed Tom. The man threw her over his shoulder and started off again. Tom forced himself to run harder. He was not going to let that mongrel get away.

*He* was sitting on the front steps of the house. Legs casually crossed as if he were waiting for good friends and didn't mind how long they took. He was even smiling, white teeth gleaming.

Jay-Tee didn't see him until it was too late. She skidded to a halt and there he was, smile growing wider. His car double-parked in the street, ready. Jay-Tee found she was too scared to move. Without thinking, she crossed herself.

"You're not going anywhere, Jay-Tee, are you?" he said as if he could see her paralysis.

*I'm not scared of you,* she told herself. But she was. She wasn't like Reason. He terrified her. She didn't ever want him to take her magic by force again. The memory of it still made her shrink inside.

Jay-Tee heard a car and turned her head. A taxi pulled up behind his limousine. The back door opened and Esmeralda got out, walked toward him. He wasn't looking at Jay-Tee anymore. He was standing, eyes fixed on Esmeralda's, like moose locking antlers. Jay-Tee could almost see a gash cut through the air between them. The hair on Jay-Tee's arms stood on end. Everything was crackling; it felt like the air was melting.

Neither moved, not even the tiniest muscles on their faces. Jay-Tee stared. They weren't even blinking. They were statues. Jay-Tee fervently hoped they would stay that way.

She heard the sound of feet pounding along the sidewalk. Danny with Reason bouncing on his shoulder. *That's got to hurt,* thought Jay-Tee. Danny smiled at her, sort of, halfway between a smile and a grimace. "You're still too fast for me," he said.

He put Reason down, who wobbled unsteadily on her feet and then looked up, seeing Esmeralda and Jason.

"Bugger," she said.

# 31
## In The Air

i could feel something in the air. It made my skin crawl, the hairs on my body stand on end. A buzzing whine cut through my head. I was completely awake now. "Bugger," I said.

Esmeralda and Jason Blake stood staring at each other. They looked dead, but the air around them was almost on fire. The ground beneath seemed to be moving, wavering like the air in the distance on a hot summer's day.

"Yeah," Jay-Tee agreed.

"What—" Danny began.

"Shhh," we both said at the same time. We exchanged an "oh, bugger" glance. I wanted to move away, but I couldn't. It was impossible to look anywhere but at Blake and Esmeralda.

"We should run, shouldn't we?" Jay-Tee said.

"Can you run? Because I can't." My legs felt like concrete.

She shook her head, then turned to her brother. "We'll explain later, I promise."

"No, you'll explain now. Why were you running away from me?"

"I wasn't. We were running away from them."

He stared at Esmeralda and Jason Blake. "Who are they?" I wondered what he saw, whether Danny could sense the electricity, hear the whine radiating from them. "What the hell are they—"

"I don't know." Jay-Tee shook her head.

"She's my grandmother," I said softly.

"Let's just go," Danny said, looking down at Jay-Tee. "You're running from them, right? Then let's go and you can tell me what's going on. Why you've been hiding from me."

Danny reached out to take Jay-Tee's hand. He pulled her into a huge hug. Jay-Tee was crying. "Reason?" she asked. "What should we do?"

I didn't respond. I was too busy recognising where we were.

Blake and Esmeralda were in front of the door that had brought me here. A man carved in the stone above, his moustache, eyebrows, and eyes crudely painted on. The moustache was bigger than I remembered, hiding any hint of mouth. He was sadder too, looked like he might cry any minute. Or maybe it was the horrible noise emanating from the two statues below him, the growing heat, that made him miserable. It was making me miserable.

The door was of a heavy wood; above it a half circle of stained glass showed a rising sun. I hadn't noticed it before, yet I knew this was the door.

I looked along the street, recognising the houses, the fire escapes, the railings. I'd've known this street straightaway. Jay-Tee had led me to the wrong place yesterday. Yet another lie.

"Do you have the key? Is it hidden here?" Jay-Tee said softly, still in her brother's arms. "Can we get through?"

"What key?" Danny asked.

I shook my head. "Lost it. Must've dropped it when I first stepped through."

"Damn," she said, pulling away from Danny.

"And if I had it? How were you planning to get past those two?"

Neither Jason nor Esmeralda had moved, eyes still locked on each other. It had started to snow, light, floating flakes like the first snow I'd ever seen, right here, only a few days earlier. The snow landed on the tops of their heads, their noses. Neither of them so much as blinked.

A woman walked past, pushing a child swaddled in sheepskin in a pram, shooting anxious glances at us all. Jay-Tee smiled, but the woman hurried past. She must've thought we were all mad.

Danny was pacing, looking about ready to explode. We definitely owed him a long, detailed explanation. I wished my head would stop pounding; the sound from the two statues, the pressure of their battle made my skull feel as though it were shrinking, pressing in on my brain, which any minute would start pouring out of my ears and nose. Did Jay-Tee feel it? She was still crying, trying to explain things to her brother, but was only managing to confuse him further.

Was it just me hearing them? If I didn't get away or stop them, I was going to start screaming. I tried to take a step, but my feet wouldn't move. Now I couldn't even walk.

Someone was running towards us. Tom. I gave him the biggest smile I was capable of (not very) and then remembered that he'd been pleased to see Esmeralda. Which complicated things. My head hurt. It would be fabulous to sleep awhile, not have to think.

"Tom," I told Danny. "He's a friend." I wondered if he actually was. "Danny." They nodded at each other, which felt weird, like we were at a tea party, not freezing to death on a New York City street half paralyzed by two witches engaged in silent fireworks. I hoped they'd burn each other's brains out before they burned out mine.

Danny turned to Jay-Tee. "Look, this is ridiculous. I've got a place where you can live now. Dad left lots of money. It's yours too."

"Would you just shut up for a second, Danny?" Jay-Tee cried, holding her ears. She was hearing the battle too.

Tom bent over, panting. "Are you okay?" he asked, while Danny continued to plead with Jay-Tee. He looked up at me. He frowned. "You look like crap."

"Ta, mate." He seemed unaffected by the two statues. Or maybe it didn't hit you straightaway. "You were looking for me with Esmeralda?" I asked. "She's the one I ran away from. She's a witch."

He nodded. "I know, but she's not what . . ." He trailed off, catching sight of Esmeralda and Jason Blake, lowering his voice. "Who's he? What's going on? What's that noise? Is he—"

"Bad," I said. "He's really bad."

I had Danny's attention too now. "Did that man do something to you?" he asked Jay-Tee.

She opened her mouth to speak, then shut it again.

Jason and Esmeralda seemed to be glowing. I could feel the

heat. I wondered if it was real or not. Even the footpath under my feet felt warmer. Underneath their feet the ground was rippling, as if its constituent elements were breaking apart. It was spreading towards the footpath, moving towards us.

The whine had become more of a whirr. It was getting louder, more insistent. I had to concentrate hard to stop from screaming.

"If he's so evil, shouldn't we be helping Mere?" Tom said, as if it were obvious.

Jay-Tee had started to shiver. Danny pulled his arm out of one sleeve and pulled her into his coat. My ears were so cold I was expecting them to hit the ground any minute, yet there was a steady warmth radiating from Esmeralda and Jason Blake—the noise they were making was getting louder. I couldn't think. I had to make it stop.

"Do you feel that?" Danny asked. "The sidewalk?"

If even Danny could feel it, then the heat must be real. We all stared at Esmeralda and Blake.

"Can you see it?" I asked Jay-Tee and Tom.

"Yeah," Tom said. "All those shapes."

"Huh? I meant under their feet. Do you see it glowing?" That wasn't the right word.

"No," Tom said.

Jay-Tee shook her head. "I feel it, though. Hear it too. I hope they both burn themselves all up. Dead."

"Not Mere," Tom protested, looking horrified. "She's my friend. She's good."

"You like it when she drinks you?" Jay-Tee asked. Her upper lip curled.

"Huh?" Tom said. "What do you mean?"

Danny looked just as dumbfounded. "Drinks you? Someone's been drinking from you?"

"She's never done anything like that," Tom protested. "Drinking me?"

Jay-Tee nodded, pointing at Jason Blake. "That one's a regular vampire."

Danny was looking at Jay-Tee and then at me. "Vampires?"

"What does Esmeralda do to you, Tom?" I asked, amazed that I could get the words out. The sound was louder, higher pitched; my brain was melting. The ground seemed to be dissolving, the crust falling away, revealing the solid mantle, rippling, glowing hot and red. The buildings around us should be crumbling; we should have melted. No one saw it but me. Was this something to do with my magic? With numbers? Fibs?

"She doesn't *do* anything to me. She teaches me about . . ." He glanced at Danny. "About, you know. How to be safe, use only the tiniest amounts. Live longer. Not go nuts. There's no drinking. She won't even let me have a glass of wine with dinner."

"She's never once tried to drain it from you?" Jay-Tee asked.

Tom shook his head. "Drain what? I don't understand."

"What if she's just fattening him up?" I said, forcing myself to concentrate on my friends, not the strange illusions around me. "Like the witch in the story." I thought about Hansel and

Gretel. Esmeralda's house wasn't made of lollies and chocolate, but there were other temptations there.

The ground was getting steadily hotter.

"Jay-Tee," Danny said. "Let's go."

"I can't, Danny. I have to stay with Reason."

I took a deep breath. "Danny, you've still got the ammonite?" I didn't have to ask. I could feel it. "The stone I gave you?"

"Sure." He pulled it out of his pocket. "Ow!" he said, startled. I took the burning stone from him; spirals went spinning out from the stone in my hand, and the sound coming from Esmeralda and Jason Blake got even louder. I recoiled. My feet moved, suddenly unstuck.

"You okay?"

I nodded, though I wasn't. "Are you really sure about her, Tom?" I made myself ask.

"Completely," he said, nodding earnestly. "I trust her completely."

"Tom believes he's telling the truth," Jay-Tee said. "Remember what *he* said to us? He said we had to make a choice. What if your grandmother really can teach us. Properly?"

"She can," Tom said. "She saved me. She wants to save you too, Reason. We have to help her."

The four of us stared at the two figures dusted with snow. I could see the cells that made up their skin and hair, the whirring of the blood through their veins, the movement of their organs. It all moved in waves like the swirling ground beneath them, yet they didn't look any different, stock-still, eyes unblinking. The noise was blasting my head open, the air was crackling, the footpath underneath us growing even hotter.

I didn't want to save Esmeralda. What about the teeth I'd found? The cat? What about everything Sarafina had ever told me? Stealing men's vital energies, sacrificing animals, eating human babies? Everything she taught me to protect myself from magic—that had all been true. As far as I knew, Sarafina's only lie was that magic didn't exist. "We could just go with Danny."

Danny nodded. "Of course. Both of you."

"And if there are others like *him* out there?" Jay-Tee asked me. "How will we protect ourselves not knowing anything? You said it, Reason, we need to know. If she turns out to be just like him, we'll run away again. We're good at that."

Danny started to talk, and Tom. The noise was so bad now it was doing my head in. I couldn't stand it. I concentrated, thought of the stars above, just as Sarafina had taught me. I took a step towards the two statues and then another. The footpath supported me. I didn't fall through to the earth's core. The other three followed, only Danny with ease.

"All right," I said, holding out my hand, not entirely sure what I was doing. Tom grabbed it, and Jay-Tee grabbed his other wrist. Danny grabbed her waist. I wondered what he thought was happening.

Feeling sick to my stomach, I reached forward and took hold of Esmeralda's hand with my ammonite between our palms. White heat. Colours. The whirring was deep inside me, pumping through my veins, pushed along by my heart, in my blood now and up my arm and into the ammonite. It didn't hurt anymore. I had stopped it hurting me. It felt good.

I saw spirals, but not Fibonaccis. These spirals were different. More erratic, slower. They swirled around me. In and out, like the petals of a flower. I looked for the pattern, but every time I thought I had it, the spirals changed, tighter, longer, then sharper, wider.

Both their patterns, Esmeralda's and Blake's, were so clear to me. I could taste the magic in them, metallic but somehow rusty on my tongue. It smelled like tobacco before it's lit. A smell of earth, not metal. I could see it too, both sharp and hazy, woven into their skin and hair, their muscles, their blood, part of every cell.

And something else, something familiar. Something of my mother. In both of them. Suddenly I knew that he really was my grandfather. I recognised his pattern.

*This* was my magic.

Someone screamed. A man's scream.

My head tilted up, met Blake's eyes: saw his confusion, his pain. No spirals in there, no patterns, just chaos.

We all staggered. Blake had collapsed, holding his head. "You," he said, not looking up. "You."

Esmeralda was the first to recover. "Thank you," she said, stepping past him, opening the door. Tom, Jay-Tee, Danny, and I followed. But Danny wasn't with us when we stepped into my grandmother's kitchen.

I was in Sydney again. I stumbled forward until I found the kitchen sink and then I threw up.

## 32
## Back Home

We sat around the kitchen table, drinking tea, water, orange juice. Only this time it was night and there were no pastries, no cinnamon rolls to tempt me. Esmeralda looked pale, but not as terrible as I had expected. Of the four of us I was the only one who seemed close to dropping.

Esmeralda insisted I keep ice wrapped in a washer pressed against my forehead and nose. It actually made the hotness go away, lessened the throbbing, but did nothing for my fatigue. Before long it started melting down my face. That felt good too.

I couldn't keep my eyes from the door, as big and wooden on this side as the other but no stained glass rising sun above it and, of course, no sad-faced, droopy-moustached man. Instead of just Esmeralda's coat, the door now held all our winter coats, gloves, scarves, and hats—a towel lay on the floor absorbing the snow melting from them. That was the only sign that New York City and winter lay on the other side. I hoped I would never have to return—then I thought of Danny. . . .

"Is Danny okay?" I forced myself to ask. Even with the horrible whirry noise gone, my head throbbed. He hadn't come through the door. Where was he? I slid my hand into my pocket, feeling for the reassurance of the ammonite. It wasn't there. Not in my left pocket either.

"I imagine so," Esmeralda said with the same fake comforting voice she'd used when she picked me up at the airport. A week ago? "He's not like us," Esmeralda continued. "He couldn't come through the door. For him it was locked. He's still back there."

"But so's *he*," Jay-Tee said. "What if he hurts Danny?"

"Will he?" I asked.

"Your grandfather is in no condition to do anything to anyone," Esmeralda said. Her tired smile said that she knew that I'd already learned who he was, and I wondered how.

Tom's mouth dropped open.

Most of the windows were open. The warm air smelled faintly of flying fox and jasmine. I thought I heard some squeaks coming from the tree, but my ears still tingled. I could've just been hearing what I wanted to hear. Outside, it was slowly getting lighter. Dawn was arriving though just a few minutes ago it had been early afternoon and New York City. *What day is it?* I wondered.

"Tom says you can help," I said, because they seemed to be waiting for me to speak again. All I wanted to do was sleep. "Teach us about magic. But you won't take it from us like Jason Blake did."

Esmeralda sipped her tea and looked at the three of us. "Who are you?" she asked Jay-Tee.

"Jay-Tee," she said. "I'm a friend of Reason's." She looked

at me and I made the corners of my mouth turn up. It hurt. "I'd like to learn more about magic too."

Esmeralda nodded. "Of course."

"So you won't take it from us?" Jay-Tee asked.

"I'll answer that question," Esmeralda said, looking at Jay-Tee and then at me, "but first I need to know what you both know."

"About magic?" Jay-Tee asked.

Esmeralda nodded.

Tom was watching us, eyes big but not saying a word. Jay-Tee kept looking around the kitchen and was now staring at the fruit bowl. I could see her wondering what the weird hairy fruits were. I still had no idea. In the morning, I decided, I'd try one. What would be the harm? Esmeralda had me now, might as well eat her food. There were three big mangoes too. They smelled ripe.

Jay-Tee peered out the window at Filomena, leaves shining palely in the moonlight. I wondered if they had fig trees like that in New York City. All the trees I'd seen had been more like skeletons.

"That it's dangerous," I said at last, wondering that I had the energy to coordinate tongue and lips. "That everyone seems to want more than they have. That it's genetic, like being left-handed. That when I lose my temper . . ." I paused. "That it's dangerous."

Jay-Tee nodded. "That it's a curse."

Esmeralda smiled sadly. "I'll tell you both what I told Tom.

What I was told by my mother when I was young. Magic is in everyone. When someone hears a phone ring and knows who it is before they've answered, that's a kind of magic. When people know they're being stared at, even though the person is behind them, that's magic too. Low level: the kind that everyone can do. In cities the air crackles with it. Certain objects, like this door, become imbued with it."

I thought of my ammonite, hoped I had dropped it on the other side of the door, that Danny had picked it up. I couldn't feel it now, thousands of kilometres and a day away, but I could remember how it had felt those few moments in my hand, burning with magic. And at the same time, the feel of it had been mixed with the feel of Danny.

"There are no coincidences," continued Esmeralda, "only a great deal of magic. Not all of it low level. Some of us are as talented with magic as a top athlete is at running or a musician with their chosen instrument. It's possible to be good without practice, but never as good or as controlled as you are with discipline and knowledge.

"Unlike music and athletics, magic is finite; there's an end to it, and at the same time it takes from you as much as you take from it. Magic sucks you dry. The more you make and the stronger it is, the shorter your life. You saw our family's monument, Reason."

She looked at me, but I was too exhausted to speak or even nod.

"Many of us don't make it much past twenty-five. For us, living to the age of *forty* is extraordinary. I am forty-five,

Reason; every day I live, I am grateful. If I make it to fifty, it will be a miracle."

"Why aren't we exhausted?" Jay-Tee cut in. "I mean, except for Reason. That was a big-ass magic fight between you and him. How come we're not all dropping right now?"

"Good question," Esmeralda said. "Because neither he nor I will ever use more magic than we have to. The battle was pitched low. It takes time, but eventually you know who's stronger, who's won. The three of you tipped the balance but lost almost no magic doing it. How do you feel?"

"Not too bad," Tom answered. "Not nearly as bad as when we did that magic together looking for Ree."

"Tired, but not magic-gone tired," Jay-Tee said. Those last words described exactly how I felt: magic-gone exhausted. Much worse than when he'd taken that small amount from me at the champagne restaurant. I wanted to sleep forever and ever. I had to force my eyes to stay open, my brain to function.

"Then why does Ree look so bad?" Tom asked.

"She tried to kill someone with magic," Jay-Tee said. "She's lucky she's still alive."

Tom opened his mouth to speak, then closed it again.

"Your grandfather?" Esmeralda asked.

Jay-Tee nodded for me.

I didn't want to talk about what had happened. Not yet. "So if you don't want to die, why use your magic at all?" I asked instead, but I knew what the answer would be before the words were out of my mouth.

"Like your mother? Like Tom's mother? If you're born with the talent for magic and don't use it, you go insane."

I knew it. Sarafina had taught me small magics, tricks like casting out with the Fib spiral, but nothing new for years now. She had stopped using hers, and now she was insane, doped to the eyeballs out at Kalder Park. I longed to see her again, but I was scared of it too. Not using magic had turned her into someone I didn't recognise.

I wished I was asleep already. I didn't want to hear any more. I'd killed a boy, tried to kill Jason Blake. How much longer was I going to live? How long did Jay-Tee have, conjuring money out of nothing every day?

"That's why Blake drank from you both. Drinking from someone who agrees to it requires little magic. You don't go mad because you're using a tiny amount of your own to make it work, and you live longer because you've gained more. None of us wants to die. Most of us don't want to go mad."

She took another sip of her tea and regarded the three of us looking back at her. "That's why I can't promise I won't try to drink from you." She looked at me, her brown eyes just like my mother's. "That's part of why Sarafina ran. I never lied to her. I told her how it might be. After all, my own mother tried to take it from me.

"Sarafina couldn't bear the idea of any of it. That's why she raised you as she did. She wanted magic not to exist, for there to be no possibility of me preying on her or her ever preying on you."

Tom gasped, but Jay-Tee's expression didn't change.

"I don't want to die either," Esmeralda continued. "I loathe your grandfather for what he's become, but I understand it. I'll do everything I can to arm the three of you against him or anyone like him. But I may be teaching you to protect yourselves against me. You have to remember that."

Tom shook his head, but Jay-Tee and I believed her. My head was a jumble of questions, but I couldn't work my mouth, keep my eyes open.

Esmeralda looked at me and smiled; I couldn't read what was in her eyes.

The first thing I saw when I woke was Jay-Tee sitting cross-legged at the end of my bed. Tom was on the desk chair. They were both looking at me, grinning. For a groggy half second I thought Jay-Tee was Sarafina.

I almost started asking her the questions I was burning with. I was so angry with my mother, yet I missed her. Once I saw her again, told her I knew about magic now, would she regret the name she had given me?

"Forty-two hours," Tom said, clapping. "You beat my record."

"She beat anyone's record. No one can sleep that long unless they're in a coma. Better give her food."

Tom picked up a plate full of pastries from the desk and brought it to me. "Cinnamon rolls. You ready to risk eating the wicked witch's food this time?"

I grinned, not because I was convinced she wasn't a wicked

witch—I wasn't sure I'd ever be convinced of *that*—but because I loved cinnamon rolls, and whether she was wicked or not, I was going to eat them. I sat up, took a huge bite, tasting sugar and cinnamon and butter. Heaven.

And then a metal taste, tobacco smell. The same as Esmeralda and Jason Blake, only it was Tom and Jay-Tee. I could see their patterns. I could see the magic in them. Just like Esmeralda, only Tom's was fresher, cleaner. Jay-Tee tasted of rust.

"What?" Jay-Tee asked.

"Nothing." I closed my eyes and Jay-Tee was just Jay-Tee, no strange smells or tastes. "What day is it?" I asked.

"Sunday morning," Tom said. Jay-Tee and he laughed.

"But it was *Thursday* when we left. . . ." I trailed off, trying to figure it out. Sunday a week ago I'd arrived here from Dubbo. Just one week. My head felt fuzzy.

"Uh-huh," Jay-Tee said, giggling. "We left New York on Thursday, but when we came through the door it was Friday morning in Sydney, but you slept all day Friday and all day Saturday and now it's Sunday morning. Simple, Math-Girl."

"I'm in the room next door," Jay-Tee continued. "It's just as big as this one. Got my own bathroom too—it's huge—and we share the balcony."

I had never seen Jay-Tee like this. She was bubbling. "It's summer," she continued. "Look at me!" Jay-Tee was wearing a tank top and shorts. Her feet were bare. The balcony doors were open, the white curtains moved in the breeze. Light streamed in so bright it made me blink. Even when the sun had come out in New York City, it hadn't been near as intense as it was here.

"Tom's been showing me around the neighbourhood, that is, when he wasn't busy. . . ." Tom shot her a look and Jay-Tee changed tack. "There are bats at night and these weird-coloured birds during the day. And everyone talks wrong like you do—"

"It's a footpath, *not* a sidewalk," Tom cut in. I felt a sudden twinge of jealousy—while I'd lain sleeping, they'd become friends. They didn't need me so much anymore.

"And it's warm and the sun's out. Oh!" she said, suddenly remembering something. "You have to tell me Danny's phone number. Mere says the door's off-limits for now. I couldn't remember it and he must be going crazy after what happened. Mere says I can call whenever I want."

I reeled off the number of Fib (33) automatically. Danny! I had to call him too. I had to explain. I ate more of the roll, igniting my hunger further, finished it, grabbed another. "What are you going to tell him?"

"The truth," Jay-Tee said. "He's seen enough growing up with my parents for it to make sense. I don't think he'll be *that* shocked. Especially after we disappeared like that. Say the number again?" I did and she repeated it.

"So have you both started witch school?" I asked, growing even more jealous.

They shook their heads. "That doesn't start until you're awake and ready."

Jay-Tee looked at me, smiling. "Mere's not *anything* like him. I'm not saying I trust her a hundred percent or, you know, even fifty, but she's been straight about everything so far. If she turns on us, well, there's three of us. Combined, we can definitely take her."

Tom looked uncomfortable but nodded. "It'll be okay, Reason."

I finished the last roll, licked my fingers, then got out of bed, managing not to stumble, though my legs were weak. "I'm going to shower. Will there be lots of breakfast waiting for me in the kitchen?"

"Heaps," Tom said. "Tons," Jay-Tee said at the same time.

"See you down there, then."

They left and I looked around the room. Fresh flowers: wattle and waratahs with sprigs of eucalyptus in the vase where there'd been lavender a few days ago. No scary smells there.

Over the back of the chair where Tom had been sitting hung something green that I didn't recognise. I picked it up. Pants with lots and lots of pockets. The fabric was amazing; it felt both delicate and strong. Tom had said he was going to make pants like these for me. While I'd slept, he'd done it. I hugged them, feeling warm and happy, then put them on. They fit perfectly, almost as if the fabric shaped itself around me.

Other than the pants and the flowers, the room was as I had left it. Light and airy. Beautiful. The blue-and-white robe was draped over the end of the bed, the matching slippers on the floor nearby.

Even my backpack was where I'd left it, sleeping bag still tied in place. I opened it, looked through my escape supplies: *Gregory's,* water bottles, dried fruit and nuts, all of it still there. I unzipped the front pocket, reached in for Esmeralda's letters. I was ready to read them now. I wondered if they would say the same things she had told us over the kitchen table. That she might try to steal our magic from us.

The letters weren't there.

I felt a chill over my entire body. So what had she said *then* that she didn't what me to know *now?*

I could grab my pack, run out the front door this very minute. I knew exactly how to get out of this room, how to get to Central, to the interstate buses, how to escape, quick and easy. Except that I couldn't. What about Jay-Tee and Tom?

I understood for the first time why Sarafina had been adamant about not making friends. I could feel Tom and Jay-Tee downstairs, imagine what they were thinking. Friends tied me down. I wasn't just looking out for myself and Sarafina now; I had to look out for them as well. Would I ever be able to escape with so many people in tow?

Not that it would make much difference, given that I didn't have long to live. How much magic had I expended? How many years did you lose for killing someone? For trying to kill someone else? Forty? Fifty? Sixty years? Was I rusted too?

I was afraid. Like Esmeralda, like Jason Blake, I didn't want to die. Would I end up taking magic from someone else so that I could live longer? I'd used magic to kill. Surely that would eat up decades? Esmeralda had made it to forty-five and she'd killed a cat. But with a knife, I realised, not magic. I felt dizzy thinking about it and sat down on the bed, waiting for my head to clear.

What a ridiculous choice: magic and early death or madness. I refused to accept that that was how things were, that there was no third or fourth or fifth choice.

There *had* to be another way, something no one had thought of: a pattern invisible to most people's eyes, but not to mine. Could the others see what I could? Jay-Tee didn't know Blake was my grandfather. She couldn't see it the way I could. I was good at patterns, at numbers, and they were intricately tied up with magic. With *my* magic.

There had to be a way to use the one to unlock the other. If I could do that, then we'd all be able to use magic and not die stupidly young. I'd save me and Jay-Tee and Tom from early deaths. Stop Jason Blake and Esmeralda from drinking anyone dry. I'd be able to bring Sarafina back from her slowed-down lonely world.

I lifted up the pillow and hugged it to my chest.

Underneath there were five black and purple feathers.

# Glossary

**ambo:** a paramedic (from *ambulance*)

**arse:** ass

**bickie:** short for *biscuit,* the Australian word for *cookie*

**biscuit:** cookie

**bloke:** guy, man

**boong:** racist term for an Australian Aboriginal person

**bottlebrush:** a tree or shrub with spikes of brightly coloured flowers

**Bronze Medallion:** system of lifesaving certificates. Almost every school in Australia teaches its students how to swim and how to rescue people if they get into trouble in the water.

**bugger:** damn. The thing you say when you stub your toe and don't want to be *too* rude.

**bunyip:** creature of Aboriginal legend, haunts swamps and billabongs (waterholes that only exist during the rainy season)

**cardie:** short for *cardigan*

**chips:** like french fries, only better

**chop, not much:** not very good; to not be much chop at something means you're crap at it

**chunder:** vomit

**croc:** short for *crocodile*

**dag:** a dag is someone lacking in social graces, someone who is eccentric and doesn't fit in. The closest U.S. approximation is *nerd*, but a dag doesn't necessarily know a thing about computers or mathematics or science.

**dob in or dob on:** to tell on. For example: "I'll dob you in if you eat all those cakes."

**dodgy:** sketchy

**doona:** comforter

**dunny:** toilet

**echidna:** a spiny anteater

**Emoh Ruo:** *Our Home* spelled backward, a common Australian name for your house

**esky:** cooler, the thing you keep things cold in if you're going on a picnic

**flat out like a lizard drinking:** busy, in a hurry

**footie:** In New South Wales and Queensland means Rugby League (Rugby Union is known as Rugby); in the rest of the country usually means AFL (Australian Football League, popularly known as Aussie Rules).

**get on:** be friendly with. For example, "Those two don't get on" means that they aren't friends.

*Gregory's:* a brand of street directory common in New South Wales (the most populous state in Australia, of which Sydney is the capital)

**grouse:** Excellent, wonderful, although it can also be a

verb meaning to complain, as in, "I wish you'd stop grousing about everything."

**gypsy cab:** an unlicensed cab

**hessian:** burlap

**H. S. C.:** Higher School Certificate, the final set of exams in high school in most parts of Australia

**Iced VoVos:** a brand of sweet bickie

**jumper:** sweater

**'ken hell:** an expression of annoyance

**knackered:** very tired, exhausted

**lend, having a:** making fun of, mocking

**lift:** elevator

**loo:** toilet

**lolly:** candy. The plural is *lollies*. Although "losing your lolly" means losing your temper.

**mad:** In Australia it means *crazy;* in the United States, *angry.*

**mum:** mom

**Pop Rocks:** a hard American candy (lolly) made with carbon dioxide bubbles. As it melts in your mouth, it feels like it's exploding. Very strange stuff.

**poxy:** unpleasant, crappy or annoying

**pram:** stroller

**recce:** from the military term *reconnaissance,* meaning to look around, check out thoroughly

**ropeable:** angry, as in "fit to be tied"

**rubber:** in Australia means *eraser;* in the United States, *condom*

**sambo:** sandwich

**skink:** a small lizard with a long body

**sloppy joe:** a cotton, fleece-lined sweater

**sossi:** sausage

**sticky beak:** a person who always sticks his or her nose into other people's business

**stinger:** poisonous jellyfish

**stoush:** fight, brawl, rumble

**ta:** thank you

**Tim Tam:** a chocolate-filled, chocolate-covered bickie

**Uluru:** a huge rock formation in central Australia, formerly known as Ayer's Rock

**Violet Crumble:** a brand of candy bar made of honeycomb coated with chocolate

**wanker:** poseur

**washer:** washcloth

**watarah:** a shrub or small tree with brilliant red-coloured flowers

**wattle:** a large shrub or tree with white or yellow flower clusters

**willi-willi:** dust devil

**witchetty grubs:** delicious, fat, white, wood-boring grubs

# Acknowledgments

An ocean of thanks to Scott Westerfeld, my first sounding board, audience, reader, editor, and critic.

Thanks also to Eloise Flood and Liesa Abrams, editors extraordinaire, for all your hard work and for continuing to push me that little bit extra. And to Andy Ball, Chris Grassi (love those snowflakes), Polly Watson and Margaret Wright.

Thank you, Pamela Freeman, Jan Larbalestier, Jeannie Messer, Sally O'Brien, Kim Selling, Ron Serdiuk, and Wendy Waring for reading and commenting on the manuscript in early drafts.

Ann Bayly for her scientific expertise (all errors are, of course, mine).

Silvia Maria Palacios and Luz Barrón for making everything run like clockwork while I wrote the first draft in San Miguel de Allende in Mexico. And to Kate Crawford and Bo Daley for letting me use their home in Annandale (Sydney) for the penultimate round of rewrites.

Thanks also to Hopscotch (Sydney), Fifi's (Sydney), Counter (New York City), La Palapa (New York City), and La Brasserie (San Miguel de Allende) for the food that sustained me while writing this book. If you don't eat, you die.

Lastly to John Bern, Niki Bern, Jan Larbalestier, and Scott Westerfeld: without your support, love, and, erm, prompting, I'd never write a word.

Here's a sneak peek at

# Magic Lessons

the second volume in Justine Larbalestier's

Magic or Madness trilogy

# 1
# Reason Cansino

Once, when I was really little, we passed a road sign peppered with bullet holes. It was pretty much the same as any of the other road signs we passed out bush, but this one I read out loud in my squeaky toddler voice: "Darwin, 350. Two times 175. Five times seventy. Seven times fifty. Ten times thirty-five."

My mother, Sarafina, clapped. "Unbelievable!"

"How old is the kid?" asked the truck driver who was giving us a lift to the Jilkminggan road. He glanced down at me suspiciously.

"Almost three." Sarafina was seventeen.

"Not really?"

"Really."

When we arrived, three of the old women—Lily, Mavis, and Daisy—sat down with us on the dirt floor of the meeting place. They gave us tucker—yams, wild plums, and chocolate bickies to eat, and black-brewed, sticky-sweet tea to drink. A posse of kids hung around, darting in and out for plums and bickies, but mostly stood just out of reach, watching and giggling.

A few gum trees dotted the settlement, their leaves a dull green, standing out amongst the dirt, dry scrub, and ant hills taller than a man. Healthier, greener trees, bushes, and vines grew farther away, on the other side of the buildings, where the ground sloped into the banks of the Roper River. The buildings were low, made of untreated wood and rusting corrugated iron. The only one with four walls, a proper door, and windows was the silver demountable where school was held— the hottest, most uncomfortable building in the settlement.

"You're that travelling woman, eh?" Daisy asked. "With all them different names?"

Sarafina nodded.

"What you want to be called now?"

"Sally. And my daughter's Rain," Sarafina said, even though my name is Reason.

"We hear about you," Daisy said. "You been all over, eh? All the way down south, too?"

"Yes," Sarafina said. "We've been all over Australia."

"Seen lots of white man places, too?"

"Some." Sarafina always stayed away from cities so that her mother wouldn't find us. "I like Aboriginal places better."

The three women grunted as if this were to be expected.

"That little one, that Rain," Daisy said, looking at me. "She's countryman, eh?"

Sarafina nodded.

"Her father countryman, innit?"

"Yes."

"Where him from?" Mavis asked. She was the oldest of the three women. Her hair was all white and her skin was so black it shone. She took a piece of chewing tobacco from behind her ear and put it in her mouth.

"I don't know."

The three women murmured at this. "Don't know?"

Sarafina shook her head.

"Who his people?"

"Don't know."

"Them from desert country? Arnhem country?"

Sarafina shrugged. "He didn't tell me."

Daisy nudged Lily. "That little one, Rain? Him amari? Him munanga, I reckon."

"True," Lily said, "but him daddy still got country." She turned back to Sarafina. "Where you meet him?"

"Out west." Sarafina gestured past the water tank resting on a huge mound of dirt, to the horizon where the sun would set.

"How long you him together?"

"One night."

They nodded at this. "Drunken fella?"

Sarafina laughed. "No."

"Him from bush or white man place?"

"Bush."

"Ah," Lily said, pleased to be given something solid. "Stockman?"

"I don't know."

"Him barefoot or got boots?"

"Boots."

They nodded again. "Stockman."

Sarafina made flashcards. She cut up an old cardboard box that had once held cartons of Winnies, and she wrote on them with a fat black Texta she'd bought in Mataranka.

She wrote the names of nine recent places we'd either stayed or seen road signs for: Darwin, Jilkminggan, Katherine, Mataranka, Ngukurr, Numbulwar, Borroloola, Limmen Bight, and Umbakumba; the names of all the planets: Mercury, Venus, Earth, Mars, Jupiter, Saturn, Uranus, Neptune, and Pluto (though she said the last one wasn't *really* a planet); and the branches of mathematics: foundations, algebra, analysis, geometry, and applied.

We sat on the dirt floor under a roof of paperbark. Occasionally strands of it would drift down and land on us. The three women sat cross-legged, gutting a kangaroo and waving the flies away.

"Sally," Daisy asked, "what are you doing with your girl Rain?"

"Teaching her how to read."

They all nodded and agreed reading was important, though of the three of them, only Daisy really knew how.

Sarafina held up the cards with one hand, waving flies away, and patting one of the dogs with the other. The sky was the intense blue that only happens when the earth is the red-brown of iron. Not one cloud. Dry season. There would be no rain for months.

"Ve-nus," I read. "Dar-win. Al-ge-bra."

Sarafina held up the next card. "Nnn . . ." I said, trailing off, staring at the card with its *n* and *g* and *k* and *r*'s and *u*'s. I wasn't sure if I'd seen it before. I didn't understand how those letters went together to make sounds.

"Ngukurr," said Lily, sliding past the *g* that had so confused me. Her people were from there. She knew how to read that one.

Sarafina put the cards down, realising she should, perhaps, have started with the alphabet. For the next two hours we sang, "A-B-C-D-E-F-G-H-I-J-K-L-M-N-O-P-Q-R-S-T-U-V-W-X-Y-Z." The old women laughed and lots of the kids joined us, some of them sneaking out of school in the demountable, with the drunken white teacher. I informed Sarafina that *f, j, q,* and *z* were my favourites.

Annie, Valerie, Peter, little Rabbit, and Dave said they liked *s* best, so Sarafina invented an *s* dance for them. This involved standing up, putting your hands above your head, pushing your hips to one side and your shoulders to the other, and shimmering like a snake.

We all *s*-danced, falling down and snake-bellying away across the ground, coating ourselves with red dirt. Everyone was good at it except me. I was too little and unco. Sarafina was the best, even though she was the only whitefella, faster and more shimmery than anyone else. We all laughed.

The dogs barked and jumped up, running in circles, trying to join in, but they weren't good at moving on their bellies and kept rolling over, trying to get us to rub them instead. They didn't look like snakes at all.

When we were all danced out and tired and the women had the kangaroo roasting amongst the coals, Mavis told us the story of the mermaid ancestor and how she'd made the land. She had many names, but Mavis said munga-munga was best.

I dreamed about her that night and many nights, but in my dreams when she made her giant path across the country, sparkling numbers and letters spilled out from her tail, littering the red earth, turning into valleys and rivers and hills and ocean, drifting up into the sky and becoming the planets and the stars.

The munga-munga has always been my favourite.

Once, when I was ten years old and Sarafina twenty-five, I lost my temper. Sarafina had always told me never to lose my temper, but she never told me why.

I'd only been at the school for a week. It was my first and last time in a real school, one where you had to wear shoes and be quiet when the teacher spoke and not leave the classroom unless the teacher said you could, but also one where there were lots of kids and games and books about things I'd never heard of. I was really hoping I'd be able to stay.

I was being called Katerina Thomas and my hair was cut short and dyed light brown, almost blonde. I still looked like me, though.

Josh Davidson was the class creep. He'd go around snapping girls' bra straps (those that had them), calling them bitches, and, when he could, cornering them and trying to touch their breasts (even if they didn't have any yet). He was taller than the other girls and boys, stronger, too.

He was a lot taller than me. He'd already tried to snap my non-existent bra, and I had a bruise on my arm from where he'd grabbed me when I was coming out of the bathroom. A teacher had turned the corner and told him to let me go before he could do anything else.

The next day in class, Josh sat next to me. He pushed his chair as close as he could. I felt fear and anger inside me like an intense heat. He didn't try to touch my breasts; instead, he put his hand on my thigh. I held my knees tight together. Put my hand in my pocket to hold my ammonite.

"Spread your legs, boong," Josh whispered in my ear.

I felt my anger getting bigger, uncoiling inside me. There was a scream, but I didn't open my mouth. The stone in my pocket grew warm and sweaty as I clutched it tightly. The rage was like a wave, starting small, then spiralling out of me. Growing bigger and bigger, as fast and beautiful as Fibonacci numbers: 0, 1, 1, 2, 3, 5, 8, 13, 21, 34, 55, 89, 144 , 233, 377, 610, 987, 1597 . . . My eyes exploded in blinding red light.

Someone yelled out, something about a doctor.

Then, for a moment, I could see. The intense light in front of me faded away. Josh was on the floor. He wasn't moving. I felt glorious, better than I had ever felt in my entire life.

Then I fainted.

It was hours before I discovered that Josh Davidson was dead. An aneurism, they thought. The blood in his head had lumped together, had stopped the oxygen getting to his brain.

Had I made his blood do that?

I didn't ask Sarafina, but that night we left. Not just the town but the state—we went all the way across the country, as far as we could get. No more school for me.

We never talked about it, but after that, Sarafina's warnings about not losing my temper came even more often. Without explanation.

I know now. I stopped that boy's blood. I killed him.

I'm magic, like my mother, but she never told me. She didn't tell me that if I lose my temper, people might die. She never told me that if I don't use my magic, I'll go mad, like her. Or that if I do use it, I'll most likely die before I turn twenty. She never told me to choose between magic or madness.

Sarafina didn't tell me anything.

# 2
# Back To The Asylum

**Sarafina didn't look any different.** She sat on one of the biggest of the ugly brown couches, still and silent, more statue than human, wearing the same white terry-towelling robe she had on last time I saw her. Only a week ago, I realised.

I wondered when time would come right again. Ever since Sarafina had tried to kill herself, it had been running either too fast or too slow. Right now it was 11 AM, but my body was convinced it was night time.

Jet lag, Tom had called it—then he'd laughed and said, "*Door* lag, really. We went by door, not jet. You get used to it. Jay-Tee and me are already on Sydney time on account of we didn't sleep away two whole days like you did."

They hadn't seemed so over it when I'd slipped out of the house, though. Jay-Tee had been sound asleep and Tom nowhere in sight. I doubted I was the only one still *door*-lagged.

The visiting room at Kalder Park was much more crowded than it had been a week ago, and hotter. The two ceiling fans didn't turn quite true and made more noise than cool air. Visitors and patients were dotted about the room, twenty-five of the first, nineteen of the latter, easy to tell apart.

Sarafina was sitting next to a much older woman with grey hair and strange, jerky movements who was trying to explain to her daughter (at least I imagined she was the woman's daughter) why Thursdays, not Mondays, were the best days for visits. It had something to do with the way $t$'s and $h$'s sounded together. Her voice was loud, carrying around the room, her cheeks red and damp. She looked exactly the way I'd always imagined a crazy person would.

Sarafina didn't look up or smile when I squeezed in beside her on the couch; her expression stayed blank and distant. I'd half expected her to tell me that I'd changed. She said nothing. She looked so much like Esmeralda. But I could see no resemblance between her and Jason Blake. It was hard to believe he was her father, my grandfather. Why hadn't she told me about him?

I reached into the hip pocket of my new pants, specially made for me by Tom, feeling for my ammonite. Just as my fingers touched nothing I remembered that I'd left it on the other side of the door, in New York City. I hoped Danny had picked it up.

Jay-Tee had called Danny yesterday. She'd chatted away with her brother for what seemed like hours, but I hadn't gotten to talk to him. It hadn't occurred to Jay-Tee that I'd want to. And Danny hadn't asked for me. I could call him later, when Sydney and New York time lined up properly, but I was too embarrassed.

Still, it was only Monday. I'd last seen Danny on Thursday.

No, *not* Thursday. That had been in New York City; it'd been Friday here in Sydney. It was three days since I'd last seen or spoken to him. I'd been asleep for almost two of those days, recovering from battling Jason Blake with magic. Maybe Danny had asked after me and Jay-Tee had forgotten to pass it on.

Did magic affect time? I'd first arrived in Sydney on Sunday afternoon and here it was, Monday, just eight days later, and yet so much had happened—I'd learned that magic was real, stepped through a door to another country, discovered other people with magic, made friends, met Danny, discovered what it is to be truly, truly cold. *Far* too much had happened in such a short amount of time—just eight days!

My world wasn't spinning on the same axis anymore. The rules of physics had been broken. Magic was real.

The grey-haired woman's daughter leaned forward to nod at me briefly before turning her attention back to her loud, unstill mother.

I stared at Sarafina's profile, counting the freckles—thirty-eight of them—on the side of her nose. I followed the line of her gaze: out the window, down to the bay, where fifteen white-sailed boats floated on the sparkling water. Did she see any of it? Her eyes were glazed over, vacant.

Just two weeks ago Sarafina's eyes had been alive, full of plans. We had been on the road together, had just decided to go to Nevertire because the name made us giggle. She hadn't been sad, hadn't gotten all obsessive, insisting she count every star or wash her hands fifty-five times in a row. None of the usual signs that she was about to lose it. But then, she'd never lost herself so completely. She'd never tried to kill herself before.

It shocked me all over again how unlike Sarafina she seemed. She'd never been a still person. Sarafina was always in motion, her face showing exactly what she was thinking. I looked at her now and saw no thought at all. It was as if she had stopped thinking, had run down and become still. All motion gone. Sarafina gone.

I tried to think of what to say. If I said, *I know about magic,* would that jerk her back to life? Not that I could say it with those two women so close by. They'd think I was one of the patients. Besides, it was hardly the best way to break the news. What if Sarafina lost it again?

A trickle of sweat ran down my back. "Hot, isn't it?" I said, just to be saying something. "At least there's some breeze off the bay."

"They never open the windows," the jerky woman said, turning to look at me. Her voice was so loud I flinched. I was glad Sarafina sat between us; white, bubbly spittle formed at the corners of the strange woman's mouth, and specks flew as she spoke. "The breeze isn't allowed in. They want us to boil."

Every window was open wide.

She tried to lean closer to me. "Did they do that to your eye?" I put my hand to my still-bruised face and shook my head. "Did they put their needles right into your eyeball?"

"Mum, hush. Leave the girl alone." The daughter leaned

forward, pulling her mother towards her, and grimaced at me—though I was sure it was meant to be a smile. She looked very tired. "Sorry, love."

Sarafina wasn't hot. My mother always stayed cool when everyone else was warm. In that way, she was still the Sarafina I had always known.

I blurred my vision until I could see inside her, down to where nothing was still, to the pumping of her heart, the blood rushing through her veins, the acid roiling in her stomach, the movement of her intestines. I could see her cells, every single one of them. Hear the roller-coaster movements in every part of her, like the ocean in a storm.

Governing it all was Sarafina's pattern with its graphic confirmation that yes, Jason Blake was my grandfather. I could see both grandparents, Esmeralda and Jason Blake, in her, traces of their DNA. Like theirs, her pattern was woven through with magic. *There* in every part of her—in her cells, in the molecules that made up every cell. The magic smelled earthy, like rich black soil, but unlike my grandparents' magic, unlike Jay-Tee's, there was no taste of rust. In its place under my tongue was a sharp sourness, like an unripe lemon. The smell made my eyes water.

Sarafina finally blinked. The movement pulled my senses back to the surface, where she was still and quiet.

The crazy woman's daughter hugged her mother, stood up, and said goodbye. Her mother started to cry.

"I'll be back, I promise." She glanced at me, embarrassed,

and then away again, avoiding her mother's eyes. "I have to go. I'll bring your granddaughter next time, I promise." She left quickly without glancing back. Her mother started to rock back and forth, her cries gradually getting louder. A nurse came to quiet her and led her from the room.

When they were gone, I moved to the other side of Sarafina and screwed up my courage to speak to her. There was so much I wanted to ask. What were the feathers Esmeralda had put under my pillow? What were they supposed to do? How did magic work? How long did I have to live? I wanted to tell her about the letters Esmeralda had slipped under my door—the letters I hadn't opened, that Esmeralda had stolen back before I could read them. I opened my mouth to say, *I've been to New York City*.

But Sarafina spoke first. "You're hers now, aren't you?" She wasn't looking at me. Her tone was flat and even, but her eyes had somehow cleared.

"No. No, I'm not." I wasn't sure, though. I was staying under Esmeralda's roof. I had helped her win the stoush against Jason Blake. She was going to teach me about magic. She had put those black and purple feathers under my pillow. Did all that make me hers?

"Then why are you wearing those pants?"

I looked down at the green pants Tom had made for me, his magic sewn into every seam. I flushed.

"You're going to die," Sarafina said. "Soon."

"Then tell me what you know," I said, trying to sound

brave, though I felt ill. "Tell me what I can do. I don't trust Esmeralda. But at least she'll tell me how magic works. If I'm going to fix this, I need you to help me."

"There's no fix. You die or you end up here. This is better."

I didn't believe that for a second. There had to be a way, a path that didn't lead to madness or early death. I was going to find it. I opened my mouth to tell her.

Instead, a question bubbled out. "Why did you lie to me?"

Sarafina closed her eyes, then opened them. Turned to look at me—*really* look at me—for the first time since she'd tried to kill herself. "I never lied."

"But magic *is* real. I've seen—"

"I was trying to make it unreal by denying it. I wasn't lying."

"But what about all those things you told me? You said there was no electricity in her house. There is. That she sacrificed babies—"

"I never lied."

"What are the black and purple feathers for? What do they do? How much danger am I in?"

But Sarafina was gone, her eyes filmed over again with the drugs they'd given her. The unripe lemon taste filled my mouth, and something sharp and jolting filled my nostrils. I gagged, my eyes watering, as I realised what it was: I could taste and smell my mother's madness.